This novel is a collaboration between, Martyn Ellington (Pen name: M.E. Ellington) a published and best-selling author, and his brother, Steven Ellington—a professional spiritualist medium. Though this is a fictional tale, the character of Jack Bright is based on a spirit Steven encountered in the Newport area of Middlesbrough, North East England, and the events described are based on actual events Steven has witnessed during his time working as a medium. Both Martyn and Steven were born and raised in North Yorkshire where they still live with their respective families.

To our eclectic group of beta readers, many thanks for keeping this on the rails...

In memory to all those killed, injured and affected by the bombing of Middlesbrough Railway Station by the Luftwaffe at 1:08 pm on 3rd August, 1942.

M.E. Ellington and Steven Ellington

THIRSTONFIELD HALT

A HAUNTING BEYOND TIME

AUSTIN MACAULEY PUBLISHERS™

LONDON • CAMBRIDGE • NEW YORK • SHARJAH

A CIP catalogue record for this title is available from the British Library.

ISBN 9781528987523 (Paperback)
ISBN 9781528987530 (ePub e-book)

www.austinmacauley.com

First Published (2020)
Austin Macauley Publishers Ltd
25 Canada Square
Canary Wharf
London
E14 5LQ

www.martynellington.com
www.stevenellington.co.uk

M.E. Ellington:

To those who have supported this journey—a sincere thank you. Long may we continue.

Steven Ellington:

To all those I hold close and dear, a sincere thank you. To James William Green. Our granddad and railway man.

Foreword

I think it's fair to say that the majority of people enjoy a good ghost story. The fact that you are reading this yourself suggests that you relish the prospect of delving into a mysterious, eerie and often frightening world.

The existence of ghosts and spirits, of course, cannot be rationally explained by mainstream science. Either because they don't know or do know and want to refrain from admitting that such a factual phenomenon that has no recognised scientific formula they can quantify actually does exist. When we experience the unknown, we become naturally frightened because we fail to understand what we are experiencing, and as with everything in life, the more we understand, the less we fear. It is, I think, important to point out that a ghost and a spirit is not one and the same thing. A ghost is nothing more than an apparition, an image, captured forevermore within the fabric of the atmosphere, rather like an image captured on a negative. A ghost, therefore, as far as witnessing its presence, will always look the same and will always do the same thing repeatedly. A spirit, on the other hand, is an actual living consciousness, an eternal energy form that continues to exist after it has discarded the physical body.

The story you are about to read is exactly that, a story, a work of fiction, a joint project between myself, a working spiritualist medium, and my younger brother, a bestselling and published author. It just felt the right thing to do. The characters, places and storyline have inhabited my head for many, many years just waiting patiently for the day to exist as written words. Like the characters, the village of Thirstonfield does not actually exist.

However, the dark, tormented spirit, central to the story, is based on a real spirit presence I encountered many years ago when conducting a spirit investigation in and around the Newport area of Middlesbrough. He was a tall and large man of unclean and dishevelled appearance, originating from the late nineteenth century and communicated to me in a very aggressive, ill-tempered manner. His energy was dark and heavy, as he told me he had served for many years in the Royal Navy. He proudly claimed, without any remorse, that he had murdered two people during his time on Earth and always carried a razor-sharp cutlass as well as relishing in the fact that everyone feared him. He was an individual that I believed was beyond redemption, and moreover, he continues to stalk the area around Newport to this day. Many of the spirit events and happenings in this story are also based on true, real-life experiences I have encountered over the years working as a spiritualist medium while investigating numerous disturbances.

So, remember as you read this story. The dark, tormented spirit and many of the sinister spirit disturbances are based on real events. And as for a house creaking at night? We're told that's the house settling after the day. This is sometimes true. However, mostly it's the spirits of the former residents keeping an eye on their home.

As I said at the beginning, everybody enjoys a good ghost story.

Steven Ellington
Spiritualist Medium

He who dwells in the shelter of the Most High will abide in the shadow of the Almighty. I will say to the Lord, 'My refuge and my fortress, my God, in whom I trust.'

You will not fear the terror of the night.

Preface

It was on the short journey back from visiting my dear old aunty in Whitby when I sat next to a young couple. I say young couple, they were by comparison to myself young. But then, as I'm now advancing well into my seventies, most are. The thing that struck me about them was not that they looked dishevelled. It was clear for me to see that the clothes they wore were of a high quality. No, what struck me was how utterly exhausted and frightened they looked and that the man was clearly injured, nursing his left arm as if it was broken. Actually, thinking back, it unnerved me somewhat though at the time that didn't register with me. Perhaps because I was so bemused why a couple, who looked like they were ordinarily of good appearance, looked so tousled and tormented.

As the train left the station, I watched them both become a little more relaxed. The further we travelled along the line, the more relaxed they appeared to be. Finally, around ten minutes into our silent journey, I leaned over and asked what had brought them onto this late and last scheduled train. As our small diesel locomotive trundled on through the storm which had blown in from the east coast and across the moors into the dead of night, she told me what had brought them to be here at this exact moment.

As with all good tales, she started at the beginning.

Part 1
The Halt

Chapter 1

October 1949

Thirstonfield Halt Station was located on the rural and beautifully picturesque line which spanned from Whitby on the North East coast of England to Middlesbrough, a large, industrial town found some fifty-miles or so away as the crow flies. Originally opened as a halt for the local farmers and Thirstonfield Estate workers, it had been improved and expanded with a passing loop and engine shed when the popularity of holidaying at the seaside increased. Taking it from a lowly halt to a fully-fledged station. But as demand for the line began to drop, at the end of the Second World War, its days, it seemed, were numbered. On the platform stood Jack Bright. In the lowing light of the autumn day, he cut a sizeable, yet lowly figure. The other passengers elected to wait for the last train in the small waiting room, but Jack stood defiantly against the chilling wind and fine mist which spread in from the East coast. His long, black coat swayed and ruffled with each gust, while his fedora hat, tipped toward the encroaching mist, shielded his face.

Jack was waiting for the train which would take him back to the small, modest home he'd grown up in with his mother, Doris. Their relationship had been one of unity against a man, Jack's father, who had repeatedly been drunk, and who had repeatedly beaten them both until Jack became big enough to fight back. After his father's eviction, by means of a broken nose and fractured collarbone, Jack's father had shouted as he limped along the narrow-cobbled street and out of sight. He'd shouted that Jack was a bastard. That he was no son of his, and that Doris was a whore. His parting shot was to announce to the street that the whore and bastard deserved each other.

It seemed to Jack those words had hit his mother harder than any of his father's punches, and when Jack had finally calmed his anguished mother, she did confess that Jack had been conceived out of wedlock, and not to the man Jack knew as his father. It had been a secret Doris had not wanted her son to know, but to Jack, it didn't matter. All that did matter was his mother. Who, or where, his father was, was of no importance to Jack. Perhaps it was for this reason, or perhaps for the reason of Jack's own vile temper as a result of the beatings he'd taken and watched his mother take, that he'd never looked for love. And love had never found him. Rather, he found solace in his mother's arms.

As Jack stood on the empty darkening platform, he wasn't looking forward to going back to Middlesbrough. Since his mother's death at the hands of the Luftwaffe during the war, Jack hated going back to his hometown. That place held nothing but demons and bad dreams. After her death, Jack had joined the British Army, vowing to kill as many Nazis as he could to avenge the death of the woman he'd held above all.

But the war for Jack ended too soon. His lust for killing and the sexual delight that came with it was not satisfied, nor was the want for the love his mother gave him.

And tonight, he had once again gone looking for it. He'd looked for it in the eyes of a young woman who glanced at him from across the bar in the small pub located just outside the village of Thirstonfield.

From her perspective, it was a courteous glance and smile, but for Jack, who had never understood the social construct of male to female courtship, it was a clear sign of love.

Jack had sat, for most of the afternoon, silently in the corner gathering the strength and courage to talk to her, but the petite, attractive woman had forgotten about the big, mysterious man she'd smiled at when she'd looked across the room to spot her friends in the crowd. A few hours after their gazes had met, she stood, said her goodbyes to her friends and left the pub. Jack put on his hat and followed her outside. He shadowed her from a distance as she crossed the high street and cut through a field toward what Jack assumed would be her home. One of the many farms that lay scattered around the moors. The scenario had played around Jack's mind since that meeting of their eyes. He would make first contact, they would talk, fall in love, marry and live in his house where she would assume the duties his mother had so devotedly carried out. Before that night when he'd run from the house.

Her rejection came almost the instant he caught up to her and spoke, and his rage came just as quick. Before Jack could think through the red mist which swirled around his mind, the petite, attractive woman lay dead in the field before him. The Kirpan knife, a treasured heirloom, had cut through her throat with ease. He'd done it again, and as always, no panic began to set in. Rather, he was calm and considered, as he wiped the young woman's blood from his hands and the blade of the knife. Without a second thought to the body that lay before him, Jack turned and headed for Thirstonfield Halt.

The mist now enveloped the platform. Jack pushed his hands deep inside his coat, his right hand still firmly holding onto the knife. Glancing up, he checked the time on the ornate station clock which hung from the wall. It read 9.20 p.m. He smirked to himself; the train was due in ten minutes. In the distance, he could hear the steam train huffing its way toward the station, and he knew before too long, he would be heading home, and in his mind at least, he would be in the clear. Besides, she had rejected him, just like the rest of the whores who smile at him and then turn him down, giving him the *come-on* only to then reject and humiliate him. His mother always insisted that no woman would ever be good enough for him, and Jack believed it now more than he did back then.

***

June 2015

Thirstonfield Halt Station now lay derelict. Closed in 1954 by British Railways, the then operators of the station, after its losses became too much to bear. The once gleaming waiting room, formerly full of Victorian charm, was now dank and overgrown. Mould crept along the floor and along the walls, and where once passengers sat waiting patiently for their trains, birds had now made their nests. The station clock which still clung to the wall on its rusting steel brackets had stopped at 1.20 p.m. The time when power had been shut off, and the station was finally abandoned. Outside, the platform had taken the worst the weather could throw at it. In winter, deep snow and the relentless wind and rain punished the facades and wooden seats, while in the summer months, the beating sun cracked and blistered the fading paint. Around the station, the once pristine gardens and small, gravel car park were now blanketed by nature. The delicate plants and flowers which needed endless care by the stationmaster had long been suffocated by the wild plants and weeds which now dominated and spread without hindrance. Nestled deep within the small valley, just off the only road between Thirstonfield Village and the market town of Stokesley, the station was disappearing back into the land it was cut from and was rapidly becoming all but invisible to passing traffic and fell walkers. Google Maps, as well every GPS software company hadn't bothered to list it. In the local communities, only those who had seen the end of war remembered it was still there, and they'd not passed on the legend of this place.

It was never to be spoken of by those who remember what happened there. Once the railway company closed the station, it was, for all intents and purposes, lost and forgotten over the decades that passed. And they all hoped it would remain that way.

Jill Goodwin looked at the clock on the Range Rover's dash. 4.11 p.m. She sighed and turned back to the view that met her from the windshield. Outside, the North Yorkshire Moors always seemed to her the most beautiful place on Earth. The rolling green hills with their patchwork quilts of farmers' fields interrupted only by the ancient stonewalls that separated them. It'd been another long day of house hunting with Paul, her fiancé and long-time best friend. Jill relaxed into the seat, smiling inside that she had made Paul drive the long, meandering journey back to their home in Hutton Rudby. After looking at another four houses today, she was far too scrambled to concentrate on the twisting, narrow country lanes the bulky SUV was now trying to navigate. Jill ran a successful web blog, helping patients who were recovering from various forms and stages of cancer. After spending a few years working as a radiographer for a local hospital, she had become one of the very people she always sought to help. The diagnosis of breast cancer at the age of thirty-four came as a bolt from the blue. She had always practiced what she'd preached: exercise, a good diet and no smoking. But her genes had other ideas. While recovering at home, Jill started the blog, not only to help her *unload* what she needed, but to offer help from both sides, Jill, the professional radiographer, and Jill, the recovering cancer patient. It had taken off, and so the decision was made to leave the hospital and focus on the blog. For Paul, this was a godsend after the fright of cancer. Running a small firm of architects out of Northallerton, he'd struggled when Jill became ill. His commitment to her was non-negotiable, but he also had his responsibilities to the partnership. With Jill working from home, the pressure was off him, and it opened the possibility of moving to their dream home.

With Jill no longer needing to commute to Middlesbrough, they no longer needed to live between their two jobs. And so, the house search had begun.

Jill was all but asleep, the heat of the day was still bearing down on them, and only the continual waft of cooled air from the Range Rover's climate control system kept the temperature inside the car comfortable. She was glad to be drifting off. The atmosphere had not been good since the last house they'd viewed in Thirstonfield. Jill felt it would have made for a lovely family home. It was quaint and homely and had that charm about it that just wanted you to make fresh bread and relax in a generous wingback chair around the open fire in the dead of winter. But, for Paul, it was too small, the ceilings were too low and the land too restrictive. She resisted

19

as much as she could, but the inevitable argument that was coming did not wait until they reached the relative privacy of their car. The estate agent had tried to brush their disagreement off, but it was clear to them both that the young man who had been sent out by the office to show them the vacant house was out of his depth, and even more out of his comfort zone. His red face and stammering while he looked for the right words had brought their argument to a premature, albeit temporary, end. Paul, ever the architect, wanted a large project, something befitting of his vision and ability, but for Jill, who was now going to be working from home as well as running it, wanted something more immediate that they could grow into, grow to love and become one with over time. She didn't want either a finished article or a money-pit of a project. After they'd both calmed, Paul did what he always did: he pushed the button on the car's audio system and blocked everything else out while his favourite band, James, played their greatest hits. For Jill, the argument was long forgotten; they had different ideas of what they needed and wanted, but she knew they would make the compromise eventually. She smiled at that thought, and after a few moments, she fell asleep.

Jill woke to find the car parked by the side of the road in a small layby. She cleared her head and looked around to see Paul standing by a rusting gate looking down into the valley they'd just skirted around. She sighed and climbed out of the Range Rover to join him. The summer heat hit her as soon as she opened her door.

"Paul?"

He turned. "Hey, hun, you're awake. Come, look what I spotted."

Jill joined him and looked to where he was pointing. In the valley below, they could see a building. It had a distinct Victorian feel about it, Jill's favourite era for building design, and it looked large.

"What do you think it is?" Jill asked.

"I'm not sure, but I'm going to look."

"Is that wise? The gate's there for a reason."

"It hasn't been opened for years. It's rusted to hell. Ya coming?" Paul said, climbing over the old gate.

"Doesn't look like I have a choice," Jill replied, switching off and then locking the car.

"Come on then, slow coach," Paul teased.

Jill caught up to Paul with relative ease. He wasn't a tall man, nor particularly athletic. That's not to say he was overweight, well, not by much, but his years of office work and his love of not exercising had certainly shaped his physique, and he was almost bald. He was at that stage where anything other than shaving his head once a week would prove futile, and Jill often tormented him if he let it grow out too long. "Going for the comb-over?" she would laugh.

Paul's reply was always the same. "It's the stress you cause me." Jill, however, was slim. With short, blonde hair and blue eyes, she was by most people's ideals quite attractive, and she'd kept herself in good shape. She followed Paul farther along the narrow track she assumed must have at one time been the main road to and from whatever this building was. As they reached the end, they came across another rusting gate.

"They certainly locked this place down," Jill said, as she clambered over it.

There was no answer from Paul, who'd already cleared it and was now standing directly in front of the main building.

"It's a station," Paul said, his smile ever widening.

"A what?"

"A station. Look, you can just make out where the tracks used to be, running back up the valley." Paul was pointing ahead.

He walked a little farther along and onto what he now knew to be the old platform. Hanging off the decaying brickwork were rusting metal flower baskets, now overgrown with dead vines and weeds. The aged wooden benches were just as rotten; the wood had split and fallen through into piles of decomposing mulch, while the metal frames fared no better. Jill looked above to the station clock. She could see it once took pride of place, hanging out for all to see.

"Huh," she whispered.

"What is it?" Paul asked.

"The clock, 1.20 p.m. Do you think that's when they abandoned this place?"

"I'm not sure. Why?"

"Oh, nothing. Just seems an odd time, don't you think? You know, not on the hour or half hour," Jill remarked.

"I don't honestly think it matters. Does it?" Paul answered, rather dismissively.

"I guess not." Jill moved farther along the platform to where Paul was standing.

They both stood back and looked at the imposing building before them. Dead centre was the main house, which had once served a duel role of the ticket office and stationmaster's house. To its left was the old, single-story waiting room, and on the opposite gable end was the parcel office. They could both tell it had been a beautiful building, built in a time when public buildings such as this had the same care and detail as private houses.

It was both imposing and grand, and yet, still radiated that charm of a simpler time.

Jill could tell Paul was starting to fall in love with it, and while she'd always been adamant that they were not going to take on any projects, and this building by any meaning of that word would be a project, she too was beginning to warm to it.

"I wonder if it's open?" Paul moved toward the double doors which led into the stationmaster's house.

He shook the door handle, but it was firmly locked. He moved to the windows, but the decades of neglect meant they were too pitted to see through. Jill looked around. Something caught her attention. A piece of board. As she approached it, she thought she heard a child singing a nursery rhyme. She stopped but the sound vanished.

"Did you hear that?" Jill asked Paul, who was still on the old platform.

"What?" he asked, moving over to her.

"Nothing, I guess. I thought I heard a child singing."

Paul chuckled. "Singing what?"

"You'll laugh if I say," Jill said sheepishly.

"Go on, I won't. I promise."

"It was the nursery rhyme 'Seesaw Margery Daw'," Jill replied.

Paul laughed. "Sorry, I lied. Anyway, why are you over here?"

"A sign, hidden behind that shrub." She pointed to a clump of bushes which had taken hold of the waiting room wall.

Paul moved over and pulled them back, revealing the sign, hidden for many years.

"Thirstonfield Halt Station," he muttered.

"I've never heard of it," Jill added.

"Nor me. It's not on the GPS. I'll check Google Maps."

Paul pulled his phone from his pocket and typed in the name.

"Anything?" Jill asked.

"No, no real mention of it. Just some black and white pictures."

Jill's attention moved to another sign. "Look." She pointed to it.

Leaning against the wall where it had fallen after the flimsy, wooden post which held it failed, lay a real estate sign. H. Yates & SONS. Telephone: 52789

"Christ, that's an old sign," Paul remarked.

"It is. The phone number is too short, and there's no web address."

"I think a web back then was something a spider made," Paul laughed and then continued, "I wonder if they're still in business."

"You're not thinking of looking into this place. Are you?" Jill asked, knowing, deep down, she already knew the answer.

"Why not? Can you imagine how grand it will be when it's shining new again?"

"Well, it's too late now to do anything. Let's just get home. We can talk about it tomorrow."

"Okay, but I'm going to find the agent and call them," Paul said defiantly.

"You do that, dear," came the sarcastic reply.

As they turned to leave, a gust of frigid air swirled around them, taking them by surprise. The long-settled leaves swirled and danced as if to strike at them, the dried out, sharpened leaves hitting them in their faces and tangling in Jill's hair.

The wind shook the station clock on its mounts, moving the pointers. Almost as soon as it started, the wind died, and the leaves fluttered back to the ground.

"What the hell was that?" Jill said, pulling her hair straight and dusting herself down.

"God knows. Could be one of those local dust devils you hear of," Paul answered, reassuring himself more than Jill.

As they walked back toward the gate and began climbing over it, Jill looked back. A cold sweat ran up and down her spine, and she shivered in the heat of the day. What neither of them noticed was where the clock pointers had settled. They read 9.30 p.m.

Chapter 2

The passengers who had elected to wait out of the weather now joined Jack on the platform, as the train approached the station. For Jack, this was the time he least liked. Surrounded by people, he felt closed in, trapped, just as he had done when he, along with what seemed far too few men, stormed Gold Beach during the D-Day landings only five short years ago. His grip around the Kirpan knife tightened, as his anxiety swelled inside him. He could hear the whistle come once again in the distance. Jack calmed himself that he didn't have long to wait and that he'd be home long before they found the dead girl.

A short, fat man stood next to Jack. Jack looked him up and down. His rotund, pasty body displeased him. He had seen many of these types of men in the war. They were all higher ranks, not soldiers, just toffs; barking orders and sending the real men to their deaths while they themselves were no more able to run and fight as a newborn infant. His disgust for this dough-ball of a man rose inside him. The little, fat man moved in front of Jack, jostling for a better seat, and now Jack stood directly behind him, looking on him from his 6'5" vantage point. He stared at his balding head, and his fat neck which oozed over the starched, white shirt collar. His gaze moved down to his small, puffy hands which held a black attaché case in one and an umbrella in the other. Jack's glare moved again to the short, stubby legs. He wanted to kill this little, fat man. He wanted to exact revenge on him for all the soldiers, the real soldiers that died because of the decisions that little fat men like this made during the war. The urge and his anger became harder to control, and with it, the excitement. The rage that he'd carried inside him for so long needed to be set free. Jack pulled his left hand from his coat. He would push this fat man in front of the train. He would shout *watch out* as he did, making all those around him believe it to be an accident.

As the train drew closer, Jack readied himself, but then came a whistle. It wasn't the whistle of the approaching train, this was different, and Jack recognised it immediately. This was a police whistle. Jack's attention turned from the little fat man, as he looked around the station. His size had always been of great strength to Jack. Not only was he tall, but he was broad and naturally very strong. Once he'd bested his father, he cannot remember a time when he had lost a fight, but his size was now a disadvantage in a crowd of average people.

Thoughts flashed through his mind. *'What if they have found the body and retraced the woman's steps to the pub? What if someone had seen him leave the pub? They would have reported a large man.'*

The train was close. It was visible as it rounded the final corner, but it wasn't close enough. Jack would have to run. He turned, pushing his way through the gathering crowd of passengers. A uniformed police officer shouted at Jack to stop.

Jack looked back. He could see two officers making their way toward him. He began running, but ahead, there were three more officers. Jack's pulse raced. Could he fight them? Take them all on and still escape? Perhaps, maybe, but then if he was caught, tried and found guilty, he would hang. His mind scrambled; he was trapped, and the police officers were closing in.

A younger officer, still full of enthusiasm, who had approached from behind a mound of luggage, caught Jack by surprise, placing a hand on his shoulder. Immediately, Jack turned and swung a hefty fist at him. On impact, his cheekbone split and his nose exploded. With the young officer on the floor dazed and in distress, Jack turned and ran. Another officer shouted for Jack to stop.

Jack darted his head left and right, looking for a route out, but the only way was across the railway lines. He looked toward the train. It was close, but he had no choice. Jack ran past the engine shed, tossing the Kirpan knife through the open door as he did. Turning back, he leapt onto the lines which now groaned in protest at the weight of the oncoming locomotive, but if he made it to the other side, he would be in the clear. He looked one more time at the officers who were now behind him on the platform. When he looked back, he saw the officers hadn't followed him onto the tracks, and he assumed it was because they didn't dare to, but it wasn't that. As Jack turned, he saw why. On the other side, waiting for him were three more officers and a well-built man in plain clothes who Jack assumed to be a detective. He had nowhere to go, nowhere to run and with the thought of being hanged racing through his mind, a moment of clarity dissolved away the red mist and chaos that swirled around him. Jack smiled at the tall detective, and then, raising his arms beside him, he turned to face the steam locomotive. As the station clock chimed 9.30 p.m., the train hit Jack.

***

Jill sat in the living room of their small cottage reading the latest novel that the book club she had joined while recovering from cancer had recommended. Next to her feet lay Charlie, a springer spaniel she and Paul had rescued as a pup. She glanced at her watch: 5.58 p.m. Paul would soon be pulling up their drive.

"Daddy will be home soon, yes he will," Jill relayed to Charlie, who, as usual, wagged his tail in excitement without taking his eyes off his favourite toy, which they called Baby.

Almost to the minute, the Range Rover pulled up. With the usual thud of the heavy, oak door, Paul entered the cottage, and then the living room. Jill could see by his childish grin that he was excited about something.

"Hi, darling," Paul announced, as he entered.

Charlie immediately sprang to his feet and danced around Paul's legs, demanding all his master's attention.

"Yes, hello to you too, Charlie," Paul said, as he leant forward, stroking the ever more excitable dog. He then turned his attention back to Jill. "Guess what I found out today?"

Jill thought he sounded as excited as Charlie. "And what's that?"

"I found out who H. Yates & Sons are, or were," he answered, now sitting next to Jill.

"Were?"

"Well, it seems old man Yates died in nineteen seventy-four, and his son closed the business in eighty-nine when he moved to Australia."

"So, what does that mean? It's not for sale?" Jill asked, rather optimistically.

"No, actually, the place is still owned by the Bradbury family, who own most of the farming land in that area," Paul answered gleefully.

"I'm not following," Jill said, trying to calm Paul.

"It turns out, the railway company, British Railways, didn't own the land. Rather, they rented it from the farm, and when they closed the station in '54, it was the Bradbury's, well, old man Bradbury, who put it up for sale. However, for some reason, he didn't sell it even though he'd received good offers for the place. After he died, and Yates closed, the building was forgotten about."

"So, that's it then, we find somewhere else?" Jill asked.

Paul chuckled. "No, I have the number for George Bradbury. I'm going to call him, see if we can arrange a viewing."

"But there must be a reason it hasn't sold, especially, if as you say, they've had good offers in the past," Jill replied.

"I guess it was the old man that just didn't want to sell. You know what that generation is like, we deal with them quite often in the practice. They don't need the money and would rather just sit on the land than see it developed."

"What makes you think this George will be any different?"

"I don't know that he will be, but if we don't ask, we will never know. Will we?" Paul answered, smiling his Cheshire cat grin.

Jill shrugged. "Okay then, give him a call. I guess it won't hurt to look. That's if he lets us."

It was another three weeks before Paul finally managed to track down and convince George Bradbury to show him the old station. Paul's first attempt had been met with a rather abrupt click when George hung up on him, but it hadn't deterred Paul who was used to dealing with moors farmers, who, by and large, liked to keep out strangers and stay away from the towns and cities. Although Paul worked for a small practice in a market town, to George, he still represented the *Yuppie Brigade* with their mobile phones and flash cars. Pop culture and modernist colloquialisms, it seemed, take a long time to reach the moors, and even longer to leave.

George had been reluctant to take Paul's calls once he understood the reason behind them. But as with many moors' farmers, times were hard, and money did not flow as freely as it once did.

Any land that could not pay for itself now needed to be cut loose, like a rotting tree branch before it killed the tree, and Thirstonfield Halt and the land it sat on was no use for either crop growing or livestock grazing. And so, hesitantly, George had, on Paul's fourth call, agreed to meet him by the old station.

Once again, Jill found herself beside her giddy as a schoolboy fiancé, as they waited for George to arrive. Though the day's temperature had only managed the mid-twenties, it was still uncomfortable standing around, waiting for someone that Jill was still not convinced would show. They, or rather Paul, as Jill wanted no part of this and was only here to placate Paul, arranged to meet George at 2.15 p.m. and as Jill glanced at her watch, the pointers had already moved past the 2.47 p.m. mark. She smiled and tapped her watch to Paul.

"See, I told you. He only agreed so you'd stop calling him. He won't show."

"Oh, ye of little faith," Paul scoffed back to her. "He'll be here. He may have been caught up with farming stuff."

"What, like, a sheep emergency?" Jill answered.

"Could be, could be one made a run for it, you know, Steve McQueen style. Pinched the old man's motorcycle and tried to jump the fence." Paul laughed at his own joke and the image of a sheep riding away on a motorbike.

"Silly sod!" Jill laughed with him.

The sound of an old diesel engine interrupted their quieting laughter. As Paul turned toward the sound, a beat-up old Land Rover Defender trundled around from behind the engine shed. It stopped sharply, and the driver's door opened.

From it sprang a lively black and white sheepdog, which immediately rushed toward them, its tail wagging furiously. Seconds later, an older man emerged and approached them, but with a lot less vigour and much less enthusiasm. He was, on the whole, what Paul and Jill expected to see. He was dressed in old clothes that they both supposed had seen many days of work on the farm. His hair was greying but thick and today at least, very unkempt.

"You must be George Bradbury?" Paul said, raising his right hand, ready to shake George's.

"I am! And are you the bloody nuisance who won't stop calling me?" he replied gruffly.

"Ah look, he knows you already," Jill whispered to Paul, smiling.

"I am, I'm afraid. I'm Paul, and this is my fiancée, Jill."

"Fiancée? And you two are wanting this to live in?" George frowned at them both.

"Well, it is the 21st century, Mr Bradbury," Jill said, rather nervously defending them both.

"Yes, yes, it is. That's used as an excuse for a lot of things wrong today if you ask me."

Jill readied herself to reply, "Well, no one did," but Paul gently pulled on her right arm. Jill swallowed her words and beamed at the old farmer.

"Guess you want to see inside it then?" George asked rhetorically, as he pulled a bunch of old, rusting keys from his jacket.

"If you wouldn't mind," Paul replied.

George didn't answer, not verbally anyway. He simply shrugged and pushed the key into the old lock. With a *clunk,* the key turned, and the heavy oak doors opened. Paul turned to Jill and smirked, then turned and followed George into the building. Inside, it was much as Paul had envisioned. The Victorian décor was still visible, though damp and mould had done its best to destroy it. The stationmaster's house was a grand affair, high ceilings with elaborate cornices and central roses exhibited an attention to detail and craftsmanship modern house builders seemed to have long forgotten, or worse, deserted. Bulky, metal radiators stood proudly, not hidden away like their modern counterparts. These radiators were on display and were as much a part of the design and style as any of the furniture which once complimented this grand old building. Jill could feel herself falling in love with the romance of this place, and she began to imagine those cosy winter nights snuggled around the open fire and the long summer days sat out on their own private platform, staring off into the beautiful views across the valley. Paul and Jill followed George through to the ticket office. Though the small room had obviously been altered throughout the station's use, it was easy to see what it once was and what it could be again.

"What do you think so far?" Paul whispered to Jill, as George led them to the waiting room.

"I think it's charming, and it would make a beautiful home."

"I knew you'd come around if we saw it."

"I didn't say I'd come around, Paul, only that it's charming," Jill answered, still wanting to resist the charm and appeal of this old building that was crying out to be saved.

George pushed open the double doors which led through to the ticket office. "There you go, that's it, well, apart from the parcel office, but it's much the same as this room."

Paul stood in the middle of the room, his architectural mind already making plans and envisioning what this old place could be. He turned to Jill, who looked blankly back at him.

"Have you seen enough?" George asked, and then continued. "I've things to sort before dark."

"I have one question," Jill said.

"Aye?" came the short reply.

"Why didn't your dad sell this place previously, and why, if it is for sale, is it not listed anywhere?" Jill paused. "Is there something wrong with it?"

Paul wanted the ground to swallow him. It had taken him weeks to get George to agree to even allow them to view it, and now, as usual, Jill was cutting through like a surgeon's knife.

George took a deep breath and sighed heavily before he answered. "It's like this, lass. We've owned this land for generations, and to be honest, I don't like change. But this land is no use to the farm, and the money isn't as good as it was in my father's time." He paused and looked at Paul. "So, the upshot is that I need to sell it, but I don't want to."

"What would you take for it?" Paul asked.

George became cool again and turned back toward the way they came in. "Make me an offer, lad. Now, I have to get back."

Without saying another word, he led Paul and Jill out of the station. Once outside, he pulled the double doors together and locked them.

"Thank you for showing us. I'll call you in a day or two," Paul said, as he went to shake George's hand.

But George didn't hold his hand out. Rather, he grimaced and held his arms still by his side. "Call if you want, but I don't think this is the place for you."

With that, George walked back to his Land Rover. As he did, he whistled, and the sheepdog which had ran across from where the tracks once were, jumped into the truck. With the diesel engine once again grumbling, Paul and Jill watched, as the Land Rover disappeared over the small hill in a cloud of black soot and blue smoke.

"What do you suppose that was?" Jill asked.

"What was?"

"It was the way he seemed to go all Deliverance on us and then tell us it's not for us," Jill said.

"I've told you, these moors farmers are hard men, and they don't do politeness as we know it," Paul said, trying to defend George, though, as he spoke, he had no idea why he considered the need to.

"That wasn't just good old-fashioned *folky-ness*, that was just weird," Jill replied, as she began walking toward the gate.

As she did, she felt something move under her foot, so she stopped and looked down. In the ground, half buried lay a crucifix. Jill was the spiritual one of the two, Paul being the atheist, and she could tell this wasn't an *off the shelf* crucifix. The last time she had seen something this elaborate, it had belonged to the priest she'd often sought council with when she was growing up. Paul noticed that Jill had stopped, and he returned to where she was stood. As he reached her, Jill picked up the crucifix and began rubbing the deeply encased mud from it.

"Who do you suppose dropped this?" Jill muttered, as she continued rubbing.

"Nuns on the run?" Paul said, trying to make light of her find.

Jill looked sideways at him. "This isn't a run-of-the-mill crucifix, Paul. This belonged to a priest. It isn't something that would be lost easily."

"Well, I think you should leave it where you found it. Until we buy this place, anything we find belongs to George's farm. Including that."

Jill nodded and placed it carefully against the gatepost. An uneasy sensation had washed over her when she'd picked it up. But she knew Paul would just make a sarcastic remark if she said anything to him, and so as they walked back to the Range Rover for the drive home, she decided to say nothing. And anyway, she wasn't convinced that Mr Bradbury, as she'd decided to call him, because George was too polite for that cantankerous old sod, was going to sell at any price.

**

The old, blue Land Rover stopped outside the farmhouse which the Bradbury family had lived in for four generations. Over time, it had been extended, modified and, at one point, almost burnt to the ground. George clambered out of the truck followed by his faithful sheepdog and made his way inside. He removed his heavy coat and hat and took a seat at the large, wooden dining table he once sat at as a child. The table was like George. It bore the scars and marks of age and use. His wife of more years than George would like to think of entered the kitchen and poured him a cup of tea and handed it to George as she sat next to him.

"Well, how did it go?" Mavis asked.

"I think they'll make an offer."

"You know we need to take it, don't you?" Mavis asked in a stern tone.

"Aye, I do." George sipped the tea and sighed.

"What is it, George?"

"You know what that place is, and you know what happened there. I'm not sure we should sell it. Perhaps it's just best to let it fall down?"

Mavis leant closer to him and rubbed her husband's old shoulders. "We need the money, George. If we don't sell off the useless land, we'll lose the farm. Time to let go. And besides, we haven't heard anything for years. Maybe all that business is over. It has been a long time."

George nodded and took another sip. "Perhaps, wife. But I remember what happened."

"That was a long time ago, George."

George sat back in the chair, holding his old, green mug close to his chest. "It wasn't just then, though, was it? I've seen things, I've heard things. The place gives me the willies."

"Well, maybe these folks will be fine, George. Besides, we have no choice." With that, Mavis stood and left the room.

George watched her go and sighed once again. He reached down and stroked the head of his sheepdog. "Perhaps she's right, lad. It could all be over now." The sheepdog looked at his master and whimpered.

***

As the Range Rover pulled onto the driveway, Jill was happy to be back home. It was fair to say she was becoming somewhat enamoured by The Halt, but still, there was something about it she just couldn't quite place, and that was before she considered its current owner, George, or Mr Bradbury. They made their way into their cottage, and as usual, Charlie fussed them like it was the first and last time he'd seen them.

"Yes, hello, Charlie," Jill said, patting her excited Spaniel.

"So, what did you think of it?" Paul asked, eager to know Jill's thoughts.

Jill stood upright. She knew exactly what he wanted her to say, and as much as she'd always insisted that a grand project was off the cards, she could see the potential. "What worries me is the restoration cost. We don't have the money to fix the place up and still live here. We'd need to sell this first."

"Yes, but we could buy it with our savings, then sell and restore."

"But where would we live?" Jill asked.

"We could rent somewhere in the village, Thirstonfield Village I mean, or even Stokesley, it's not that far. Or we could buy a caravan?"

Jill frowned. "A caravan? Over the winter, in the middle of the North Yorkshire Moors? Now I know you really have lost the plot."

"Winter? It's summer now," Paul said, in futile retaliation.

"And by the time you deal with Mr *fucking* Congeniality and then put in the restoration plans to the planning office, and we sell this and then complete the work, it'll be four summers from this one. I've seen too many people on too many TV shows attempt what you want to do, and it always takes more money and time than they think it will," Jill replied more sternly than she intended. She sighed and continued. "Listen, see what you can get it for, I'll go along that far. If it's not listed and there aren't too many planning restrictions and hoops to jump through," she sighed again, not believing what she was about to say, "we'll sell this place and rent. However, I am not, I repeat, not living in a caravan."

Paul grinned and walked toward her, wrapping his arms around her and pulling her close. "Thank you. I promise it will be beautiful when it's done." He kissed her on her forehead and then pulled back. "Let's take Charlie for a walk, then we can have tea."

Chapter 3

March 1931

Jack Bright was a boy of twelve, and once again, he was walking as slowly as he could home after another day at school and after yet another beating at the hands of Paul Stokes, the largest boy in his year and the boy who had took it upon himself to make Jack's life as miserable as he could. Jack often asked why him, as the blows came from Paul's clenched fists while he pinned Jack down, but he only ever got the same answer. It was because Paul's dad told him that Jack's father was a drunken fuckwit, and his son was no better.

On this particular day, the beating was over quickly, but only because Mr Harrison, the aging Physical Education teacher and the hardest man Jack thought he had ever known, had intervened and pulled Paul off him. Jack had then managed to slip by Paul at the end of the school day, but he knew the same would be waiting for him the next day and every day after that. As he rounded the corner and entered the street which would take him to the small terrace two up-two down street house he'd always known as home, another feeling of dread rose inside. While Saturday and Sunday, as well as the school holidays, provided some respite from Paul's indignation, Jack, had no such break from his father's.

As Jack stood on the doorstep, he waited, listening for his father's voice. Usually, he would be at the pub at this time of the day, but not always. He moved his face closer to the door, turning his head, pinning his ear to it. He could hear nothing. It was a sweet relief, and Jack knew if he could get in, have his tea and hide away in his bedroom, he may just have, what he and Doris called, a safe night. Which meant he'd escaped his father's wrath. This wrath was not because of Jack, nor his mother, who endured the most of his father's rage. What his father was mad at was the rest of the world. After an accident aboard a Merchant Navy ship left him with a damaged leg, the man with no education found it impossible to find any form of useful employment. His wife, Doris, however, did secure a job on the railways and became the household's only breadwinner. To Jack's dad, this was emasculating and the reason he could be found at the local pub whenever it was open. It's also the reason why he would tell anyone who would listen his woes to try and blag a free a drink, and why, when he returned home, he vented his frustration at life on Doris, and if he was to hand, Jack. But there was also a deeper reason why the resentment by Jack's father had been growing.

While in the Navy, and before they'd wed, Doris had cheated and became pregnant. To Jack's dad, he saw only two choices out of it. The first was to admit that Doris had strayed away from his bed, and that would be like admitting he couldn't satisfy her. The second was to marry Doris and claim the unborn baby was his. In his mind, this was the only option that didn't undermine his manhood, either in his own eyes or perhaps more importantly, the way he perceived others saw him.

But this union of convenience for his pride had not been the life he wanted, and after the accident, the rage had built up inside him until, finally, he had let it out. With one swipe, he had hit Doris and knocked her off her feet. In that moment, he felt the power he once had before she'd *gone off* with the other man and before the iron anchor chain had mangled his leg.

Every time he felt belittled, he drank, and he lashed out, and it was always Doris who apologised after, and it was always Jack that comforted his mother when his father had, at last, fallen asleep in front of the fire.

Jack made it to the relative safety of his room by the time his father staggered home. He listened as his father berated Doris, accused her of ruining his life and told her she was worth less than a pint of his own piss.

He listened as his mother said nothing, after learning shortly after Jack was born not to antagonise the drunken man, but to stay quiet and not make eye contact. Sometimes, this worked, and he would fall into a drunken sleep before the beatings started. Sometimes, it worked, but tonight, it didn't.

Jack listened, as the first slap hit his mother and she cried out in pain. He listened again when the second and third struck her, and when finally, he stopped, she thanked him. But for Jack, the sound he feared the most was the sound of his father's heavy boots, as they thumped up the steep staircase. He counted them: one, two, three, until they reached twelve. Then he counted the steps to his bedroom door: one, two, three, until they reached six. And then, the bedroom door flung open.

Jack trembled, as he watched his father remove his belt. He knew tonight was not going to be his safe night.

***

"Yes, I understand, George, sorry, Mr Bradbury. Yes, I'll come over to your farm tomorrow, so we can seal the deal then." Paul put his phone on his desk and sighed heavily.

"Sounds like he was giving you a hard time?" Jeff, Paul's business partner, commented.

"You have no idea. He won't do any final negotiation over the phone. It all *must* be done face-to-face, as he says. Belligerent, old sod."

"You're sure you hung up. Right?" Jeff said, smiling.

Paul nodded, and as Jeff turned back to face his own desk, Paul glanced swiftly at his phone.

"Made you look," Jeff said, laughing, still with his back to Paul.

"Fuck you," Paul replied in kind.

Paul sat back in his chair, contemplating what the station could be like. He already had great plans for the old place. Of course, it would keep its Victorian charm, but inside, it would be contemporary and clean, but most of all, everything would be bespoke.

From the fitted kitchen and bedrooms, through to the home office he'd started planning for Jill. He was determined to take everything he had learned as an architect and make their forever home their perfect home. All he had to do now was convince the *old git,* as Paul had come to call Mr Bradbury, to sell him it at a price that would allow his grand restoration. And so, the meeting was set, and by this time tomorrow, Paul hoped to be the new owner of Thirstonfield Halt Station, at least in principle. And though this elderly moor farmer was generally a pain in Paul's arse, he knew his type. And once hands were shaken, that was as good as exchanging the contracts. All he had to do now was convince Jill beyond all doubt. And that, he thought, may be just as difficult as dealing with the *old git.*

Jill had not long been back from taking Charlie on his daily field run. Anyone who has owned or owns a Spaniel knows that this particular breed of dog not only likes to run but they like to run the longest distance between any two points, and also the muddiest. It often confounded Jill how Charlie managed to find a muddy puddle in the height of summer when all around was dry and the field they ran in was largely scorched. The grass had long-since lost the lush-green of spring for the yellowing gold the sun turned it during the hottest of summers, and this summer was a hot one. They entered the kitchen, and Charlie made instantly for his water bowl, lapping as much water on the floor as he did into his mouth. Jill shook her head, as she watched her beloved four-legged friend spread a mixture of water and saliva around the kitchen floor. "You are a messy boy." Charlie lifted his head from the bowl and shook, spreading his *Charlie gloop*, as Paul liked to call it, over Jill's clean windows.

As she wiped clear the mess, she heard the Range Rover pull onto the drive, and she checked her watch. "Christ, is that the time?" Though why she asked it aloud, she wasn't sure. First, it obviously was that time, and secondly, Charlie was far too busy cooling himself to be concerned with such trivia as timekeeping.

As Jill entered the hall, Paul came in looking as excited as he had done a few weeks ago when they'd first seen the station.

"You spoke to him then?" Jill asked.

"Who?"

"Mr Bradbury," Jill sneered.

"I have."

Paul's goading of her was becoming tiresome very quickly. It was too hot. "Just tell me what he said. It's too damn hot for your antics. I've been out with Charlie, I'm sweaty and I need a shower before tea."

"I'm seeing him tomorrow."

"What? I thought we'd only agreed to talk about a price. Why are you seeing him?" Jill was a little concerned. She had relented and agreed to go as far as the negotiation. But no further.

"He won't talk over the phone. He said *it's not the way it was done in his day, bloody phones.* So, I have to go to the farm tomorrow morning."

Jill sighed. "Okay, see what he says. Let me know tomorrow."

Paul grinned at her in a cheeky way. "So, you're having a shower?"

Jill returned the smile. "I am. Why? What have you got in mind?"

"Well, I could maybe rub your back, wash those hard to reach parts?"

"Tell you what you could rub," Jill said seductively.

"Go on." Paul began pulling his tie off.

"Well, I'm thinking breasts." Jill leered while she unfastened her blouse.

"I'm listening. What would you like me to do?" Paul walked a little closer.

Jill smirked. "Take the chicken breasts out of the fridge and rub in the garlic butter. Put them in the oven, and I'll be down in a few minutes." She began to laugh while closing her blouse.

"You had me going then. Look." Paul pointed to his groin.

As Jill walked past, she tapped the bulge in his trousers. "Well, you two can have a cold shower after me."

As the summer day came to its end, Jill and Paul sat in their back garden. The dying fire in the chimenea was trying hard to keep the encroaching chill away, while the small lights around the garden kept the darkness at bay. Charlie lay in his bed asleep, and Jill sipped on a glass of white wine. They had moved into this cottage together, it was their first home, and they had both come to love it. The quiet village of Hutton Rudby suited them both. It had the local shop, a village green and, of course, the local pub, or to be more accurate, two local pubs. But after Jill's recovery from cancer, they also both remembered the time when Paul was nursing her and the days she couldn't get out of bed. They had decorated since then and even moved bedrooms, but it still hung over them. And so, though they loved this place, they also needed to move on.

Jill took one last sip to empty her glass. "What time are you meeting him?"

"He said to be there no later than nine-thirty," Paul answered, emptying his own glass.

"What do you think would happen if you were a little late?"

"Oh hell, I reckon I'd get a lecture about how things ran like clockwork in his day, and it's just rude and a sign of the times to be late," Paul chuckled.

"I reckon you're right," Jill replied with an Americanised southern drawl.

"You know it's the North Yorkshire Moors I'm going to and not bloody Texas or wherever that accent is from," Paul sniggered.

"And you wonder why you couldn't join me in the shower. Men." With that, Jill stood and went inside, closely followed by Charlie.

Paul watched the dying embers of the fire and finished his wine before joining Jill in the kitchen. As he locked the door and the night closed in around them, he felt satisfied and full inside. He looked down at Charlie.

"Another day done. See you in the morning."

Charlie lay in his bed, and in the way only dogs seem able to, he instantly fell asleep.

At 9.28 a.m., Paul sat at the top of the long track which led to George Bradbury's farmhouse. He sat watching the time pass on the dash clock. "Half-nine exactly you want, half-nine exactly you'll get," Paul muttered to himself. As the clock hit 9.30 a.m., he slipped the Range Rover's auto gearbox into D and gently drove along the undulating and pothole riddled track. Now he understood why the old git continued to drive his boneshaker of a Land Rover. In that, at least the track wouldn't feel any different. As he pulled up next to the aging Land Rover, George Bradbury opened the farmhouse door and watched Paul as he brought the SUV to a stop and climbed out.

"That's a fancy thing," George said, lifting his green mug and pointing to Paul's Range Rover.

"You think so?" Paul answered, trying not to get pulled into a false modesty trap before he'd even stepped foot in the farmhouse. In secret, however, Paul was very proud of his Range Rover autobiography. When he'd ordered it, he also ordered every conceivable option, along with the supercharged V8 engine.

George took another sip. "Aye, very fancy. Don't suppose it would do well with a few bales of hay in the back, mind. Wouldn't last long doing a day's work either, I reckon. Not around here anyway."

Paul took a deep breath. "You're right. I think that old Land Rover you have is just perfect for you, Mr Bradbury."

George pondered what Paul had said for a second, and then smiled. "Come on in then, let's hear what you've got to say."

George led Paul into the kitchen and pointed to the large table. Paul pulled out a chair and sat. As he did, Mavis entered and sat opposite him.

"This is Mavis, the wife," George said, pointing to the stern looking woman who was half-smiling at Paul. "This is Paul, err, oh, seems I don't know your surname, lad."

"Sullivan, Paul Sullivan. It's a pleasure to meet you, Mavis."

George sat next to his wife, and Paul found himself in some bad dream. Sat at a long table in a dark, old farmhouse that had long seen its best days and staring at two of the most unsociable and surly people he'd met in quite a while. He'd had dealings with farm-folk on numerous occasions, and he thought he'd seen them all, but these two, dear God, if it wasn't for what he'd come for, he'd be happy to just get up and walk away. But as the temptation inside him to do so grew, the image of The Halt shooed it away.

"Okay, Mr and Mrs Bradbury. First, thank you for letting me come here to see you. I've looked at the value of old working buildings from similar eras to the station, and I think I have come up—"

George cut across his well-prepared and rehearsed sales patter. "Just tell us what you think the old place is worth, lad. We've no time to listen to all that claptrap."

Paul took a deep breath. "Two-hundred thousand. Cash," he answered bluntly.

George looked to Mavis. Neither of them spoke, but Paul could see something between them, a look, a gesture, but it was neither a nod nor a shake of the head; it seemed almost a resigned look.

"Okay, lad, but we use my solicitor, David Smith, he's been with us for years. I don't trust any of those fancy city types," George said.

Paul held out his hand. "Okay, I'll be in touch in a few days."

After a few seconds, with his hand still pushed out and no sign of George or Mavis wanting to shake it, Paul pulled it back and stood, expecting that George would follow him to the door. But he didn't, rather, he simply said, "Show yourself out, lad, and be sure to close the door."

Paul did just that and made his way back to the Range Rover. Once inside, he smiled to himself, started the engine and drove off the farm. When he joined the main road, he hit the voice dial. "Jill." A few seconds later, she answered.

"Hello?"

"Hi, hun, it's me," Paul said, excitedly.

"How did it go?"

"We got it." This time, trepidation replacing the excitement in his voice.

"What do you mean, we got it?"

"Okay, okay, I know I said I would call, but listen. I started to give him my sales patter, and I was going to offer two-hundred and fifty-five like we said. But the old sod cut across me, so I thought bugger it, I offered two-hundred, and they took it. I couldn't walk away at that. Even if we don't move in or do a damn thing to it, we could sell it and make fifty-thousand."

A heavy sigh came down the phone. "I suppose. We'll talk about it in detail tonight. What time will you be in?" Jill's mood lightened.

"The usual, around six."

"See you then."

Paul pressed the red *end call* button and headed back to his office.

***

George Bradbury watched as the Range Rover trundled along his farm track and then turned onto the main road. Once it was out of sight, he returned to the kitchen where Mavis was still sat.

"Well, wife, that's that done," he said, as he sat at the table.

"When he signs the papers with Mr Smith, make sure he signs them all. You know what I mean, George?"

"Aye, wife, I do. He'll sign it, don't worry. He's desperate for that place, thinking he could swag it for a pittance. Good riddance is what I say. He could have had it for half what he offered."

"If it means an end to all that trouble, he could have had the old place for even less, husband," Mavis answered.

George picked up his old, green mug. "Is there a brew going?"

* * *

Jill took the homemade Cottage Pie out of the oven and placed it on the side. Charlie watched her intently, as she moved it. From the moment, Jill had opened the raw packet of minced beef and all the way through the cooking process, the smell had sent Charlie's olfactory receptors into a frenzy, and Jill could feel his eyes burning into her back.

"You can have a bit when we do," she said to the drooling dog, who did not move, save for his gaze, which just darted between her and the cooling food on the kitchen counter.

As Jill set out the table, she heard the familiar sound of Paul's Range Rover pull onto the driveway and the thud of the heavy door.

"Hi, I'm home. What's for tea? I'm starving," Paul announced as he entered.

"Hi, hun. Cottage Pie tonight," Jill replied, kissing him on his cheek.

"Bloody lovely," Paul said, sitting at the table.

"So, how did it go with t-farmer?" Jill asked, as they began to eat.

Paul sniggered. "What a strange pair they were. His wife's just like him. Honestly, I thought I'd entered the bloody Twilight Zone."

"But they accepted the offer?"

"Without hesitation," Paul confirmed, putting more Cottage Pie onto his plate.

"Doesn't that seem a little strange to you?"

"Not really. I mean, look. They're farmers who keep themselves to themselves; he even made a comment about my car, trying to get a rise out of me. They don't know how these things work, and besides, we know they need the money, so it's a win-win."

"What did he say about your car?" Jill asked, somewhat perplexed.

"Oh, said it was too fancy, and it wouldn't be up to the job on a farm. I didn't take a lot of notice, to be honest. Once I've sorted things out with his solicitor, I doubt we'll have much to do with them. If anything at all."

Jill stopped eating. "His solicitor?"

"They insisted that I use their solicitor, a David Smith. It's not a big thing."

Charlie shuffled closer to the table, licking his lips.

"Doesn't that strike you as a little odd? What if there's something wrong with the place? They could cover it up."

"I know the practice, Smith and Dawson. They've been in Stokesley for years, and they wouldn't be a party to anything untoward. And besides, I've dealt with them before," Paul answered, trying to reassure Jill. And himself.

"So long as you know what you're doing," Jill said, finishing the meal.

Paul helped her clear the dishes. Charlie's patience was rewarded when Jill scraped the leftovers into his bowl along with his own food. Jill set the dishwasher, and they both retired to the living room, where the summer sun hung a low orange light through the generous bay window, illuminating the room in a soft, warm glow.

"This is my favourite time of the day," Paul said, as he slumped into the larger of the corner sofas.

Jill smiled at him. "Mine too."

"Imagine the station when it's finished on a summer evening like this one," Paul said.

"I thought we'd get to this at some point," Jill replied, quite churlishly.

"What's that tone for?"

"Well, you did buy it without calling me."

Paul's tone became defensive. "But I told you, we stole it from them, and as I said when I *did* call you, we can sell it without doing a thing and make money."

"Well, see how it goes at the solicitor's. Knowing that old sod, he could change his mind again."

"Yes, dear."

Jill glanced sideways at him. She hated that *yes dear* comment. It was so patronising, but it was a perfect, summer's evening. The soft glow still lit the room, and the cross breeze from the open front windows and kitchen door, which the light mesh curtains billowed in, caressed her tenderly, cooling her from the heat of another sweltering day. In fact, it had been such a beautiful day, Jill didn't want to end it in an argument over something she knew would make a gorgeous home, even if it was going to be a huge project, the one thing she'd insisted they wouldn't start. Inside, she smiled to herself. Life was good, and she was very content. If Paul wanted this, if this was to be their forever home, then she would allow him his project.

"When are you seeing the solicitor?" Jill asked.

"This coming Monday," he answered, nervously.

Jill grinned. "Okay then, let's do it."

"Really? You mean you're not thinking of backing out or selling it for a quick profit?"

"I know you better than that. I know that was spin to soften the blow of you buying it. You didn't want to move it on, did you?"

"No, I guess you're right," Paul admitted.

"See, I know better than you think," Jill joked.

"Mm, and you know what I like too," Paul replied, smirking.

Jill laughed. "Don't push it. You're lucky you're not sleeping with Charlie tonight."

Chapter 4

July 1933

It was the last day of school for Jack, and from tomorrow, he would be expected to work and help Doris to run the home. He was too young to join the army, though if he could, he would and escape his father's tyrannical temper. However, Jack's mam had already lined up a job on the railways as an apprentice engineer, and while it wouldn't allow Jack to escape, it would teach him a skill and put money in his pocket and this, at least, would give him some freedom. As the last lesson drew to its close, Jack knew he had one last thing to go through before he would be allowed to leave. Paul Stokes, whom Jack had begun calling *Ninnyhammer*, had promised Jack a beating on the last day, and he'd also promised it would be an appropriately harsh beating, as it was to be his last. Paul Stokes was to leave Middlesbrough tomorrow; he was joining his father in the Merchant Navy, and it would be very unlikely they would see each other again.

Over the last year, Jack had gone through what the doctors told Doris was a very unusual growth spurt. He'd gone from being of average height and size to being over six-foot with the shoulders and muscle mass to match. It didn't surprise the family doctor. His birth weight had been nine pounds and four ounces, though his growth had been slow. Until now. But Jack still hadn't adapted to his new size, and to himself, at least, he was still the same average, and somewhat scrawny, boy he'd looked at every day in the mirror. As the teacher lifted the old bell and rang it, ending the school day and Jack's school life, he stood and made his way toward the gates, ready to receive what was coming. And it didn't take long to arrive.

Jack dropped his school bag and turned to see the Ninnyhammer running toward him. As the first punch landed on Jack's left cheek, he stumbled backward, but this time, he didn't fall, rather, he stepped out from under the punch and remained upright. Another punch came, and again, Jack remained standing. The usual crowd that had gathered were used to seeing Jack collapse under the impact of the first strike, then the Ninnyhammer would sit atop of Jack and humiliate him, but something had changed, and as he squared up to Jack again, Jack became aware of what it was. He was now taller and bigger, much bigger. As the next punch made impact with Jack, he didn't move. The Ninnyhammer's punches had lost their power. He wasn't used to the resistance and had put everything he had into the first two punches. Jack could feel his own fist tighten. He swung it upward, catching the bully of all of his school life by surprise. As Jack's tightly clenched fist hit his adversary's face, the gathered crowd heard a crack. Paul Stokes' eye socket had split with the force levelled by Jack, and this time, it was he that now lay dazed on the floor. Jack straddled the disorientated boy and began raining blows upon him. By the time the sixth or seventh blow landed, the Ninnyhammer was unconscious, and the teachers were dragging Jack from him.

Jack looked down on the boy who had made his school life nothing but a misery and an extension of the despair he felt at home whenever his father was there. Even when he wasn't, Jack's time was spent worrying when he might turn up and what mood he would be in. Paul Stokes lay beaten and bloodied.

On his last day of school, he would leave without fear and knowing he beat him. And for Jack, who was now only beginning to realise what his emerging size meant, he felt another thing waken inside him. It was confidence, something he'd not experienced before. As the Ninnyhammer began to come around, Jack spat on him and walked home.

It was a little after nine when Jack heard the front door to their small street house burst open, and his father staggered in in yet another drunken stupor. He listened from his bedroom as his father once again began scolding Doris.

But after the events of today, Jack felt differently. He wasn't hiding in the corner, waiting to count the footsteps, rather, tonight, he promised himself that he would, for the first time, stand up to his father and protect his mother. Jack stood from his bed and began creeping down the stairs. He could hear the garbled, drunken words become louder, as he got close to the bottom of the tight, steep staircase and the half-glass door which led into the front reception room. Through the frosted glass, he could make out the back of his father's outline. He stood over Doris, who cowered in the wingback chair placed next to the open coal fire. Jack watched, as his father raised his right arm. As he did, Jack burst into the room.

His father twisted around, his arm still raised. Jack clenched his fist and swung it as hard as he had that afternoon, and he caught his father square on the chin. This time, there was no crack, no downing of this tormentor and no quick and easy victory. Jack took a step back. He was in shock; this wasn't how it was supposed to go. Why was his father still standing when the Ninnyhammer had gone down so easily? Jack didn't have time to consider his next move. The reprimand for daring to protect his mother came quick, and before Jack knew what was happening, he was laid on the floor, bloodied and dazed. Jack looked past his father who stood over him, and to his mother who sat perfectly still, frozen with fear and with tears running freely down her cheeks. He looked back to his father, his fists still clenched, the anger in his eyes still burning brightly and Jack knew he'd been beaten, physically and figuratively. He pulled himself back to the staircase, and with one last defeated look to his mother, he crawled up the stairs like a dog castigated from its pack.

From his bedroom, he heard the cries and the blows, and there was nothing he could do to stop them.

***

51

Paul pulled into a parking spot on the high street in Stokesley's market square, across from the offices of Smith & Dawson: the solicitors George had insisted they use to complete the sale. The old building hadn't changed in the four-hundred years it had stood. He exited the Range Rover and made his way into the small reception area. He mused to himself how it hadn't changed on the inside either. The old, wooden floor and chairs had likely been here when old man Smith had started the practice long before the current Smith had taken over and brought on-board his partner, Cyril Dawson.

The reception desk still had the original phone system, and Paul found himself wondering how the analogue apparatus that still sat proudly on the desk could work with the digital exchanges everywhere now used. There was also a clear absence of any kind of PC. *'Perhaps it was in the back room somewhere,'* he thought to himself. The receptionist, who Paul chuckled to himself, must be as old as the building, probably insisted that the infernal machine was kept away from her, as she wanted nothing to do with such new-fangled things. His thoughts drifted to wondering what type of computer it might be and if it used Binary or Basic. He was convinced it would be nothing as modern as a Windows machine.

The receptionist interrupted his thoughts. "Mr Smith will see you now, Mr Sullivan."

Paul stood and made his way along the dark corridor to the first office on the right. On the frosted glass was proudly displayed, in gold lettering with a dark-green border: Mr D Smith. Paul knocked and waited to be invited in.

"Enter," came the surly voice from behind the glass door.

Paul walked into the office and smiled politely at Mr Smith, who was sat behind a rather imposing dark wood table. Around him were what seemed like decades of paper files and the fake wood-effect cardboard boxes that once seemed to be the staple of the office. Paul sat and noticed that as with the reception, there was an obvious lack of any form of modern office equipment.

There was no PC or even a laptop, and the phone on his desk was the smaller brother of the exchange he had wondered about while waiting to be called in. Mr Smith leaned forward, and his large, ox-red leather chair groaned as he did. Paul watched, as he opened one of the files on his desk and began to shuffle through the papers.

"So, you've bought the old station?" Mr Smith asked, not looking away from the file.

"I have."

"And you're paying cash, so there's no mortgage. Is that correct?" Mr Smith asked, this time looking at Paul over the top of his thin-rimmed, round glasses.

"Yes, two for two," Paul answered, trying to lighten the mood. But he failed.

Mr Smith grimaced at Paul. "Well, then, there's just these to sign today. Once the bank transfer has gone through, Mr Bradbury will release the deeds. Once I have them, I'll call you, then it's all yours."

He handed Paul a small pile of papers which were neatly stacked and had little, coloured sticky notes on them, indicating where he should sign. Paul signed through them hastily. He was used to what he was seeing and understood the process completely. He turned over the last piece of paper and stopped. He hadn't seen this kind of contract before.

"What's this for?" Paul asked, as he pushed the contract back to Mr Smith.

"It's a simple waiver to say the sale is final, and no matter what you may encounter when you begin work or move in, my client is in no way responsible."

"What I may encounter? Just what are you expecting I may encounter, Mr Smith?" Paul asked.

Mr Smith shrugged. "Mr Bradbury was insistent you sign this, and without signing it, he won't sell you the property."

"What does he know? Is there subsidence, something wrong with the land or the building?"

"No, in fact, Mr Bradbury had a rather extensive survey completed only a few months before you showed interest. I have it here, and you are welcome to have a copy."

Paul became more confused. "So, there is nothing wrong with the building? Nothing wrong with the surrounding land? And there's no indication that Tesco are going to build a supermarket within spitting distance? Yet, he still wants a waiver signed in case I encounter something?"

"Yes, that's about the size of it," Mr Smith replied.

"Well, if that's what it takes to keep the old man happy." Paul snatched the waiver back and signed his name. After he'd handed it back, he pulled out his phone and transferred the agreed amount of money to the bank account of Smith & Dawson. "If you check your account, you'll see I've transferred the two-hundred thousand."

"My secretary will call into the bank later today when she's cashed up, and I'll call you then."

"Just check online now. You do have a computer? Internet access?" Paul was becoming impatient and agitated.

"Yes, Mr Sullivan. We do have a computer, it's in the back office, but I'm told it can't connect to the internet, something to do with compatibility. To be honest, I don't think it's been switched on for quite a while now."

"How the hell do you do business?" Paul snapped.

"As we always have done, Mr Sullivan, and that's how we always will do. Now, if you'll excuse me, I have another meeting." Mr Smith stood and held out the flat of his hand, which Paul knew wasn't an attempt at a handshake, but rather, a five-finger point to the door and the exit.

"I'll wait for your call then," Paul answered, as he left the office.

***

Mr Smith waited until he heard Paul leave the building. The small bell that had been attached to the main entrance door since he'd been an office junior under his father rang the all clear.

He sat back behind his desk and picked up the discoloured phone, which had once been a fashionable cream but was now more of an off-yellow.

"George?" Mr Smith asked when he heard the phone he'd called being answered.

"Aye, is that David?"

"It is, George. Paul Sullivan has just left."

"Did he sign everything?" George asked him.

"He did, including the waiver," David Smith confirmed.

"That's grand. When is he to pay for the place?"

"Says he has. He pulled his mobile telephone out and did it in my office."

"I'll bring the deeds over tomorrow, David. The quicker he 'as 'em, the quicker I'll be shot of it all."

"I'll see you tomorrow, George. Pass my best on to Mavis." David Smith hung up and put the forms Paul had signed back into their folder and then into the fake, wooden box.

***

In the old farmhouse, George put down the receiver and picked up his green mug. Smiling, he turned toward the living room and entered where he found Mavis sat watching their old Ferguson TV set. "Well?" she said without lifting her gaze from the screen. "Did he sign it?"

"Aye, wife, he did," George answered before sipping from the tin mug.

"So, that's it then. We're free of it?" Mavis said, only now turning toward George.

"We are, wife. We are."

"And what of his bunkhouse in the barn?" Mavis asked.

George pondered her question. "Best leave it be."

***

The *waiver,* as David Smith had called it, troubled Paul as he returned to his office. *'What an odd document,'* he thought to himself. In the years he had dealt with solicitors over properties, he'd never come across such a thing. It wasn't so much the way in which Mr Smith seemed to have placed it at the bottom of the pile, perhaps hoping that Paul would just sign it without thinking, it was more the wording. And the more he thought about it during the twenty-minute drive, the more it confused him. One sentence in particular stuck in his mind.

The previous owners, Mr and Mrs George Bradbury, will not be responsible for any unforeseen acts of disturbance, violence or disruption. Whether they be manmade, natural causes or otherwise.

First, Paul couldn't understand why it particularly listed disturbance, violence and disruption, and secondly, what precisely did *or otherwise* mean? Other than what? What could there be other than manmade or natural causes? God? Perhaps. He pondered this sentence until he reached his office whereon he decided that he would pay it no more mind. It was nothing more than that daft old git being kitschy. He had also reached another decision, and that was not to tell Jill. After all, she was the spiritual one, and anything like that spooked her. It occurred to Paul that if he went home and told her about it, she would immediately pull the plug on his dreams, and he'd put up with too much shit from the old git for that. No, it was for Jill's own good, more than for himself that this would remain a secret.

As Paul entered his office, the familiar face of Jeff met him. "All done?" Jeff asked.

"Christ, give me a chance to get in the door."

"Well, you're in now, so," Jeff pushed the question.

"Yes, all signed and paid for. Thirstonfield Halt Station is now all mine. Well, ours."

"You're lucky, sods," Jeff chuckled.

"We will be when it's finished. I have so many ideas on what to do with the old place." Paul became more excited.

"And a large bank balance too," Jeff laughed.

"Well, we will when we sell the cottage. Jill is seeing to that today, and then we need to find somewhere to rent in Thirstonfield while the work is completed."

"When will you be on?" Jeff asked.

"On what?" Paul replied, puzzled by such an ambiguous question.

"You know, *Grand Designs*, with whats-his-face, Kevin something," Jeff chuckled.

"Yeah, yeah. Sod off, you're just jealous," Paul sniggered back.

"Well, I hope it all works out for you. You both deserve it after Jill's cancer." Jeff became serious.

Paul nodded to him. "Thanks, mate."

***

Jill hated having people in their home. She hated having repairmen in, she hated having decorators in, in fact, anyone of any trade. It wasn't because she was afraid, or that she was inimical in any way, in fact, she was very much the opposite. It was just that she always found she couldn't relax and do her normal day stuff. She always believed as if she needed to be just as busy as they were, or she felt lazy and guilty at the thought of someone working hard in her home while she wasn't. And it was the same now while the real estate agent poked around their lovely home, being nosy, and in Jill's mind, judging their choice of decoration and taste. Jill hated that everywhere should be *neutral and contemporary,* which was just a posh way of saying modern. Their home wasn't either of these things. Neither of them liked the neutral look; they found it cold and hotel-like. They wanted their home to be decorated to their own tastes. It was, in fact, very traditional, or old, and that suited them fine. The cottage itself was around four-hundred years old, though no one was sure when it had been built and modified. All they did know was that during its life it had been an inn, a village shop and even a small school. Jill watched as the snooty lady, as Jill had decided she was, continued to poke around and write notes. After the snooty lady had taken measurements and photos on her iPhone, another thing Jill hated, the way people flocked to things because it's the thing to be seen with or in, rather than on the merit of it, she closed her folder and grinned her snooty smile at Jill.

"What do you think?" Jill asked.

"I would market this property around four-hundred and sixty-five thousand, perhaps four-hundred and forty-five, for a quick sale," the snooty lady replied.

"You know one has just gone for more than that? Same house as this, almost, and it went for closer to five-hundred. I'm sure they bought it from your office. John and Samantha Andrews. They have a little boy, Mickey, I think he's called. Do you know them?"

"I can't discuss other sales. Would you like me to offer it for sale?"

"Well, yes, we need to sell. Put it on for four sixty-five. See what interest you get. We can always come down, I guess," Jill replied. All she wanted now was to have her home back. They'd bought The Halt, as her and Paul now called it, for fifty-thousand less than they had budgeted, so, if they got around four-fifty for the cottage, they'd still be *quid's in*, as Paul often said when he was sounding like a used car salesman.

"I'll arrange it as soon as I'm back in the office."

Jill watched as the snooty lady headed along their garden path and climbed into a convertible Audi A3. "Figures," Jill said to herself, as she closed the door. As she turned, Charlie sat waiting for her. Like Jill, he too had watched this intruder from his bed, which, as always, was by the radiator in the kitchen, and like Jill, he hadn't liked her. But now, she had gone, and it was just him and his master. This strange looking figure which fed him, walked him and most bizarrely, to Charlie anyway, picked up after him when he'd marked his territory.

"She's gone, yes, she has," Jill said to Charlie, in her best *dog-fuss* voice.

Charlie wagged his tail eagerly and headed for the garden.

After all, now that the other strange looking thing had gone, he had to protect his masters from anything else that dare to pass by the gate or overhead. And that included those noisy things in the sky which left their white trails behind them.

As Jill entered the kitchen, the phone rang. "Hello?"

"Hi, darling." It was Paul. "It's all done. I've signed the papers, and we should exchange contracts within the four weeks."

"I can't imagine it would be that straightforward, what with the way he's been up to now," Jill replied.

Paul thought for a second, he thought about the waiver, and then decided that his original plan not tell Jill was still the best one. "No, everything was straightforward, no surprises." He hesitated and then continued. "Have they been to value the cottage yet?"

"Yes. She's just gone. Didn't like her, too much bling, with her designer phone and fashion accessory of a car," Jill scorned.

"Just because you don't like people in our house," Paul laughed. "What did she say about the price?"

"I said to put it on at four sixty-five."

"The old rectory just went for five-hundred, and ours isn't that much different. Did you mention it to her?"

"Yes, Paul, I did, and she said," Jill did her best impression of the snooty woman, "'I can't discuss details about other sales'."

Paul chuckled. "You really didn't like her, did you?"

"No, I didn't."

"We better get looking for somewhere to rent in Thirstonfield." Paul changed the subject.

"Shouldn't we hold off and sell this place first?" Jill asked.

"No, we can afford the rent if we just get somewhere small. Besides, we should be closer to The Halt when work starts."

"You mean I should be closer?" Jill confirmed.

"It was the royal we, darling," Paul sniggered.

"As it usually is, darling," Jill teased him back.

"Okay, gotta go. I'll go online later, see what's for rent."

"Okie dokie, see you when you get home. Love you," Jill replied, before hanging up.

Paul put down the receiver of his desk phone and leaned back in his chair. *'Another step closer to The Halt,'* he thought to himself.

Jill pulled the summer casserole from the oven and placed a generous pan of new potatoes on the gas hobs. By the time Paul arrived home, they would be lovely and soft, just how he liked them. As usual, Jill's biggest fan, Charlie sat motionless while she cooked, and only his eyes moved as they darted between the pot of *fantastic smelling stuff* and the kitchen counter where his master was doing something he couldn't see but smelt just as wonderful. Almost to the minute, Jill once again heard the Range Rover pull onto their driveway, followed by the closing of its door, and then the opening and closing of the cottage's door. Jill smiled, as he entered the kitchen, and again, he kissed her on her cheek, smelt the food, commented on how hungry he was and how great it all looked and smelt, and then fussed Charlie, who, as usual, fussed Paul while keeping one keen eye on the *fantastic smelling stuff.*

By the time eight o'clock had come around, they had eaten, changed, cleaned the kitchen and the dishwasher was running while they relaxed in the cosy conservatory which overlooked their country garden. And as always, Charlie lay asleep, full and content. This had been their routine since they had moved into this cottage, and it was one they were happy with. For Paul, he saw no reason why this shouldn't continue when The Halt was finished, and they'd moved in, but Jill had her reservations. The Halt was much bigger, and the cosy, warm feeling she often experienced in their modest home would be lost in the sprawling rooms and spaces of The Halt. After all, at its peak, the station could handle around forty-five passengers and their assorted luggage. Once they move in and opened it up, there would be only herself, Paul, and Charlie, of course, but he didn't take too much room. Jill looked around as the sun began setting below the large trees which grew at the end of their garden, and she thought to herself that she was lucky to have lived in such a beautiful place as this.

She saddened a little, as she remembered her battle with cancer, and in her mind's eye, she could see Paul bringing her his magic homemade soup while she recovered in the seat in which she now sat. The cancer had taken more from her than it could in mere medical terms. It had not only invaded her body but her home too. The place where she felt entitled to be safe, secure and without worry. She looked across to Paul, who was engrossed with his iPad, and her smile returned.

She had agreed to The Halt because it was what he wanted, and it was what they needed. A fresh start and a challenge to leave behind the ghosts of Paul bringing her soup, and of Charlie howling for his master while she lay ill in bed. Maybe the new custodians of this quaint little cottage in this quaint little village could live as they had once dreamed of doing. And perhaps when The Halt was finished, and they moved in and became its new custodians, they too could, at long last, have the peace and tranquillity they once sought here.

Jill placed her cup down and moved over to the couch Paul was sat on. She took hold of the iPad and placed it on the low coffee table.

"Hey, I was looking at that," he said.

She sat across from him. Leaning forward, she kissed him gently. Paul responded, and she sensed his hands on her sides. She leant back and smiled at him. "Wow," he said. "That was nice." Jill slid down him and kneeled in-between his legs. As she unfastened his trousers, she tossed her hair back.

***

"Morning," Jill said, as Paul entered the kitchen.

"What got into you last night?" he said, smiling like a smug cat.

"Other than you?" Jill replied. "Oh, you know, just wanted to show you how much I love you."

"I think you showed the neighbours too. First time we've done it in the conservatory. What would Mrs Beatty say next door?" Paul sniggered.

"Well, give the old woman something to talk about. Besides, I bet she's done worse."

Paul drank his coffee. "Actually, I think it was poor Charlie who got the biggest fright."

"Charlie won't say anything." Jill tossed a scrap of bacon toward the waiting dog. "Will you, boy? No, you won't."

"I'll see you tonight for more of the same?" Paul said in a hopeful tone.

"What, you want a summer casserole again?" Jill answered, teasing him.

"You know what I mean."

"Go and make lots of money so we can pay for this grand design of yours." Jill smacked him on his backside, as she frogmarched him out of the cottage.

Paul waved at Jill, as he backed the Range Rover out of their driveway and onto the small, narrow lane which separated the row of cottages from the road which ran through the centre of the village.

Jill waved, and then after looking around, she quickly opened her dressing gown, allowing Paul to see her in her short, black nightshirt. He flashed the car's headlamps and blew a kiss toward her.

She smiled back at him, fastened her gown and went back inside. As she locked the door, she could hear the Range Rover pull out onto the road. She entered the kitchen where Charlie was sat waiting for her. "We'll go for a walk soon, Charlie." Charlie wagged his tail enthusiastically; that was one of his buzz words and one on a very concise list that would bring him around from a deep slumber to full consciousness almost instantly.

Jill did what her normal daytime routine demanded. After clearing the breakfast pots and stacking the dishwasher, she vacuumed and dusted, set the washing machine for the next pile of never-ending laundry, and then showered and dressed. Next, she would take Charlie for his run around before settling in her study with a coffee where she would begin writing her blog and answering questions and emails from her website. If she had time, later in the day, she would treat herself to an hour on the sofa with a cup of tea and a piece of cake before the chore of starting the evening meal. And as she had no need to go food shopping, and she had no errands to run, Jill fancied that today could be a cake day.

***

When Paul arrived at the office, he noticed a large, brown envelope on his desk. After slipping off his jacket and grabbing a coffee, he sat and pulled it open. Tipping its contents out onto his desk, he sniggered to himself when he realised what it was. Before him were the deeds to The Halt and a copy of the paperwork he'd signed. And though this seemed to have happened unusually quickly, he was glad all the red-tape had been completed. Now he could get on with the project, or at least make a start on it. Without the sale of their cottage in Hutton Rudby, they could only afford to clear the site and prepare for the restoration. Still, he thought to himself, the sale shouldn't take too long. As he began to bundle up the paperwork, to place it back in the envelope, which was held closed with a brass eye and string, typical of something from the old solicitor, he kept the waiver he'd signed to one side. Sticking to his decision of keeping this from Jill, he slipped that particular piece of paper into the top right drawer of his desk where he had decided it was to stay.

Paul pulled the refastened envelope close to his nose and sniffed. "Fuck, it even smells like the old place," he whispered to himself.

***

By the time Jill had completed her to-do-list, it was closing in on three-thirty, and if she had any chance of having some cake time, it would need to be now. Charlie, who was still asleep following his exercise, snored softly in the kitchen and Jill had taken up her relaxing position on the generous corner couch in the living room. She picked up the TV remote and pressed the button. The wall-mounted flat screen came to life, and as if it was just meant to be, her favourite daytime TV show was beginning. She picked up her coffee and took a sip. "Just perfect," she said to herself before taking the first bite of her cake.

She placed the small plate which held what was left of the cake and a large pile of crumbs on a small table and sat back, determined to savour it and not just shovel it in the same way Charlie attacks his food. As Jill got herself as comfortable as she had been for a long time, her phone rang. "Oh, Christ, who the hell can that be?" she said, exasperated.

"Hello," came the voice, and Jill recognised it immediately. It was the snooty woman.

"Hello," Jill replied in kind.

"Is this Ms Goodwin?"

"Yes, this is Miss Goodwin."

"Oh, hello, Miss Goodwin, I hope I'm not disturbing you." Jill looked to the TV and then her cake before the snooty woman continued. "I have someone interested in your cottage, but they can only see it today. Would it be okay to come around in say, thirty minutes?"

Jill took a deep breath. Of course, she'd say yes, how could she not? But boy, she truly didn't want to do this today. All she wanted to do before Paul came home was enjoy her TV, coffee and cake. Jill simultaneously shook her head and smiled. "Yes, that's fine, of course, it's perfect timing. I'm home and available."

"Oh excellent, we'll see you soon." The snooty woman's voice became more excited and higher in pitch.

Jill put the phone down and looked back to the kitchen. Disturbed by the phone call, Charlie had come into the room to investigate. Once inside, however, any thoughts of protecting his master had been banished by the smell and sight of the half-eaten cake. Jill looked at him and placed the plate on the floor. "Go on, you may as well enjoy it," Jill said. Charlie had no thoughts of savouring it, and in two bites, it was gone. Jill picked up the plate and her cup and walked to the kitchen. After she had pushed them into the dishwasher, she wiped the worktops again and emptied the small swing bin. Almost to the second, and thirty minutes after she had called, the snooty woman pulled up outside with a second car behind her. Jill guessed these were the prospective buyers. She watched as the young couple climbed out of their BMW X3. Jill didn't know too much about cars, and to be fair, she wasn't that interested, but she recognised what it was because she and Paul had considered one for her, though she turned away from the idea after being tailgated by one which had been driven by a particularly aggressive woman. *"If these types of people are buying this type of car, I'm not,"* she remembered telling Paul. Before she had chance to snatch back from remembering that incident, there was a knock on the door, and putting on the best honest smile she could, Jill answered it.

***

As 4.45 p.m. came around, Paul was at his desk signing off on his latest project. It had taken three years to go from the initial meeting with his clients to having the plans approved by the belligerent local planning office. But finally, Mr and Mrs Sayers could now build their dream home on the land they'd bought four years previously. As he closed the file, his phone rang. He recognised the ringtone as Jill's.

"Hi, darling," he answered.

"Hi, guess what I've done?" Jill sounded excited.

"I couldn't possibly."

"Well, I've only gone and sold our cottage."

"What? Honestly, so suddenly?"

"Yup. They called this afternoon, came around and made an offer while they were still here."

"How much?" Paul asked, his fingers crossed tightly.

"Four sixty-five, on the nose. Their property was flooded and declared dangerous, and the insurance has paid out. So, they're cash buyers, and there's no chain," Jill said.

"That's great. Looks like after our fight with cancer, our luck is beginning to change. Things will only get better from now on, Jill. That much I promise," Paul said, tears filling his eyes.

"I hope so, hun. I'm off to do tea, see you when you get in," Jill said before hanging up.

Paul sat back in his chair and smiled to himself. Jill's battle with cancer had been a tough time for them both, and though the prognosis had always been good for a full recovery, the road to it had proved to be difficult and testing. He now perceived a sense of calm. It seemed to him their universe was aligning again. They had secured The Halt for far less than they had hoped, the sale had gone quickly and now they held the deeds. And to top it off, their cottage was sold. Everything was in place for their fresh start. Turning back to his PC, he began to look for rental properties within the village of Thirstonfield.

Chapter 5

August 1936

It was Jack's 17th birthday and his mother, Doris, had, as always, laid on a celebration tea for Jack and his friends, who were becoming fewer with every passing year. Most had moved away when they had left school. Joining the Merchant Navy had taken most of them, and a few more had travelled south seeking better employment chances. Of all his friends from school, only three had remained in the North East, two worked on the railways with Jack and the third had found work in the steel foundry with his father.

The mood across Britain had become darker over the last few months as the build-up of Germany's forces, under its leader, Adolf Hitler, continued. Jack listened to the older men at the railway yard, some of whom had fought in the last war, The Great War, and they were convinced beyond doubt that Germany would not start another war, not so soon after being beaten the last time. But the younger men, who, by comparison to Jack, were older than him, but who had missed the last war, were not only convinced war was again coming, but it seemed to Jack at least, were actually wanting it. They felt they'd missed out the last time around, and they wanted their turn at beating The Hun.

Jack's three friends, who gathered around the small table while Doris lit the candles on the cake, were split. His railway co-workers wanted a war, while his oldest friend, Tommy, wanted nothing to do with the notion of it. Jack took in a deep breath and blew out the three old candles which he'd used every year since his 11th birthday. But, as always, Jack had more pressing matters. While his father allowed this *celebration of a bastard,* as he called it, he had always insisted it was over and that all traces were gone by the time he came home from the pub. Jack thanked his friends for coming and watched as they meandered along the street, joking and laughing with each other. He wished every time he blew out the candles that he had a life like theirs, that he hadn't had to listen to and witness his mother's beatings at the hands of his drunken father, and he wished he himself hadn't had to suffer them too.

As the boys rounded the corner and disappeared, Jack went back into the modest street house and closed the door. Inside, Doris was, as usual, clearing away and preparing his father's supper. He watched this sad woman as she seemed to move without thought, without consciousness, and it seemed to Jack that the older he'd become, and the more aware he became, that she was, in fact, living every day on autopilot.

Jack felt sorry for this woman. He had no idea why his dad seemed to hate them both so much. He was aware of his dad's accident, but neither of them was to blame for his misfortune. He sighed and began to help his mother clear the last of the dishes away and dreamt that one day, they would find peace.

The night passed without incident after his father returned home. As he always did, Jack stayed awake until his return, and then, while trembling inside as his adrenaline coursed through his body and his heartbeat in the back of his throat, he listened for the shouting and hitting and for the cries of his mother. But none came that night.

After his father had stumbled in through the door in his usual drunken stupor, he had, for the most part, been quite decorous, and had soon fallen into a deep and snore-filled sleep. The following morning, Jack and Doris left the house to head for the railway station where Doris would work in the canteen and Jack would continue with his apprenticeship. Doris had kept a close eye on the events that were building in Germany. She knew that, should war come again, Jack would be called up, but if he'd finished his apprenticeship before then, he would be safe from conscription.

The railways, as with the previous war, were seen as being essential to the war effort, and the men and women who ran them were every-bit as important as any serving soldier, pilot or seaman. Jack only had eighteen-months left, and then he would be safe, should the world go to war once again. Doris prayed every time she turned on the BBC World Service that another day would pass without war.

Jack was working on an old *shunter* locomotive in one of the many workshops which were scattered around the yard. The last couple of days had been, by Jack's standard, good days. He'd begun talking to Molly, a somewhat shy girl of similar age who worked with Doris, and while Jack hadn't had a girlfriend before, even he knew things were developing between them. Even so, he hadn't yet gathered the nerve to *call upon her* and ask her to the Friday night dance. Molly was a small girl in stature, and quite slim with blonde hair and brown eyes. As with Jack, her mother worked on the railways, but unlike Jack, her father worked in the nearby steel foundry and was not a habitual drunk. After the celebrations of his birthday and the calm night his father had given both Doris and himself by falling asleep by the fire, Jack felt quite happy. It was a feeling that was not strange to him, rather, it was an infrequent visitor, and one Jack wished he could meet more regularly. He would often look around at the people who passed him by or rode on the tram with him and wonder how their lives were being played out. Did they too have dark secrets which must be kept hidden? Did they carry invisible crosses of their own which could not, and must not, be seen by anybody else, and yet burdened them with the same weight as Jack's own invisible cross? Perhaps this was a punishment for a past sin. One which was so odious he must suffer not only in this life, but it would also follow him after death. The thought of this, along with the reality of his home life, sometimes left Jack feeling that he was trapped and that no matter what his penance may be, in this life, or the next, it was carrying some kind of burden, he may never rid himself of it. And if this was to be the case, why bother to pay the penance at all.

His thoughts came back from the darker places of his mind. Tonight, he'd arranged for Molly to meet him by the main engine shed when their shifts had finished. There, after gathering the courage, he would ask Molly to the dance, and if she said yes, then nothing, including his father's temper, would spoil his week. As the day, which had dragged like no other he could remember, eventually came to an end and the sun was beginning to sink, Jack cleaned himself from under the layers of engine oil and soot, changed his clothes and made his way to the agreed meeting point. Though the sun had started its descent and the air was beginning to cool, Jack felt a spring in his step and a smile which spread across his face. If things went well with Molly, then perhaps, just maybe, they could begin courting, become engaged and marry. And then he could move himself and his mother out of that house and leave his father to what was left of his drunken, miserable and angry life.

Jack arrived a few minutes early, but to him, that didn't matter. Before his father had had his accident, he'd once told Jack that when it came time to meet the *ladies,* he should always arrive before they did, and never, ever after. Jack stood holding the modest bunch of flowers, checking the time on the grand clock which hung over the engine shed. When he heard the footsteps behind him, he spun around, excited and expecting to see Molly. But it wasn't Molly who stood before him, it was Paul Stokes, the Ninnyhammer from school Jack had beaten a few years earlier. As Jack cleared his mind of confusion, he realised that Paul Stokes wasn't alone. Jack backed away, clutching the flowers, but Paul and his two friends approached him, and Jack knew he had only one option. He placed the flowers down and removed the jacket Doris had cleaned for his special meeting with Molly. The first of the Ninnyhammer's friends rushed him. He was shorter than Jack but still broad and heavily built. Jack swung out at this milk-jug of a man, catching him on his jaw and sending him sideways and off balance.

Jack turned to face the next aggressor, but they were too quick. The blows came hard and fast, and Jack couldn't block or deflect them all. With his nose blooded and his clothes torn, he found himself laying on the floor. The Ninnyhammer picked up the flowers and began pulling them apart, and Jack could do nothing but watch him. The larger of his two associates then whispered something to him, and a smile as evil as Jack had seen spread across the Ninnyhammer's face. The three of them approached Jack, and while the two abettors held Jack down, the Ninnyhammer pulled off Jacks trousers and underpants. When he stood and moved away from him, leaving Jack spread-eagled on the floor, Jack caught sight of Molly, who had arrived in time to see Jack's humiliation. The Ninnyhammer threw Jack's trousers at Molly while he and his two accomplices walked away laughing.

Molly stood rigid, tears in her eyes, and for a brief moment, terrified as the three men walked toward her. Once they had passed, but not before making obscene suggestions to her, which were loud enough for Jack to hear, she picked up Jack's clothes and moved toward him. Jack was still on the floor. He was battered and bruised, but worse than the physical injuries, which he was used to, he had been degraded. Molly was the first girl who had ever shown an interest in him, and she had seen him like this. Crumpled on the floor, naked from the waist down, she had seen his most private and intimate area, and he felt a shame he didn't believe was possible. Jack drew his feet up and cupped his hands over his groin. She moved a little closer, but Jack turned his back toward her and shouted that she should leave. Molly dropped his clothes and ran from the yard in tears. As Jack pulled on his trousers and picked up the shredded flowers, he swore to whoever might be listening that he would never again allow himself to be so vulnerable.

Over the days and weeks which followed, Jack replayed that afternoon in his mind, looping it around like a reel of film, and the more it went around, the more malevolent and distorted it became until Jack's manhood was no bigger than that of an infant child, and Molly herself stood with the Ninnyhammer while they pointed and laughed at his tiny, flaccid appendage. Eventually, the rage which built inside him, as the movie reel continued playing, became too much for Jack to contain.

***

Jill took one last look at the cottage they had called home before she followed Paul and the removal truck to their new, albeit temporary, home in Thirstonfield Village. The sale had proceeded with only a few minor niggles, one of which was a small argument over the holes which had been left in the wall above the original fireplace, where Paul had insisted the flat screen TV *just had to be mounted.* Jill reminded him that she foresaw the day when hanging the bloody thing there would bite them in the ass, and she also took delight in proving herself right. Again. The compromise was to leave the bracket fastened to the wall, allowing the new owners to hang their TV in the same place. For Jill, this was the best outcome because she was damned sure it wouldn't take pride of place in their new home, no matter how high the definition was on the oversized, over-priced and far-too-big piece of *man crap*, as she called it, was. TV-Gate aside, the sale was mostly cordial and easy. She turned to Charlie who sat next to her, wagging his tail in eager anticipation of where this journey would take him.

"C'mon, Charlie, let's start our new adventure," Jill said as she pulled away.

For now, their new home was a delightful three-bedroom end-terrace cottage, located in the centre of Thirstonfield Village. Paul had secured a twelve-month lease from Thirstonfield Estate, which was the manor house the village had originally grown up around to service the ever-increasing agricultural needs of the area. The estate had been in the same family since the late 18th century. Though most of the land had been sold off over the years to private farmers, the Bradbury's being one such family, the Thirstonfield Estate, or *Thirste,* as the locals referred to it, still held influence in the village and owned fifteen properties it leased out on short-term agreements.

Today was the big day, the day when the restoration of The Halt began in earnest. The plans had been approved, and the materials for the initial phase sourced and delivered. Paul and Jill were to meet with their project manager, John Watts, in an hour, and their excitement at beginning the real work of transforming the dilapidated station into a home fit for the 21st century was washing over them both in equal quantities. The plans were sympathetic not only to the original Victorian design but also to the heritage of the station. The station clock had been removed and was away at a restorer. Jill was adamant that the clock not only used its original movements, but it looked in place too, and for her, that meant a slight patina look and not the out-of-the-box look Paul had wanted. She was pleased when the restorer and John Watts had agreed with her.

Other sympathetic alterations included the adjacent engine shed which was by any standard rather considerable in size and had posed a particular quandary and a few arguments during the design stage. Paul, as he would, wanted them converting to become the perfect man-cave, housing his yet to be bought classic car collection and a bar as well as a four-lane bowling alley. Jill, however, saw it as accommodation, an annex allowing friends and family to come and stay when, and for as long as they wanted. In the end, it was decided the shed was big enough to meet with both their way of thinking, though Paul lost his bowling lanes and his classic car collection was cut to two cars. A Datsun 240z Samurai and a Triumph Stag. The shed itself would look much the same on the outside as it had when it had been in use.

The clever design incorporated the accommodation inside the shed, with the two classic cars being in a fictitious setting, making it look as though they were parked at the side of an imaginary road and the bar Paul managed to keep would be behind a façade, much as you would see in an indoor heritage museum, where old-fashioned streets and buildings were accurately recreated. But this would be phase two and wouldn't begin until phase one, The Halt, was all-but finished and habitable. And that still seemed a long time away.

The track which led from the road to The Halt, which they had first stumbled along over a year ago now, had been cleared, and on the whole, resurfaced to allow the various trucks, diggers and, eventually, a large crane to drive along without the risk of becoming stuck. As Paul and Jill pulled up in what was once the car park, John came over towards them smiling.

"That's a good start," Paul said to Jill, switching the engine off and unbuckling his seatbelt.

"What is?" Jill asked.

"He's smiling. That's good, isn't it?"

Jill followed Paul out of their SUV and met John who was standing at the front.

"We broke ground today. Just waiting for the heavy machinery to arrive," Jill heard John explaining to Paul, as she joined them. As she did, John turned to her. "Morning, Jill, how's you?"

"Fine, excited and nervous," Jill replied, smiling.

"'Tis always a nervous time starting a project like this. Never know what we'll find till we get cracking," John said, smiling back at her. "I did find this, though," he continued, as he pulled the crucifix from his pocket that Jill had stumbled upon when they'd originally found The Halt.

"I'd forgotten about that," Jill said excitedly, as she took it from him.

"Aye, looks silver to me, and it'll look grand cleaned up, I reckon."

"It will, I can hang it somewhere." Jill rubbed the silver cross, but the dark tarnish wasn't coming away.

"It'll need a silversmith. There'll be one around somewhere," John said before turning back to Paul.

Jill walked away from Paul and John while she continued to look at the tarnished crucifix she held in her hands. As she turned it over, she noticed a partial handprint on it. It was a large hand, and she assumed by the size of it that it must have been a man's hand, but even so, it was still big. Larger than any Jill had seen. She pushed the crucifix into her pocket and paid it no further thought, as she looked across to the rear of

The Halt from the car park. She wished to herself that their bad luck was coming to the end of its run. She was sure from here on, the universe would be kind to them.

A scream, a shout of pain and of help startled her. Jill spun around, trying to pinpoint where it came from. It came again. The engine shed. Jill could see workers running over to the workshop, John, and Paul in pursuit. Jill, too, began to run over. "Call a fucking ambulance," she heard, as she approached.

As she reached the door and pushed through the small crowd of workers who had gathered, she was met with the sight of a young man lying in an old inspection pit and in a pool of his own blood. She climbed down the concrete steps and knelt beside him. He was half conscious, dazed and in obvious distress. On his left side, under his lower rib, a handle protruded from his thoracic area. Jill's knowledge of anatomy told her he'd punctured his lung and very likely perforated his spleen as well. Moving closer, Jill whispered, "Don't worry, you'll be fine, just take it easy."

**

Darren Pratt was working to impress his new boss. He'd been given an apprenticeship, and his first involvement with the building firm was the renovation of an old station. His work-mates, mostly made up of older, balding men with broad backs and stomachs to match, had told him his main duty on this job would be *S.F.T.* He'd bitten and asked what *S.F.T.* stood for, and they'd all delighted in explaining it meant *Sweeping and Fuckin' Tea making*. Darren wasn't bothered. His dad had been a builder, and his dad before him back in the boom days when you could walk out of one job and into another without crossing the road. But things were much harder now. Cheap labour had decimated the chances of working for the mass-production building firms who pushed up modern homes as if they were pre-fab. His best chance had come with the prospect of working for a local company who specialised in renovation projects and wanted to employ local trades who knew the history of the local buildings and how they were constructed. His task today: to begin clearing the old engine shed of the heavy engineering needed to service a fifty-four-tonne steam train. After arriving on site, Darren had begun sweeping and clearing the main shed. Years of old dust and debris which had been whipped in by the wind and then stuck to the years old oil had made this task the obvious choice for the new *sprog,* as he was known to the rest of the crew.

After climbing the fold-away ladders to better reach a shelf which still clung onto its oil cans and other various equipment once used, Darren thought he'd heard a voice.

He turned and looked to the far of the shed. He squinted and moved his gaze left and right.

In the dapples of sunlight which breached the shed's aging roof, he thought, just for a moment, he could see a man, a large man dressed in dark clothes and wearing a hat, but Darren couldn't decide if it was a trick of the light or not. He leaned a little farther, struggling to see through the waterfalls of dust he'd swept up. He removed his hardhat and safety glasses. The figure seemed to move and sway in the dust, and then it vanished; nothing but the empty shed met his now straining gaze. He shifted his weight back onto the ladder.

"What the fuck was that?" he asked himself, as he began pulling back on his safety gear. The voice came again, this time behind him. It startled him, and Darren lost his balance. He fell backward and readied himself to scream, but there was no time, and he hit the ground hard, smashing through a wooden board which had been laid over an inspection pit which in turn was covered in decades of dirt and dust until it was as fine a trap as the best hunters could create.

The impact of the board had winded Darren, but the impact of the concrete below was worse. He stopped falling with a dull thud, and no more than a silent wince from his deflated lung as plumes of thick, greyish stale dust rose above him and then cascaded down. Covering him in a fine layer.

He lay, disoriented, unsure of what had happened, and in the beams of sunlight which found their way into this pit for the first time since before this young man had been born,

Darren thought he saw the man looking down on him. He reached up his right hand. "Help me," he gasped, but the figure disappeared again, wafting away as a soft summer breeze came over him. He lay for a moment longer until he'd regained his thoughts and put them in an order he could use. He moved, and as he did, a sharp pain, like none he'd suffered before, sent a white-hot bolt of lightning through his body. His lungs, now somewhat replenished, allowed a scream to escape his mouth. Darren reached around and felt something, a handle. It was curved and moved when he took a breath. He followed it along its curve. The cold, smooth handle became steel, which became his body, and Darren realised he'd been impaled on something, and he was in trouble. He took as deep a breath as his lungs, and pain threshold, allowed and shouted, "Help me."

Sooner than he might have imagined, but still longer than he'd hoped, a crowd of his colleagues gathered around him. "Call a fucking ambulance," he heard through the din of the worried and panicked faces. Then he felt a soft touch as someone gently removed his safety gear, brushing his hair from his eyes. "Don't worry, you'll be fine, just take it easy," he heard, as he slipped into unconsciousness.

Darren woke to the sounds of the air thudding in his ears as his eyes adjusted to his new surroundings; he could only see the sky and a man in a green uniform looking at him. Jill stood next to Paul, as they watched the air-ambulance take off. The rest of the builders had dispersed once the paramedics had arrived in their fast-response cars, and it was them who had called for the helicopter. The knife was deeply embedded, and because of its curved blade, the damage it had done was far worse than they had seen in some time.

Jill turned to Paul. "I'll head to the hospital, see how he is. I'll call you later."

Paul didn't reply, not verbally anyway, he just nodded and watched Jill head back to the car. As she pulled out of the car park, Paul turned back to the engine shed and made his way into the inspection pit.

On the ground by the dark stain and drying blood were shards of broken wooden floorboards which had covered the pit. Paul looked back up and then around the pit, his mind scrambling to work out how such a weapon could have been placed here and by who. A shout from above brought him back. It was John.

"The lads are a bit shook-up, so we're calling it a day."

"Yeah, sure, that's fine. Be back tomorrow, John. Early start," Paul answered.

John didn't answer verbally. He just nodded an acknowledgement and left the shed.

Paul climbed back out of the pit and closed the hefty doors to the shed. This wasn't how he wanted the build to go; an accident like this so early in the build might spook Jill.

He knew how superstitious she could be. He knew he should be thinking of Darren, but as much as he knew that, and as much as he tried, all his mind could concentrate on was the project and what cost this delay could have.

He shrugged and made his way back up the lane. In his haste and confusion, he'd forgotten they'd come to The Halt in the same car, and Jill had just taken it. But it was a lovely afternoon, and the village wasn't that far away. *'An hour, maybe a little less, and I'll be home,'* he thought to himself, as he began to walk.

***

Jill had arrived at James Cook Hospital thirty minutes after the helicopter. By the time she'd parked and made her way to the ward, Darren was being prepped for emergency surgery.

The knife had caused severe internal bleeding, and for now, all she could do was wait and hope that her former colleagues could repair the damage and save his life. She must have fallen asleep in the warmth and comfort of the relatives' waiting room she had been hastily shown to by an over-eager young nurse. Even though Jill had protested that she wasn't, in fact, a relative, the young nurse had opened the door and left Jill standing inside the room before rushing away. As she came back to full consciousness, she became aware that she was no longer alone. Sitting opposite her were a man and woman who wore an all too familiar expression of worry and dread. Jill had seen this look before while working with cancer patients. She assumed them to be Darren's parents. She looked up at the white, plain wall clock; four hours had passed. She must call Paul and let him know what was happening. *'He'll be worried,'* she thought to herself. Jill stood and left the room. She pulled her phone from her pocket.

"Paul?"

"Yes, hi, how is he?"

"He's still in theatre. The knife caused horrific injuries."

"How did it get into the pit?"

Jill paused. "I don't know, but we need to be careful moving on, as there could be anything lying around. Dirty needles, animal droppings, even dead animals." A cold shudder travelled along her spine at the thought of it.

"Let me know when he's out," Paul replied.

"Yeah, will do. I think his parents are here."

"Best speak to them, let them know our thoughts are with them and him."

"Will do," Jill confirmed before ending the call.

She took a deep breath before re-entering the room, nervously twiddling her phone around as she did. "Hi, are you Darren's parents?"

The man looked up. "We are."

Jill stretched out a hand. "I'm Jill. Darren was on my project when he had the accident."

The man, who was middle-aged, of slightly shorter stature than would be considered average, and had a weathered look about him, took hold of her hand and gently shook it. "Do you know how it happened?"

Jill pulled her hand back. It seemed a little strange to her that he didn't introduce himself at first, but then, why would he? His son was in theatre, so why would he concern himself with such insignificant formalities? Jill decided not to answer his question with one, and instead decided he looked like a

Keith. "To be honest, we don't know. He was beginning to clear the old engine shed when he fell through an inspection pit, which had been covered for decades, and fell onto a knife. That's all we know so far."

Keith sat and took hold of who Jill had decided was his wife and Darren's mum. Jill thought she would be called Susan for no other reason than she looked like a Susan Jill had known as a child. "Okay, thank you for coming over," Susan said, softly.

Jill sat opposite them. "It's fine, honestly. I want to make sure he's okay."

A quiet fell over the three of them. Keith and Susan sat silently, their heads bowed, while Jill felt a sense of guilt. She didn't quite know why she should, but there it was anyway, that sense of responsibility where none actually existed. As if on cue, a surgeon, still in his green scrubs and wearing a pulled down facemask entered the room. Susan spoke first.

"How is he?" The question came with more hesitation than Jill had heard anyone deliver.

The surgeon looked at them with as much reassurance as Jill thought anyone could. "Darren will be fine. We've stopped the bleeding, given him a blood transfusion and he's in recovery. We'll move him to a ward soon. Go have a coffee and then you can see him."

Keith's and Susan's relief was more emphatic than the hesitation, and their smiles even more so. They nodded politely to Jill and then left the small room. Jill sensed a smile begin to spread across her face. It hadn't crossed her mind yet, she hadn't allowed it to, but had this young man died, she didn't know if she could have carried on with the restoration, and she knew that would cause trouble between her and Paul. But it was a good omen. He was going to be fine, a full recovery, wonderful, marvellous, tickety-boo, Jill thought to herself. She stood to leave the room and drive home. As she did, a young and rather tall police officer entered holding a clear plastic bag.

"I understand this was on your land?" he asked Jill.

Jill looked at it. Inside was the knife, she recognised the handle, but it was the first time she'd seen the blade. Still somewhat stained and rusted, it was six inches long and curved around on itself.

A shudder went through her at the thought of the pain Darren must have suffered.

"Yes, it seems it was. It was hidden in an old inspection pit," Jill answered, wary of where this conversation might lead. "What will happen to it?"

"It'll be destroyed unless you're Sikh?" the tall police officer answered.

"Erm, no I'm not, we're not."

"I'll take a statement from Mr Pratt when he's well enough, but I doubt you'll hear anything further from us."

"Okay, thank you," Jill replied.

The tall officer left the room, and Jill headed back to her car, exhausted. She was ready for home and her bed.

As Jill pulled onto the drive of their rented cottage, all thoughts of the knife had slipped out of her conscious mind. She was exhausted, beaten and she just needed this day to be over. She switched off the engine and climbed out of the SUV. The remaining heat of the day hit her, as she left the air-conditioned cabin. In the main window of the house, she could see Charlie eagerly bouncing around on the armchair, waiting to greet and fuss her.

"Hello, hello," Jill said, as she entered, and Charlie ran around her feet, panting.

"Hi, how is he?" Paul entered from the kitchen.

"Thankfully, he'll make a full recovery, so it looks as if work can continue."

"What does that mean?" Paul asked. A puzzled look came across where his smile had been.

"Well, if he'd died or been permanently injured, we couldn't have gone ahead. Surely?" Jill replied.

"You're joking, of course? We've sunk our entire savings and the proceeds of our home into this. We couldn't have just walked away because of an accident," Paul snapped.

Jill thought before she spoke. This *could* explode, this *could* become a huge argument. She would, of course, have the moral high ground, but the point about the money was a valid one, even if it was made in a cold and entirely mercenary way. She decided to swallow the fight, bury it and eventually forget about it. Darren was going to be fine, and that's all that mattered anyway. "It's a moot point, as he's going to be fine. Let's just eat, have a drink and start again tomorrow," Jill replied, smiling disarmingly.

"You're right, of course. I'm sorry if I seemed a little crass."

Jill knew he was being charming because she'd backed down. But she would take it. "It's fine. Call John, see when they can be back on site."

"Oh, they're back on-site tomorrow. Eight-thirty sharp," Paul answered, as he headed back to the kitchen.

Jill muttered under her breath, "You are a twat sometimes."

Another red-hot day awaited them at The Halt when Jill and Paul arrived a little after nine. John and his team were, as promised, already on site and picking up from where they'd left off the previous day after Darren had had his accident. The task of clearing the shed had now been given to one of the more experienced builders, while the rest of John's team continued clearing and preparing the main building for the restoration.

As they pulled into the car park, John walked over to meet them.

"Morning," John said.

"Morning, have you heard from the hospital?" Jill asked.

"I spoke to his parents late last night, and his dad said the strangest thing."

"What?" Paul asked.

"He said Darren fell off the ladder because someone spooked him. He saw a man, a big man, dressed in black with a large hat in the shed."

"Well, who the hell would that be?" Paul asked.

"Buggered if I know. No one else saw anyone like that. Could've been the heat; if he hadn't drunk enough, could have been a little dehydrated. You know what young'uns are like," John remarked.

As they turned to head toward the main building, Paul heard the rumble of a diesel engine. He turned to see a truck approaching, and he recognised it as the clocksmith's truck. "You go ahead. I'll catch up with you," Paul said to John, as the truck pulled up. John turned and headed away. He had enough to do without being dragged into this project as well. The older-looking man removed the station clock from its protecting crate and manhandled it back to its rightful place. While the clock was off-site being repaired, the elegant cast iron bracket, which supported it, had been stripped and repainted in the original dark green. Jill watched excitedly as the clock was mounted and connected. For the first time in decades, the second had swung around the big face, and the grand clock once again took pride of place above the old platform.

"Doesn't it look wonderful," Jill announced, as she stood under it.

"It's coming together," Paul replied and then continued. "Okay, I'm off to the office."

"Can you drop me in the village? I've found a silversmith I'd like to take a look at the crucifix."

"Of course, I just need five minutes with John," Paul replied.

"I'll wait at the car."

Once he was sure Jill was out of range, Paul approached John. "This thing about the man in the hat, keep it quiet from Jill, in fact, anything that you may consider a little strange or weird will spook her. She's into all that ghost and spirit shite. If she thinks there's something off here, she'll pull the plug. And if she does that, it'll ruin us." Paul was trying hard to get John on side with his request. So much so he'd stepped over the line he always promised he wouldn't. He's was deriding her and her beliefs. And he could tell John wasn't comfortable.

"If you say so, Paul, you're the boss." John's acceptance of the request had come with an unease.

"Cheers, you know how women can be." Paul continued to try and get John on side and was perhaps being too open with John in his desperation to keep anything a little strange from Jill. "Thing is, I've overspent somewhat. She doesn't need to know, and I can make it back up, but if she gets the heebie-jeebies over something like a fucking man in a hat before this is finished, well, it goes without saying."

"Like I said, you're the boss," John said politely. But it was a cold, 'I know my boundaries' kind of reply.

"I knew you'd understand. See you tomorrow," Paul said before turning away.

Paul walked over to their car. "That's that," he said.

"What did you need to talk to John about? Looked important," Jill asked.

"Oh, nothing. Just keeping things right on the site. You don't need to worry, but it may be best to bring your own car from now on, that's if you want to come. Honestly, I can run this if you'd prefer to concentrate on your blog." Paul kept his eyes straight ahead, as he pulled onto the main road, avoiding eye contact with her and hoping Jill would see the logic in his request and begin staying away from the site.

"I could do with writing a little more, I guess. And I need to begin sourcing the fixtures and fittings. So long as you're sure it's not too much for you," Jill answered.

"Nope, I can manage," Paul replied.

Jill arrived at the silversmith's and presented the crucifix to him. The blackened, tarnished silver cross had lay where it was dropped, undiscovered and partially buried close to the gate. The hot sun of summer and countless winter storms had battered and beaten it, but still, the large handprint had survived.

The silversmith was an aging man and had lived in the village of Thirstonfield all his life. He'd attended the local school and followed in his father's profession as so many did from around these parts. He took the crucifix from Jill and inspected it closely. He rubbed it lightly, mumbling and grunting to himself as he did before placing it on the old, heavily scratched glass counter. Removing the thick-rimmed glasses which helped his aging and weary eyes to continue what they must, providing the old man with his sight, and in turn his livelihood, he looked back to Jill. "Where did you find this?" he asked, as he cleared his throat.

"On a property we've just bought, well, outside, actually, by a gate," Jill answered.

"Oh, you're the one who bought the old station," the old man said. Announcing it to Jill much more than he was asking her.

"Yes, that's right. I'm Jill. I expect I'll be in the village quite a lot now." She smiled at him. His expression didn't change.

"Leave it with me. I think it's beyond what I can do, but I'll do what I can. Come back in a few days."

"Thank you, I hope you can make it presentable," Jill said, smiling through her words.

"I expect I can," the old man answered, as he turned his back and walked through the open doorway behind his counter, which she assumed led into his workshop.

Jill left the silversmith's shop, next on the list was the local butcher's. Tonight, she'd decided, they would have prime steak, sourced locally and cooked bare until it was just turning from red to brown. As she entered the butcher's, two local women were standing at the counter, talking with the butcher's wife. A hefty woman, who Jill had bought meat from a few times since they'd moved to the village. And though by-and-large Jill had found her professional, she wasn't what Jill would call gracious or customer focused. Jill moved a little closer to them, as she began to overhear their gossiping.

The older of the two women seemed to have the most to say, a *head gossip* as Jill's mum would have likely described her.

As Jill approached the big woman behind the counter, she cut her conversation short and turned to her. "Yes?"

"Two large sirloin steaks please," Jill answered.

"Be two minutes. I'll need to slice them." The hefty butcher's wife announced, wiping her hands on the once-white, and heavily bloodstained piny before heading through to the cold storage room where the sides of cattle hung from substantial, stainless-steel hooks.

The head gossip turned to Jill. "Are you the couple that bought the old station?"

"Yes, well, I'm one of the couple, two people, well, myself and Paul." Jill flapped a little, not expecting an ambush. "I'm Jill."

"I heard there was an accident," the head gossip asked.

"Yes, unfortunately, there was, but he's fine." Jill stopped, keeping the answer short.

"Well, after all that's happened at that place, I'm surprised old man Bradbury managed to sell it," the other woman, the subordinate gossip, said. "But then, he was desperate to get rid, I heard."

"What do you mean, all that's happened?" Jill turned to her, asking her directly.

The head gossip stepped across her junior, blocking Jill from making direct contact with her. "Tell me what you mean by that," Jill pushed her question.

This time, the head gossip answered, while glaring her groupie down, who dutifully backed away. "Well, if you didn't look into its past before you bought it, what with all the awful things that took place there, I would suggest you do. You know, before it's too late. But then, you are an outsider, so it's no surprise you're ignorant."

Jill felt winded by this remark, and caught off guard, she wasn't sure how to respond.

"Two sirloins." The hefty butcher's wife had returned. "That'll be ten pounds, eighty-six."

Jill took the wrapped meat from her and tapped her visa card against the small card reader which chirped that the transaction was complete. Without saying anything more, she left the butcher's and made her way back to the relative peace and safety of her car.

Chapter 6

March 1937

In the eight months since Jack had suffered the devastating humiliation at the hands of the Ninnyhammer, and in front of the only girl that showed an interest in him, Jack had withdrawn into himself. Molly had, as best as she could at least, avoided Jack, though it had been inevitable that, at some point, their paths would cross. When they had, Jack had tried to initiate a conversation, a look, a smile or even a spoken word, but Molly had blanked him completely. In the modern day and age, a victim of such a heinous act would be counselled, they would be coddled, told that they were the stronger person for not fighting back, and they would be befriended by all those who felt offended on their behalf. But this was a very different time and talk of another world war had pumped up the resolve of every individual who knew what that would mean. You were expected to fight back, to stand up for yourself, as Jack had once done on the last day of school. Back then, the Ninnyhammer had been by-and-large on his own and unprepared for Jack's attack, but the subsequent beatings by his father had knocked out whatever it was Jack used that day to have his victory. As for Molly, a man who would allow himself to be degraded like that without trying to fight back would be no good as a father to her children. The primal instincts buried deep in every human being always, on a subconscious at least, influenced what men and women look for in a potential mate. A list of must haves, and must nots, and what Molly perceived to be cowardice on that day was a definite must not.

After the attack, Jack had run home. He was once again a nine-year-old boy who had been beaten at school, and the only person who could make it all go away was his mother, Doris. Jack had burst into his home, holding his trousers, gathered around his waist, his nose blooded and his shirt torn. He fell into the arms of Doris who cradled him, stroked his hair and told him it would pass, that she suspected Molly was not the right one for him anyway, and that no woman would ever be good enough for her gorgeous little boy. That only she could love him the way he was meant to be loved, and that only she could ever take care of him properly. His mother's words stuck in his mind and calmed him as they always had, and eventually, after she'd prepared his favourite meal, he'd gone to bed, once again convinced by Doris that he was too good for them and that their hostility toward him was nothing more than misplaced jealousy. But, that was back then, and since that time, Jack had begun to have other thoughts. Ones of revenge and what he'd do if he was to ever see the Ninnyhammer again, and as more time passed, the darker these thoughts became. During one such dark storm in Jack's mind, he made his way into the attic where he found what he'd gone looking for: his grandfather's war chest from 1918. He pried open the lid and began looking for a particular item. He remembered his grandfather showing him it with immense pride. It had been given to him in France at the end of the Great War by a friend who'd served in the Indian Expeditionary Force. Jack pulled it from its resting place, his eyes widening, as he pulled the curved blade from its sheath. The intricately carved ivory handle felt glorious in his hands as he tightened his grip around it. He swished it through the air, one way and then back again before touching his finger to the tip of the blade. It pierced his skin with ease, and Jack watched, as his own deep red blood ran along the curve of the blade. He simpered to himself while sliding the devastating Kirpan knife back into its protective, leather sheath.

His chance for revenge came unexpectedly in the form of an overheard conversation between co-workers. The Ninnyhammer would be coming home after six months at sea.

That's why Jack had not seen him about. After the attack, he'd left for Portsmouth. Jack listened to the details. He would be on the last train from Whitby next Thursday, calling at Thirstonfield at 8.30 p.m. Jack knew this stop; he'd worked track repairs up there the previous summer. It was a small station, and it would be likely there would be few people around, and in March in the northeast of England, it would also be dark, and the small station didn't offer much in the way of light.

As the days rolled around, Jack's hunger for revenge swelled inside him; like the appetite of an apex-predator, it had to be satisfied. Firstly, he would need a reason to be there at that time so he could cover himself in case his plans didn't go as they should. The alibi he would need was given to him by his manager, Jim Green, or as Jack had been instructed to call him, Mr Green. One of the old Victorian signals had begun to stick, and Jack was told to go through and fix it. He jumped at the chance, but not before telling Mr Green it would be Thursday before he'd finished repairing the old shunter he'd been working on. Mr Green wasn't too bothered. This signal was on one of the rarely used lines, which is why he'd given the task to Jack. No one further up the food chain in the yard fancied the journey to Thirstonfield. The roads were narrow, steep and slow, and the old Morris repair truck wasn't the most comfortable of things.

Thursday rolled around, and his plan was set. He would travel to Thirstonfield after lunch, the journey itself taking around forty-five minutes. He would fix the sticking signal and then lay in wait. Once the Ninnyhammer was off the train, he would approach him, offer him a friendly ride home. He would, of course, say yes, at least in Jack's mind, and for his plan to work, he would, then Jack would have his chance for revenge. He would beat him, strip him and make him walk the rest of the way back naked. Then, and only then, would Jack's honour be satisfied, and with that, Molly would come back to him. It was settled, this was the plan and that is indeed how it would go.

Over and over, the plan played in Jack's mind, as he made the journey to the small station. He arrived a little after two on a warm spring afternoon. The deep-blue sky was only broken now and again by the sight of RAF aircraft flying above. More people were becoming convinced that another war would soon be upon them, as Adolf Hitler continued his rhetoric about German superiority. Jack hadn't paid too much mind to it: he'd been told by his grandfather that the Great War was the war to stop all wars. The levels of human suffering had been so great that any idea of another war, so soon after at least, was nothing more than poppycock, and this Hitler fella was just beating his chest. But still, it seemed the RAF were building their numbers, and more and more army vehicles were passing through Middlesbrough Station on the back of transport trains bound for the south.

By the time Jack had completed the repair, it had gone 6.30 p.m. He had nothing to do now but wait for two hours until the final train of the day made its way into the small, isolated station. In the days before mass CCTV and mobile phones, keeping a low profile just meant keeping away from the people who were around you. There were plenty of hiding places for Jack in this quiet station, but the best place to hide would be in the large engine shed behind the main station building.

It was obvious that it had been some time since this shed had been used for its main purpose of servicing and repairing steam locomotives. While the inspection pit wasn't fully covered, enough of it had been to suggest it was no longer required. Jack stepped into the dimly-lit pit. The small, narrow stairs were shallow and very steep. The pit itself was only just wide enough for Jack's sizeable frame, and the once gleaming white painted sides were now a dull-brown from the years of oil and grease. He placed his hand gently on the left wall. It was cold, as was the grey concrete floor. Jack walked to the far end, the end mostly covered over. It was dark there, and the smell of the grease and oil was the strongest. He lowered himself, sitting on the cold floor with his back resting against the far wall. He liked it down there; it reminded him of himself. He too felt largely abandoned, neglected and unloved. Jack drifted in and out of sleep in his new hidey-hole.

After one such long snooze, he woke to find that darkness now encompassed everything outside of the pit. He checked his watch 8.12 p.m. He would soon be here.

Jack waited until the last train began pulling out of the station. He'd watched his prey get off the train and head to the waiting room with four or five other passengers. Jack hadn't counted how many, it didn't matter to him anyway, because at some point, he would have to get the Ninnyhammer on his own, and it didn't matter if there were a hundred people or just a single person with him, there couldn't be anyone around that could place Jack at that time. One by one, he watched them leave. He observed them, trying to figure out who they were, what their reason was to be on this last train. The older couple, no doubt from one of the farms, by the way they were dressed. The younger man, slim and smart with slicked-back hair, a future spiv if Jack had ever seen one. And the last to leave, a younger couple smiling, holding hands and giggling to one another, no doubt a courting couple planning a quick fuck somewhere in the open night air before returning to their respective homes. That just left him, the one Jack had waited for. As if his plan had been well-rehearsed by all participants, the Ninnyhammer stepped out into the night air. He stood under the clock and single light which shone as if a stage spotlight was trained on him. He lit a cigarette, unknowing that Jack was stalking him. Paul Stokes began to make his way towards the gate near the car park which would lead him up to the main road. From there, he would walk into the village and find a room at the local pub before catching tomorrow's train to Middlesbrough. As he approached the gate, he heard his name called. Startled, he turned to find Jack standing a few feet away.

Jack could see his quarry. He seemed surprised and bewildered. Jack had gone through his plan in intricate detail, but now this, this absolute fucking bastard was standing there, without his friends and off guard, Jack's plan evaporated, and with it, any and all control Jack might have had left. He flew at him, hitting him hard. The Ninnyhammer stumbled backward, hitting the gate hard, and as he did, he slipped, losing his balance. He fell onto the gravel path. Jack struck out again, catching the side of his head, then his chest, as he rained down blows on him, his fists striking out with no target in mind, just raw power. Most missed, those that did land hurt him, but none of them made the knockout blow they needed to. Jack was exhausted. He'd let the last seven-month's rage out in one three-minute barrage, but his lack of precision had meant his opponent was now able to begin his fight back. He stood, spitting blood from his cut lip, as he taunted Jack. Calling him a limp pricked mummies-boy, that when he got home, he would fuck Molly, show her how it was meant to be done, after which she would only ever think of him while Jack fumbled uselessly with his child's tiny, flaccid dick.

Jack flew at him again, but this time it was the Ninnyhammer who landed the first blow, sending Jack to his knees. The Ninnyhammer climbed over Jack's back and began punching the back of his head, stopping Jack from getting back to his feet. Hit after hit came and Jack could feel himself losing another battle. The fear of what that might mean sent Jack's brain scurrying for ways to win this. And then it came to him: the knife, he'd forgotten about the knife. In his rage and anger on seeing him, all rational thought had left him. As another blow came, Jack reached into his coat pocket and pulled out the curved blade. From the corner of his eye, he saw the Ninnyhammer step back and kick out at him. Jack moved, the leg passed him and Jack thrashed at it with the blade. The cries of pain from his tormentor pierced the still night air, and Jack rallied to his feet, his head cut and sore, but the Ninnyhammer was on the floor, and a deep laceration across the back of his calf muscle meant he couldn't stand. Jack stood over him and without saying a word, slashed the blade back and forth at the outreaching arms and hands of this now crying and pleading tormenter. Jack stopped the unrestrained attack. His former bully lay beaten. His hands and arms covered in deep slashes, blood oozed from each of them, and Jack felt he could leave him here defeated. But he remembered the last time he thought he'd beaten him. This time, Jack decided, he wouldn't leave it to chance.

Jack straddled across his chest and swiped the curved blade across the Ninnyhammer's throat. As his victim gargled and choked on his own blood, Jack stood over him and watched. As he did, he experienced a rush of excitement, as adrenaline coursed around his body. But it was different to the rush before he'd fought. This was a pleasurable rush. He tingled all over, and he became hard, as he watched his prey take his last breath. Jack sensed a surge of sexual delight, and he ejaculated into his trousers. Jack checked his watch; he wanted to know the exact moment he'd taken his last breath. It read 9.30 p.m. Jack was now clear in his own mind. He wasn't a limp pricked mummies-boy with a small child's dick. Killing this worthless asshole had given Jack his manhood back. And with it, his power, and a sexual delight he'd never-before experienced. Jack unzipped his trousers and cleaned himself as best he could before he dragged the dead body over to the engine shed. He wrapped the body in old tarpaulin and pulled it across the floor until it lay under the overhead crane. He fastened the body to it and then winched it until it was at the height of the metal girders which supported the crane. After climbing up, Jack pulled the body to the far of the shed where he slid it between the metal beams that supported the glass roof and the metal roof joists. Jack knew there would be no need for anybody to be up here unless either the roof fell off or the building was being demolished, and by then, Jack was confident the body would be unrecognisable. The local wildlife would make short work of the discernible features needed to identify a corpse.

The drive back home was a satisfying one for Jack. He walked into his home around midnight to find Doris asleep by the dying fire. He crept by her, eager to hide the stains of his dry ejaculate. He changed and put his clothes in to soak, by morning the blood and semen would be gone. The following day, work came and went without incident, and no fuss was made around the yard of the missing lad who was supposed to have returned home on the morning train. Molly, as usual, ignored Jack who now didn't care. The satisfaction he had gained last night was much more than she, or any woman, could give him. For all Jack was concerned, she could disappear from his world, and he would pay her no more mind than a fly he would swipe from his arm.

Day turned to evening, which turned to night, and, as always, that meant getting home, eating tea, bathing and listening to the radio before bed. The radio broadcast once again focused on the rise of fascism in Germany and the possible threat to world peace.

Jack was woken sometime in the early hours by the cries of his mother and the shouts of his father. After his beating of the Ninnyhammer, Jack had decided he would no longer allow his mother to be beaten by this drunken coward, and so Jack calmly got out of bed and walked down the narrow staircase and into the small parlour where he found his father standing over his mother. His father had heard Jack enter the room, and as he had before spun around ready to beat him as well, just as he had a few short years ago, the only other time when Jack had dared to stand up to him. He let go of Doris's hair and stepped towards Jack, his left hand clenched in a fist and raised, ready to bring it down. Jack threw the first punch, his drunken father too slow to react. It hit him, sending him sprawling onto the small settee which sat along the back wall. The rush flooded Jack again, and he unleashed his rage. Finally beaten, his father pleaded for Jack to stop, which he did on one condition. That he would never again step foot back into their home again, and that he would move away and stay away. He agreed, but not before publicising the truth about Jack, as he limped along the street and out of their lives.

To Jack, what he'd said, and what Doris then confessed to him meant nothing. He'd protected his mother, set her free from her own tormentor, so it meant now the two of them could be together. Jack's world was complete for the first time he could remember it being so. The replay of the fight with his dad and subsequent victory made him feel aroused again. As he lay, erect in bed, he remembered his mother's words, and he decided he would call upon the woman who said she was the only one who could fully love him. Jack climbed in to Doris's bed behind her, still erect. She was asleep and stirred only a little when he pushed up against her. His hand moved around her front, cupping her breasts. She woke, shocked and still somewhat disorientated. As Jack knelt up beside her and unfastened his bottoms, Doris screamed for him to get out, to cover himself up and stop. But Jack was too aroused to respond rationally, and he forced himself on her.

***

The steaks sizzled on the cast iron grill plate while Charlie lay in patient wait, knowing that once his masters had finished consuming the best of the meat, he would be thrown the tough parts it seemed these upright beings didn't like to chew. Jill plated the steaks, allowing the meat to relax and the juices flow, as she pulled the home-cooked fries from their bath of boiling oil. Paul, she thought, must have smelt her plating their food, because as she did, Jill heard the slamming of the car door moments before he entered through the kitchen. Charlie, confused about what to do, couldn't decide whether to risk losing his chance of meat by fussing his male master or continue to shadow the female, who it seemed was in charge of the feast. In the end, he chose the latter.

"Mm, steak and chips. Lovely," Paul said happily, as he sat at the table.

"How was your day?" Jill asked.

"Nothing really to report. The station clock was hung and connected, so it's once again keeping time."

"Anything else?"

"They've finished clearing the engine shed, now we can get access to the roof for the first time. Looks like that'll need new joists, and there's a few broken panes of glass."

"What about Darren?" Jill asked, taking another mouthful of steak while Charlie watched.

"At home, resting and out of danger."

"Well, I had an interesting conversation today. Want to hear it?" Jill asked.

Paul knew the tone. This was a trap whichever way he answered. He chose to answer it in the way he believed would cause him the least amount of pain. "Of course, darling."

"I was at the butcher's. There were two women, locals, and they let me know quite clearly that they were. Anyway, the older of them told me a lot has happened up there, meaning The Halt, and that old man Bradbury was desperate to get rid of it."

Paul swallowed his steak. "They say anything else?"

"No, I just paid and left. What do you suppose they mean?"

"I have no idea. I wouldn't take any notice of idle gossip. Just likely locals who don't want *outsiders* like us buying up the local properties and land," Paul tried to sound as relaxed as he could. His mind flashed back to the peculiar waiver Smith the solicitor had insisted he sign. If Jill found out about that before they moved in, coupled with the accident, she would put a stop to the whole project. "Honestly, I wouldn't take any notice. They're just jealous."

Jill took the last piece of meat from her plate and swilled it down with a gulp of wine. She wasn't entirely settled by his dismissive response, but he was almost certainly correct. At least if she convinced herself he was, she would feel a little more settled. Jill stood and took her and Paul's plate from the table. "Aye, you're probably right," she said.

She scraped the leftovers into Charlie's food bowl before mixing it with his usual food and placing it on the floor.

While Charlie devoured the mixture as hastily as he could, convinced as always that his masters would try and take it from him, Jill made coffee and returned to the table.

"How does the clock look?" Jill asked, taking a sip.

"It looks great, the restorers have done a wonderful job, just the right amount of reinvasion and not restoration," Paul answered, knowing it would bring approval, and somewhat of a smug answer from Jill. But that was fine, he could keep her off the topic of The Halt's past.

"See, I told you it should be a tad patinated," Jill scoffed, holding the outsized coffee mug to her mouth.

It had worked. Jill had forgotten about the gossips in the butcher's. "Yes, as always, you're right, that's why I love you."

"Has John said when the building will be ready?" Jill asked.

"He says The Halt will be ready for decoration and moving into within the next few weeks. The engine shed, maybe another six months. Once the roof is fixed and its weather tight, it'll need decontaminating before it's habitable."

"Just as well, the lease on this place is up soon, and I'm not sure the estate will extend it month-by-month, and we can't afford to sign up for another twelve months just to have The Halt lay empty."

"No, it'll be ready to move into when we need to move out of here. That was always part of the contract with John. Any delays and he pays a penalty."

"That's good then." Jill finished her coffee and began clearing the kitchen.

The following morning, Jill and Paul stood outside of The Halt admiring the façade and the platform restoration work. The old building looked young again, and Jill began to imagine, once the site was cleared and the building works paraphernalia had gone, what it would like look.

She looked at the clock. "Uh, that's strange," she said to Paul.

"What is?"

"The clock, look, it's stopped."

Jill and Paul looked at the large station clock. Jill was right, the second hand had stopped dead on the twelve.

"Ah, for fuck's sake, I'll call them now," Paul said angrily, as he pulled out his phone, pressing the speed dial.

After a few seconds, it answered. Jill listened in on the conversation. "Hi, yes, this is Paul from The Halt. Yes, that's right, yes, it was fitted yesterday. Well, it's stopped, dead on nine-thirty. I think last night; the small indicator is pointing to the pm. Today? Yes, that would be great, thank you. Yes, bye." Paul slid his phone back into his pocket.

"Well, what did they say?" Jill asked.

"She said he'd be back out today, maybe after lunch."

As Jill looked back to the clock, she felt a cold chill run along her back, as if a frigid wind had targeted only her.

She couldn't describe it, but if she had to take a swing at doing so, she would say it felt like ice-cold fingers running up and down her spine, and for just the briefest of moments, she felt unwelcome in this place she was soon to call home. She shook, which didn't go unnoticed by Paul.

"Someone walk over your grave?" he asked, sniggering.

Jill didn't answer. She knew what Paul thought of her spiritual side and how upset he became if she seemed to let it influence her in any way.

He'd often argued with her that in the 21st century, with the existence of God being unprovable, governments in developed countries at least should take away religion's protections, recognition and tax breaks. *'Why should the lives of people who don't believe in such old world and out of date doctrines be bound by laws made to appease and protect people who believe that which cannot be proven to be real?'* Jill could hear his arguments rolling through her head. No, she would keep this uncomfortable moment to herself. As she turned away from the building, Jill took one last look at the clock. This time, she sensed no frigid wind or chills. She shrugged and made her way to the engine shed to join Paul and John.

As she approached, Jill could see that scaffolding had already been erected inside the shed, ready to begin the much-needed work on the old and deteriorating metal roof. Around the concrete floor of the shed lay shards of the glass which were once panes in the ceiling. After decades of neglect, the metal frames which held them were rusting away, allowing gravity to begin claiming them one by one. Standing in between Paul and John, she watched the roofers make their way along the interior of the roof while they surveyed what it would need to become weather proof and habitable. Each roofer wore the usual high-viz jacket, hardhat and a plethora of harnesses and ropes. The shed roof was high; it had to be to accommodate the engines which were once worked on and to allow ventilation. As they continued around the structure, John's walkie-talkie crackled.

"John, it's Mat. It's not looking good up here." Mat, the senior of the men John had called in to repair the roof was, like John, an expert in his field, but not so good with diplomacy. "It's a fucking mess here, mate. It's gonna take longer to fix this shit-hole than you first thought."

John, somewhat embarrassed, replied abruptly, trying to stop Mat from saying anything further. "Mat, I hear you. I'm stood with the clients, and they can hear you too."

The radio crackled for a few seconds. "Shit, sorry, mate, didn't realise. But never-the-less, it is a fucking mess."

Jill smiled to herself at his honesty, though she also suspected that this honesty was going to come at a price.

John's radio crackled again. "Hang on, mate, there's something up here wrapped in an old tarp. Give me a minute." There was a crackle and then silence.

Balanced on the leading edge of the scaffold, Mat and his long-time friend, Simon, leant over the dirty, old, blue tarp. Decades of weathering had almost transformed the stiff material into stone. Moss had begun to grow over it, and it had stench the likes of which neither Mat nor Simon had smelt before. Mat reached out and pulled on the corner flap which stuck upright. Leaning back as he pulled on it, the tarp began unravelling.

As it did, the smell became worse, and both men began to retch as the odour hit the back of their throats. Simon leaned in with Mat, taking hold of another piece of tarp which had disentangled itself. Both men pulled hard, and the tarpaulin revealed its secret.

Jill had heard a truck pulling up, and when she turned to see who it was, she recognised it as the clocksmith. Leaving John and Paul, she headed outside to meet him.

"Hi," Jill said, as she approached the small older man.

He nodded to her while unloading his ladders. "Your husband said it's stopped?" the older man asked before walking toward the clock.

"Yes, it has. Do you think you'll get it going again?" Jill asked.

He leant his ladders against the wall directly under the clock. Jill watched him, as he made his way up. "Not sure why it's stopped," he replied, as he examined the main wiring which fed into the back of it. "Looks like I'll have to take it down."

"Well, if that's what it needs," Jill replied, not sure of what other responses would be appropriate. "Will it take you long to do that?"

"I'll need a few minutes," he answered. Gruffly.

"Okay, I'll leave you to it." Jill took the hint from his tone, though she believed it was more from embarrassment that his repair hadn't lasted a day than it was directed at her. She turned and began to make her way back to the shed, and as she did Paul came out, looking somewhat unnerved.

"Don't go in there," he said to Jill, as she approached him.

"Why, what's happened? Not another accident?"

"No, it's just, well, they found something in the eaves."

Jill was puzzled. "What is it?"

"A body. Looks like it's been there a few years. It's in a bad way."

Jill walked past Paul and into the shed where she found John and Mat standing over the decaying corpse. Clearly, this was, at one time anyway, a man. Though there wasn't much of him left. She turned to John. "Have you called the police?"

"Simon is on the phone to them now." He sounded shaken.

"Who the hell put him up there?" Mat asked, still holding his hand over his mouth.

"I guess whoever killed him," John said, quietly.

"How do you know he was killed?" Jill asked.

"Why else would someone go to the trouble of gift wrapping him, and lifting him up there, if not to hide the body?" he answered without moving his gaze from the skull which seemed to stare back at him.

"How long do you reckon?" Mat asked.

"I'm not sure. In medical school, we did study decomposition, at a guess, and by the clothes he's wearing, I'd say sixty, maybe seventy years, or so," Jill answered.

"Shouldn't he be bones by now?" John asked.

"Not necessarily. The tarp he's been wrapped in may have slowed the process," she answered. Though even as she spoke, she wasn't sure herself it would have had any effect on the decomposition process.

"The police are on their way," Simon said, as he re-joined them.

"There's nothing more we can do here, so let's clear out and wait for them," John replied.

As they exited the shed, the older man, carrying the station clock, passed by Jill. "I'll work on this tonight, give the shop a call tomorrow," he spoke, as he walked briskly, clearly in a hurry to be away. "Oh, I think someone is looking for you. I saw a man hanging around, wearing a large hat. A big bugger, bloody weird if you ask me."

By the time Jill had understood what he'd said, he was out of earshot. Jill wasn't expecting anyone to visit, either in a professional capacity or a friend. And besides, none of her friends wore a hat. *'No doubt a friend of Paul's,'* she assumed. She looked around but saw no one. Dismissing it, she paid it no mind. Instead, she turned her thoughts back to the ill-fated man that lay in their shed. As she watched the clocksmith load the broken clock into his truck, she saw the police car turn off the main road and onto the track. Simon had now joined Mat, Paul, John, and Jill, and the five of them watched, as the response car came to a stop close by, and two uniformed police officers climbed out. One of them Jill recognised. He was the tall officer from the hospital. *'Great!'* She thought to herself.

"I know you, don't I?" the tall officer said directly to Jill, as he approached the group of five.

"Yes, I was at the hospital," Jill, replied.

"And here we are again," the tall officer said, smirking.

The second officer, an older man with sergeant's stripes on his short-sleeved white shirt, took over the conversation. "Where is the body?"

John pointed into the engine shed. "Just in here."

Jill, Mat and John followed the two officers into the shed. The tarpaulin had been placed back over the body by John, he felt this was respectful, though he was in no way a religious man. He simply presumed it was something you were supposed to do.

The sergeant squatted, pulling the tarp back, uncovering the young man's face. "Fuck, that's a smell," he said, trying to push back down his gag-reflex.

"Any idea who he is or how he came to be here?" the tall officer asked.

"None," Jill answered. "Mat found him wedged into the metal roof supports in the far corner. I reckon he's been there a while."

"One thing is for sure, he died long before any of you were born, so we can rule you out," the sergeant said, covering the face and lifting himself upright. "Who's got the keys?" he asked, looking between them.

"I have, why?" Jill answered.

"Well, because this is a suspected crime scene. We'll need to bring CSI in, so it's best if you go home today. We'll secure the shed when we leave."

Mat scoffed, "Is that Miami or New York?"

"Yup, we get a lot. Unfortunately, that's what it's called. More Americanisms for you," the sergeant replied, with obvious frustration.

"How long will we be locked out?" John asked.

"A day, maybe two or three, depends on how rapidly we can comb the shed, look for the weapon, or some clue to who he is, and when and what happened."

"Can we continue to work on the main building?" Jill asked.

"I can't see why not. I'll inform the coroner and call the local undertaker to remove the body," the sergeant replied before turning to the tall officer. "Make sure the S.I.O is informed. He'll need to be here. I believe it's Inspector Bailey that's on duty."

"Do you think he's been murdered?" Mat asked.

"We may never know with a body this old. It's more likely it'll be put down as an unexplained death," the sergeant answered.

"Will you be able to find out who he was?" Jill asked.

"Perhaps. We'll come back to you if we need anything further."

Following the sergeant's instructions, they exited the shed and made their way back to the main house.

"Something is off here," Jill said quietly to Paul, as John, Simon and Mat began securing their equipment for the coming night.

"How do you mean?" Paul asked.

"It hadn't clicked earlier, but when the clock guy left, he said someone was looking for me, a man in a hat. I thought it was a little strange but forgot about it."

"And?" Paul shifted his feet.

"Didn't Darren say he thought he'd seen a man in a hat in the shed just before he fell?" Jill replied.

Paul shrugged, electing not to reply verbally.

"We're off; see you tomorrow," John shouted over as he, Mat and Simon climbed into their building truck.

Paul grabbed the opportunity to shift Jill's attention away from what had happened and her connecting of Darren's accident with what the old clocksmith had said earlier. "Yes, okay guys, see you tomorrow," he replied, as he turned away from Jill and walked toward his SUV.

Jill stood a moment longer, the uneasy sensation she'd had since Darren's accident wouldn't leave her. If anything, it was becoming stronger. Her mind scrambled to find the rational explanation Paul always said existed. It's an old building, and old buildings always had secrets to give up, they were by their nature more perilous places to work, unsecure brickwork and decaying foundations.

Something, in fact, that John had warned them about. Yet, it still niggled her. Taking one last look around while the two police officers began wrapping the shed doors in police tape, she wondered who this man in the hat was. Jill heard the Range Rover's horn, Paul's signal that he was becoming impatient. She turned and headed for the car.

***

The older man lay the clock on the counter inside the workshop he'd spent every day of his working life in since leaving school some fifty years previous. Opening the case, he could see no obvious explanation that would explain why the movements had stopped at nine-thirty dead. There seemed no blockages or failing parts. He turned the movement of the clock, and as he suspected it would be, it was effortless and free of any obstructions. He checked his own watch; it read 8.55 p.m. Setting the clock, he closed the case and powered it up and watched as the second hand clicked its way around. Satisfied to a point, he went into the small *Bate-room* where he and his colleagues, who had now all left for the day, took their breaks. He made a cup of tea, broke open a packet of biscuits and sat at the small, round, wooden table, where he began reading today's local paper.

As the clock on the wall began closing in on 9.25 p.m., he folded the newspaper, swilled his cup in the old stainless-steel sink before placing it upside-down on the drainer and then made his way back into the workshop. He checked the time again on his watch and the clock which hung on the wall, before checking them both against the station clock. All three read 9.28 p.m. He watched, as the second hand continued its mechanical march around the face. The older man preferred this type of second hand to the ones which swept silently around the clock face. He felt more secure with the mechanical assurance of the tick-tock of the second hand.

The three clocks passed 9.29 p.m. He scrutinised the station clock as the second hand made its continuous march around, passed the nine, and then passed ten. As it reached the twelve and the minute hand hit the six, it stopped. Frustrated, he checked his own watch. It too had stopped, as had the clock on the wall. All of them at 9.30 p.m. Stymied, he walked into the front of the small shop. Every clock had stopped, and all of them precisely on 9.30 p.m.

He was worn-out, it had been a long day and he'd stayed back only to make sure the station clock made it past nine-thirty. He sighed heavily and noticed that in the warm shop, he could see his breath escape his body. He felt cold and unnerved. A man now in his sixties, he didn't scare easily, if at all, but he detected a chill run through him the likes of which he'd not felt ever in his life. Even in its most challenging times.

In the dull glass of the old display cases, he saw a movement, a reflection and realised with a sense of overwhelming dread he had seen this figure before. It was the large man, wearing the hat he'd seen at the station. He spun around, ready to confront this intruder, but he was met with an empty shop. He walked pensively through to the workshop, and still, the large man was nowhere to be seen. The air became cold, and every breath he exhaled left a trail of condensation, as he moved cautiously through the small workshop and into the cramped parts room. Still, there was no sign of the large man in the black hat he'd seen earlier that day.

He relaxed. Perhaps the clocks stopping in unison had spooked him, and with his imagination fired up, he thought he'd seen the man because when he'd seen him back at the station, he'd felt unnerved then. There was just something about the figure. Apart from his apparent size, it was his clothes, all black topped off with a fedora.

One second, he seemed to be standing at the end of the platform, the next, he'd vanished, as if he'd wisped away in the breeze. Still, that didn't explain the cold and his breath. He shrugged. "Something wrong with the fucking heating again," he mumbled to himself, trying as best he could to reassure himself that's all it would be.

He relaxed, convinced he was just too tired, overworked and still a little shaken from earlier, he made his way back to the workshop. "I'll sort this tomorrow," he said aloud, as he closed-up the station clock's casing. Picking up the electric screwdriver, he began feeding the screw through its guide hole. Lining up the screw head, he pulled the trigger. As the chuck began to rotate, he sensed a breath on his neck. Startled, he looked around and saw the baleful apparition of the large man in the fedora hat. The older man dropped the screwdriver and turned to flee the workshop, but the shock had been too much for him. With one final beat, his heart stopped.

As he lay dead on the floor, the station clock, along with every other timepiece, began up again.

Chapter 7

March 1937

Jack stood at the end of the bed, the craze-induced lust satisfied. As his mind began to clear, the red misted fog which had swirled around him, clouding his cognitive thoughts until his ability to reason with himself, as well anyone he may encounter, had been diminished to a point of indifference, he began to understand what had taken place, what he'd brought upon the only person in his life that had loved him. He looked at Doris, his mother who now looked at him with more terror than she ever had his father. He looked down and saw that his pants were still around his ankles, his now flaccid penis still wet. A feeling of repulsion for himself and for his actions swelled inside him. What had he done? Panicking, not knowing what to do, he grabbed at his pants, pulling them up to hide his shame, he ran from his mother's room and to his own. A mist came again, a different mist, not the red mist of anger or of lust; this was a blue mist, and it brought with it shame, regret and humiliation. It began swirling around as his mind scrambled to understand what had taken place. He didn't remember anything past beating his father, yet it was obvious to him what he'd done and who too.

Jack changed, pulling on his work clothes, he pushed what other clothes he had easily to hand into a small case and without looking back to his mother's room, he ran down the stairs and out of the house. It was all a blur, and in his head, the sounds of confusion, of crashing cymbals, a banging and a pulsation he'd not heard before. Jack covered his ears, as he staggered along the street his father had retreated along only a few hours earlier. As he passed the sign, *Tavistock Street,* he had only one place now he could go where he would feel safe. Thirstonfield Halt.

A little after midnight, Jack reached the station. He knew the last train had already gone, and the stationmaster would now be in his bed, oblivious to his presence and intention to sleep there for the night. Jack made his way into the engine shed and into the inspection pit and under the locomotive which sat atop of it. Down there, he was safe, calm and reassured that with his back to the wall, facing the only way in or out, no one would be able to catch him off guard while he rested, and his mind cleared.

As the morning sun crept through the stained and dirty windows of the engine shed and found its way under the locomotive and into the pit, it warmed Jack's face, and he began to wake. Before his eyes had opened, he recognised the smell of his environment, and as his eyes adjusted, he saw the familiar and safe surroundings he'd fled to the previous night. How he'd got there and at what time, he had no idea, but he'd found refuge and solace in the inspection pit and under the enormous locomotive. Standing, he stretched and yawned loudly. It didn't matter, he knew the routine of this place, he knew the stationmaster would likely still be having his breakfast, and there wouldn't be any paying passengers for at least another few hours or so. He stepped out of the pit and made his way outside. As he did, the reason he was there began to invade his mind again. What he'd done the previous night brought waves of repulsion over him. How could he have done that to his mother?

As hurriedly as the waves came, a realisation soon followed, a realisation that he could never again go back to the small two up two down street house he'd known as his home from his earliest memories. His job at the train yard was also now behind him, and with it, the safety it brought from the draft should war, once again, come to the world.

Jack picked up the small, brown case he'd packed in his blind panic and walked out of the engine shed. He passed the stationmaster's house, and across the car park and over the fields which surrounded the small station. He wasn't sure how long he'd been walking through the spring air or how much distance he'd covered before he felt the need to stop and rest.

Jack sat on his crumpled jacket, the one he'd worn the night he was to meet with Molly and thought about where his life would now lead him. With no home, no family and no job, he'd become a street urchin, destined to sleeping rough and begging for money, with the guilt of what he'd done forever haunting him, following him and with him. Perhaps it would be easier to end it, to bow out of this existence which had been one struggle after another for as long as he could remember. After all, what else was there for a partially-trained steam locomotive mechanic other than joining up? And if he did that, then surely the truth about the Ninnyhammer and his mother would come out. As the spring sun climbed higher above him, a clarity followed it across his mind. With no other options, Jack would return to the station tonight and throw himself under the last train. It would be painless, and it would be best for all.

As Jack imagined the scene, he heard a voice shouting to him. He stood, wiping his trousers clean from the damp mud and grass. He turned to see an older man walking across the field, waving at him. Jack picked up his jacket and case, ready to run if the need came. As the man came closer, Jack realised the man was not shouting at him to go away, indeed, he was asking him to stay put. By the time he reached him, the old man was all but breathless. His rosy cheeks puffed while his rotund stomach heaved under his brown, corduroy trousers and rough, cotton shirt. After catching his breath, he introduced himself as Thomas Bradbury, the farmer who owns the land Jack was on, as well as the land the station sat on.

After a short conversation, Thomas invited Jack back to his home for a warm meal, and reluctantly, at first, Jack agreed. As they entered the old farmhouse, after what Jack thought to be a fairly long walk, Thomas introduced his wife, Anne, and his three-month-old son, George.

Jack felt cosseted by this stranger; there was something about him he couldn't put his finger on. The man he had just met, this Thomas Bradbury, had a warmth about him which disarmed Jack's usual predisposition to be defensive and suspicious. After eating a full meal, the kind man, Thomas, led Jack outside and showed him the farmyard. The mixture of out-buildings which held most, but not all, of the farm's livestock were scattered around in a higgledy-piggledy jumble of sheds and barns. Unsure why the kind man was showing him this, Jack followed anyway. He had nothing to do now until the 9.30 p.m. train made its appearance back at the station. After showing him the last of the buildings, Jack assumed he would be sent on his way by the kind man. When Thomas offered Jack a job on the farm as a labourer, Jack was taken aback. Perhaps, Jack thought to himself as Thomas waited for his answer, this kind man was sent to allow Jack to make up for his transgression towards his mother and perhaps even the Ninnyhammer.

After accepting the job, Thomas showed Jack to a barn which had been partly converted for human habitation. After thanking him, more than once, Jack settled into his new surroundings. For the first night in as long as he could remember, Jack sensed a feeling of peace as he drifted to sleep. He wasn't sure what time he woke in a cold sweat, the blue mist once again swirling around his mind. The image of Doris curled up in her bed, frightened and pulling her sheets over her played in his mind. He was, once again, standing at the end of the bed. Naked and shamed, he ran from the house, while lined up along the stairs were Molly, the Ninnyhammer and his father, all pointing and laughing at him. The dream had come while he was in his deepest sleep, and to Jack, it seemed real, as real as any experience he'd had. Sweating and sitting bolt upright, he heaved for his breath as tears ran from his eyes, and his nose-dripped mucus.

He wiped himself clean with the back of his hand and sat motionless, waiting for the blue mist to dissipate. After calming himself, Jack lay back on the bed staring at the high-vaulted wooden ceiling. Could it be that his curse in life was to be troubled in his sleep? Perhaps this would be his own penance for what he'd done to the only person who had ever truly and unconditionally loved him.

As the days turned to weeks, and they in turn became months, Jack watched as the seasons passed him by. The blue mist still came to call on him, but its visits were becoming less frequent as the days on the calendar were ticked off. As for the red mist, Jack had not felt its presence after that night. Life on the farm was a busy one. With limited mechanical machinery, much of the back-breaking work was still done by hand, and this suited Jack's large, powerful build. The tasks Thomas could no longer manage, Jack took over with ease. The kind man would often comment that Jack had the strength of three men and the stamina of ten. Life was good, and Jack felt he'd found *his* place. No one bothered the farm, they were, for the most part, left alone, only the odd trip into the village meant that Jack had to deal with others, and that suited him.

Rhetoric from Germany had become more intense over the last few months, and though the Prime Minister, Neville Chamberlain, had delivered a speech the previous September, promising peace for our time, only the most wishful and naïve of people truly believed it.

Certainly, Thomas didn't, and he could tell Jack was worried about the possible outbreak of war. The kind man was *world-smart*, he'd known it when he first laid eyes on Jack, laying on the ground, that this was a man running from something. He'd heard the cries from the barn in the dead of night, and he knew conscription would be problematic for him. He'd never asked Jack what it was, or who it is, he was running from; he figured Jack would tell him in his own time if he wanted to. For Thomas, it didn't matter; he knew we all have our past, the demons we keep locked away from everyone and that only come out when we let down our guard, and for most of us, as it was with Jack, that was normally when we're asleep. When the news came of Germany's shelling of Poland almost a year to the day after Neville Chamberlain's speech, Thomas knew that war was once again unavoidable. And so, on September 3 1939, Britain declared war on Germany. After hearing the news, Thomas reassured

Jack that he would keep him from conscription. After all, like the workers on the railway, farm workers were seen as being vital to the war effort. For now, at least, Jack would be safe

**

Late August 2017

Jill had collected the now fully refurbished crucifix from the silversmith and was making her way to The Halt. Moving day had arrived, and her excitement was only matched, or more accurately surpassed, by Paul's, and perhaps Charlie's, who had been sent to the local kennels to keep him out of trouble. This had been a pet project for Paul since he had first laid eyes on The Halt two years previously. The main house, car park and gardens were now finished, along with the driveway which meandered from the main road and along to the parking area. The engine shed was, as expected, behind its scheduled date. The finding of the body had seen that project put on hold while a search had been carried out to try and ascertain who the deceased was and how and why he was there. So far, he had not been identified, though this was not so surprising given the length of time they now expected he'd been in the roof space. Work on the shed was expected to begin in the new year, and for now, Jill had requested that John and his team clear the site so that she and Paul could enjoy the remainder of the summer and the coming winter in peace and quiet, which was, after all, the main reason they had bought it. John had, by-and-large, been happy to accommodate this request.

The Halt had taken its toll on him and his team, with the injury to Darren, as well as a few other rather bizarre occurrences which he'd been under strict instructions from Paul to keep from Jill.

As Jill turned off the road and started down the driveway, the old station looked splendid nestled in the shallow valley. The heavy machines and work trucks were all gone, and for the first time, she could see what Paul had seen in his mind on that first day. The main house, as they now called it, principally because that was how it was referred to in the architectural drawings, sat proudly in a moat of landscaped gardens. Hanging baskets full of the local wildflowers hung from the four corners, while the old platform now began its new life as a porch, complete with fire pit, barbeque area and seating. Below it, where the tracks once were, a green trail led away and along the gentle slopes on each side of the valley.

To the east, the walk would take you to the seaside town of Whitby, and to the west, Middlesbrough. But here, in the beautiful surroundings of the North Yorkshire Moors, with a deep blue sky above, both seemed a world away.

As Jill entered the house, holding the crucifix, Paul came in from what once was the waiting room but was now the main hub of the house. A large, contemporary, kitchen-diner with space to entertain in the summer and look out at the wonderful views in the winter when the moors would turn white. As she stood in the hallway, the entrance opened in front of her. Ahead was a sizeable staircase which split, allowing for a vaulted landing which led to the master suite to the left, and the guest bedrooms and bathroom to the right. Where Jill stood, and to the right of her, which was once the stationmaster's house, was now their main living room, along with a drawing room and study for Jill. And to the left was the kitchen-diner. Paul had taken the opportunity to install the latest tech, which included underfloor heating, water purification systems, heat exchangers, air filtration systems and enough photovoltaic roof tiles to allow the building to be self-sufficient during the summer months. The control systems for these were to be found in the small plant room, which Paul had hidden behind the kitchen-diner as a small extension.

It was, as Paul had promised Jill it would be, a beautiful, modern and yet charming home which managed to keep the charm of the Victorian era, even down to the bulky, metal radiators, which though they now served no purpose, they'd kept maintaining the charm and splendour of the building. Paul's skill was clear for Jill to see. All the high-tech that made this building fit for the 21st century and to be autonomous in its heating, cooling and security was completely hidden from sight. Jill grinned at Paul as he walked past her, and she noticed the haughty look of self-congratulation on his face.

"Yeah, okay, smug man, it's gorgeous, you were right," she said, smirking.

"I told you, trust me. I'm an architect," Paul sniggered, as he walked out the door toward the car park.

Jill noticed the fastener she'd asked John to put up for the crucifix. Carefully climbing up the small stepladder, she hung it above the door where she had decided would be its rightful place. "Bless people on the way in and bless them on the way out," she'd told Paul. Who, as usual, had shrugged and made no comment.

As she put the ladder away, Jill heard a horn from the car park. Eagerly, she rushed out to meet the truck. Today was the day when the station clock was being hung after being back at the clocksmith's. She watched, as a younger man than before unloaded the clock and made his way over.

"Where's the older guy?" Jill asked the younger man, as he manhandled the clock onto the porch.

"Keith? He's not with us anymore," he answered.

"Ah, did he retire?" Jill asked, as the younger man placed his ladder below the bracket.

"Retire? Didn't anyone contact you? He had a heart attack in the shop, that's why your clock is a little delayed."

"Oh, I'm sorry to hear that. No, no one has been in touch, I am so sorry." Jill responded the only way she knew how and the only way she could. With compassion and shock.

"Thanks, we're all a bit shaken, but things have to keep on, I guess."

"I'll leave you to it," Jill said, as she made her way back into the main house, unsure of how to proceed any further without her own excitement seeming callous.

As she continued to unpack, Paul joined her in the kitchen.

"Did you know the old guy who came to fix the clock has died?" she asked Paul.

"No, why would I?" Paul replied, a little defensively.

Jill shrugged, "Oh, I don't suppose you would, but it's a little strange, don't you think?"

Paul kept his back to Jill. "Why, what do you mean, strange?"

"Well, first Darren's accident, then the body in the roof and now the clocksmith."

"Think it's called coincidence," Paul replied, and then changed the subject. "What time are we picking up Charlie?"

"I told them anytime today, just when we're ready for him."

Paul didn't answer; he kept unpacking the cutlery box with his back to Jill. Still, in his mind, what Jill had said and the way she'd summed up the three incidents played on his mind. After a few moments, he pushed it to the back of his thoughts. Besides, they were nothing more than coincidence. It was Jill's agenda behind her questioning that had unsettled him. Soon enough, his logical brain placed things back into the order he liked.

"Hi, it's all done," the younger man said, as he looked diffidently through the open door. "The clock, it's up and working again."

"Thank you, do you know why it had stopped?" Jill asked, as she walked over to where he stood, seemingly too polite or nervous to enter the kitchen fully.

"No idea. When we found Keith, the clock was working, so it looks like he'd fixed it before he—" the younger man stopped mid-sentence.

Jill understood why and didn't push him to finish it. Rather, she thanked him and walked back to his van. "Well, thank you for fitting it anyway, and again, we're sorry about Keith."

The younger man, who had still not introduced himself to Jill, climbed into the van. With a rather fleeting wave, he drove out of the car park and away along the drive. Jill watched him as far as the main road before she headed back inside.

She found Paul in the drawing room hooking up his high-end hi-fi. A passionate audiophile with a wide-ranging taste in music, the hi-fi system was to take pride of place in this room, with the valve amp sitting proudly next to the granite-based turntable. Next to it, on the bespoke cabinet, his impressive and carefully catalogued vinyl collection.

"I think it's safe to pick Charlie up now."

Paul looked over to her while bi-wiring the floor standing speakers. "Would you? It's just that I'm a little busy," he said, holding onto the thick, copper cables.

Jill shook her head. "Yeah, okay."

"Thanks, darling, you're the best."

"You too," Jill replied, with the same sardonic tone Paul had just used.

By the time Jill returned, Paul had finished the drawing room and was setting up Jill's study, where she would work on her blog and website. Charlie, seeing this new home for the first time, did what any self-respecting Spaniel should. Race around sniffing every nook-and-cranny until he zoned in on the one room in which he had that special interest. The kitchen. As the day wore on, and the heat of the afternoon climaxed at a high twenty-eight degrees, both Jill and Paul decided to call it a day.

They had, by any measure, achieved more today than they had thought they would, and with the hot weather forecast to continue, there would be plenty of time over the coming days to finish off *operation clusterfuck,* as Paul had seemingly aptly named it.

Jill and Paul sat on the porch. The summer sun now hung around the left side of the building, casting a long, cooling shadow across where the seating area was located. Paul had spent time, too much time, Jill often thought, working out where the seating, fire pit and barbeque area should be. But as she cooled from the sun, she was again forced to admit he'd got this right too. Though she wasn't about to tell him that. Not yet, anyway. Paul poured her another glass of white wine and sat next to her while Charlie laid at her feet, his stomach full thanks to the feast Paul had cooked up on his new state of the art barbeque. The sun's evening rays stretched out across the deep green of the moors, and Jill felt content at what they'd accomplished between them. As the temperatures began to fall, and a cooling breeze picked up through the shallow valley, they both decided to head inside, beaten and worn out from the physicality of moving as well as the mental exhaustion of getting to this point over the last two years, it was time for an early night. Jill tapped her leg and called to Charlie who eagerly followed them both. As Jill passed under the station clock, it read 9.12 p.m.

With the house secured and Charlie in his new sleeping place, Jill and Paul followed their customary routine for bedtime and eventually, climbed under the light, summer covers. The air-conditioning systems Paul had had installed kept the air quality and temperature of the house at that perfect setting of utmost comfort for both its human and canine occupants. Jill turned on the TV and set the sleep timer for sixty minutes. As she lay in her usual position, laid, to some degree, on her left side, facing away from Paul, she felt a hand move tenderly around her stomach, and then a loving kiss on the back of her neck. As the station clock outside reached 9.30 p.m., Jill responded to the advances, and with her eyes closed, she turned and gently began kissing the mouth which had caringly nuzzled at the nape of her neck. She felt his hands move down her body, reaching inside her shorts and she responded in kind. As what seemed to Jill the most affectionate and passionate lovemaking Paul had ever brought to her reached its climax, she felt the weight of him, which she only now recognised as being more than it would usually be, lift from her and move to her side. Almost in unison, the TV switched off. Jill turned her head to look at Paul and opened her eyes for the first time since she had felt the soft hand on her stomach.

In the darkened room, with the sun's light now long since extinguished, Jill's eyes scrambled to decipher the image before her. In the split second her mind jostled with the confusion of what she saw, a million thoughts flooded her. The primary thought being, she did not recognise the man lying next to her. In the dim light, he seemed larger than Paul, much larger. After the split second had passed, Jill screamed and jumped back for the light switch, blinking frantically as she did.

"What's wrong?" Paul's soft voice said.

The light illuminated him, Paul, lying where she had assumed he would be and where the large man she thought she'd seen had been. Jill sat, pulling on her nightshirt.

"It's nothing, I must have dosed off."

"You gave me a fright when you yelled," Paul said, moving over to her and placing his hand on her shoulder.

"It's okay, just weary. I'll be fine in the morning," Jill said, as she turned off the light, pulling the Egyptian, cotton sheets back over her.

As Jill closed her eyes, the image of the man she'd seen when she had looked to her fiancé became more detailed. She did not recognise this face or his size, which she would remember if she'd met anyone matching that description.

She pushed it back from her mind. She was likely right, overtired and with too much on her mind given the ever-increasing to-do list. As Jill fell into slumber, the station clock, as with all the timepieces, slipped past 9.30 p.m. And in the hall above the door, the crucifix dulled.

The following morning, Jill woke before Paul. She had not slept easily, the image still forming in her mind of the strange, large face which she'd seen. Even in the bright sunlight of another hot August day, it still formed in her mind's eye like some sort of manifestation which was not yet ready to fully reveal itself. Charlie brought her thoughts back to the pressing matters of the here and now, as he scratched at the kitchen door. Jill stood, still holding her morning coffee and opened it for him. Charlie sprang from the house and ran toward the car park, barking and then disappeared. "Charlie," Jill shouted. Still, he barked out of sight. "Fuck," Jill whispered, as she put down her coffee and headed out the door.

She followed the barking around to the front of the house, where she found Charlie sat under the station clock barking directly at it. "Charlie!" Jill demanded the dog's attention, but she was greeted with indifference and ignored. She moved a step closer. "Charlie!" she shouted again. Once again, Charlie ignored his master's voice. "What the hell are you barking at?" Jill looked to the clock. She saw nothing unusual. The second hand was sweeping around the face, and it read 6.38 a.m. Jill looked closer at the clock face, making sure she'd read the time correctly. She had. She pulled her phone from her night-robe pocket and touched the screen. 7.38 a.m. Jill remembered she'd switched her phone off when they had gone to bed. *'Has it not corrected its time when I switched it back on?'* she wondered. Jill moved back to the house and checked the wall clock in the kitchen. 6.38 a.m. Mystified, she checked every clock in the house, including Paul's phone, and they all read the same. They were all one hour behind. A thought occurred to Jill; she had set the TV timer to one hour when she'd gone to bed, and it had switched off at the exact moment their lovemaking had finished. She hadn't paid it much heed at the time, other than she thought it rather humorous that should Paul know it lasted an hour, he would consider himself the world's greatest lover. But the humour of it was now gone. And the thought of the swirling image of the large man came back to the front of her mind.

Jill tried to connect the dots that now ricocheted around her mind. Had there been a power cut? But even if there had, that wouldn't affect Paul's mobile phone. The cars. Jill walked to the two parked cars and checked them; they both read the correct time, now approaching 8.00 a.m. It was only the clocks located in the house or switched on that precise time. What time was it? She tried to remember. "Yes, nine-thirty," she said to herself, as she remembered that *Veep*, her favourite American satire, was just starting. But, still, why an hour? Why only that precise hour? Jill sat with her coffee. Charlie had since stopped his complaining at the station clock and had returned, satisfied that he'd once again protected his territory and humans from whatever perceived threat he had sensed. Paul interrupted her thoughts and caused a disconnect from the mystery that, for the time being, at least, only she knew of.

"Hey, you're up early," he said, entering the kitchen.

"You might want to check the time again," Jill replied, sipping her coffee.

"What? Why?"

"For some reason, and don't ask me, I have no clue, every clock in the house is an hour slow."

"You sure?"

"Yup," Jill confirmed.

Paul placed down his toast and coffee and reached for the small remote and pointed it at the wall-mounted flat screen. As the BBC news came on, the time showed in the bottom corner of the screen. "They look okay to me."

Jill looked at the screen. 8.27 a.m. She turned to the wall clock, 8.28 a.m. She turned back to Paul. "What time do you have on your phone?"

"What?"

Jill raised her voice, a note of panic resonated in it. "What time do you have on your phone?"

Paul pulled it out of his pocket. "Eight thirty-one. Why, what's the matter?"

Jill slumped back into her chair. Had she just imagined it? Had they all been an hour out, or like the large man beside her in bed last night, was it some kind of stress-induced reaction to everything? The moving, the accidents and the dead body?

"Are you okay?" Paul asked again.

"Huh, yeah, sure. I think I'm a little bushed. I expect I'll be fine when we're totally put straight." Jill smiled as reassuringly as she could. Then returned to drinking her coffee.

"Okay, I have to pop to the office. I'll be back later, but are you sure you're okay?" Paul asked while finishing his morning coffee.

"Just go, I'll take a shower, I'll be fine. I promise."

"All right then."

"What did you mean when you came in?" Jill stopped Paul from leaving.

"What?"

"When you came in you said to me, I'm up early. What did you mean?"

"Nothing, it's just that it was a little before eight. I didn't expect to see you out of bed yet," Paul answered.

Jill became confused again. "No, you put the TV on, it said eight-thirty on the screen, I remember."

Paul looked sideways at her. "Honey, I made coffee and toast before I put the TV on, don't you remember? It was almost eight when I came in, I remember seeing the clock."

Jill didn't reply. What had happened to the time, half an hour had passed while Paul made, and ate his breakfast, and she couldn't remember it.

"Are you sure you're okay, hun?" Paul asked again.

Jill dismissed him with a wave. "Yes, you go, and I'll get started."

"See you soon. I love you," Paul said, as he left the kitchen.

Jill looked back at the clock. 8.43 a.m. Had she genuinely had a time slip? Not the sci-fi-alien abduction time slip she'd seen in countless movies, but a mental lapse so peculiar she had actually missed the half hour between saying good morning, as Paul entered the kitchen to him then eating his toast and leaving for work. And what of the hour? She had checked all the clocks in the house, even the electronic ones, hadn't she? Could it be as simple as physical and mental exhaustion? The last few months as the development had begun to come close to its completion had been a very stressful time and moving in hadn't been easy. There was still lots to do, all the small, finicky finishing touches that seemed to take an age and in which she would go around in ever decreasing circles. Yes, the to-do list seemed to be getting longer the more she did. Jill resigned herself to the latter explanation. She didn't conceive of how she could simply lose an hour and a half, and so she put it down to stress. She cleared away the breakfast pots and cleaned the kitchen before making her way to their new master suite. After making up the bed, she stripped and got into the generous walk-in shower.

After switching off the shower, Jill exited the glass enclosure and wrapped a large, soft towel around herself. She felt cold, the hairs on her arms stood erect and she felt goose bumps raise over her body. She shivered and left the en suite bathroom. In the bedroom, Jill sat at her dressing table and began combing her hair. Today was more functionality than style, and while she felt cold now, she knew the day would be another hot one. There was no need to spend time drying and styling, rather, she combed it through and still wet, tied it into a ponytail. She stood and dropped her towel.

Making her way to her wardrobe, an uneasy feeling came across her as if she was being watched. She looked across at the window. She knew the curtains were open, but there was no road or houses on that side of the house. It wasn't rational to think anyone would be outside looking at her; there would be no reason for anyone to be there on their land. The view was clear, as she imagined it would be. She felt the chill again, and again, she shivered. Shrugging both the chill and the thought of some voyeuristic stranger watching her dress, she put on her clothes and made her way back to the kitchen and the waiting Charlie.

"Is it time for your walk?" Jill asked the waiting dog in her best *get Charlie excited* voice.

Charlie, as always, carried out his ritual dance of circling his bed and darting to where his lead was kept while yapping excitedly. Jill fastened the long, retractable lead to him and left the house. As she did, the heat of the morning hit her. This was the first house she'd had with a fully autonomous climate control system. Even so, she thought, it seemed it was working a little too well. The house didn't feel comfortable in the heat of this August, the hottest on record the BBC kept repeating; it was keeping it too cold. She would look at it when she got back. While it was very much Paul's domain, she knew how to check the setting at least. Jill walked around the front of the house, below the patio and onto the green track. Turning west, she began her first long walk with Charlie on what was now their land. Allowing the lead to unravel, she watched as the ever-more excited Spaniel sniffed his new territory and began marking it, still cocking his leg, even though he'd long-since emptied his bladder.

She pulled her phone and headphones from her pocket and put on the album, *Alone in the Universe*, which was rapidly becoming one of her favourites. As the track list played through, she turned a corner and came across a bricked-up tunnel. This, it seemed, was where the green lane ended. On either side was a steep embankment, too steep to climb in her everyday trainers, anyway. She turned back. "Come on, Charlie, looks like we're heading home." Charlie stopped halfway up the steep incline to her left, lifted his leg for one last dry piss, and then scuttled down to join her.

Jill entered the house via the utility room located at the back of the kitchen. The temperature inside was a sharp contrast to the heat. For a short while, it was refreshing, but Jill knew that to keep the house this cold, in this heat, would cost them a small fortune, even with the self-sustaining energy systems Paul had built into the build. After giving Charlie a bowl of cold water, which, as usual, he managed to get at least the same amount as he consumed on the floor, she headed to the small plant room where the control systems for the underfloor heating and climate control were found. Jill checked the reading. The settings were correct. The house was supposed to be kept at a stable eighteen degrees Celsius, and according to the readouts, that is what it was, but it felt much colder to her. Paul had said there could be minor teething issues with a system this new and advanced, and so Jill decided to call out the engineers. After all, it wasn't a cheap system, and if it was reading falsely, she wanted it fixed and bug-free before the winter came.

Dutifully, the engineers arrived and checked the system. Much to Jill's frustration, they found no defects or bugs. Rather, the system was working at one-hundred percent efficiency, and when they entered the house to check the temperature with a stand-alone device, not only did the interior now feel comfortable and not cold, but the device read exactly as it should. Jill thanked the two men and watched them leave before closing the door. She turned and made her way through the house. She needed to finish setting up her study. She had announced that she would be taking a break from blogging and updating her website while she moved, and in general, her readers and fans had been supportive. But Jill knew that if she left it too long, they would desert her to get their fix for information elsewhere. As Jill passed through the hallway, she noticed the crucifix had a dark tarnish across it. Pulling over one of the armchairs placed either side of the staircase, she climbed on it and reached up.

Licking her thumb, she rubbed it across the crucifix. The dark tarnish came off, leaving a shining streak.

"That's strange," Jill muttered to herself. She lifted it from the nail on which it hung and walked to the utility room with it, rubbing it as she did. Taking a cloth, she wiped the dark tarnish from it and placed it on the countertop while she put the cloth away. When she turned from the cupboard, the crucifix had dulled again. "What the hell?" Jill scolded. She picked it up and looked closely at it. She rubbed her thumb across it again, and again, the tarnish came off. Placing it down again, she studied it. Nothing happened; the clean streak she'd made with her thumb remained. Charlie barked, and she turned. It was unusual for him to bark a warning, as he was used to people coming and going. She felt cold again, a shiver the same as this morning, and now Charlie growled. A deep, guttural growl of a pending attack. "Charlie?" Jill moved closer to his bed where the Spaniel sat, his gaze fixed on the hallway. Jill moved around the island in the kitchen, and as she did, the hallway came into view. Through the frosted glass on either side of the front door, a shadow.

A man, a large man, and Jill saw the outline of a hat. She moved guardedly toward the door, Charlie's growling becoming more aggressive. She reached the door, but the shadow hadn't moved.

Jill reached for the handle, turning it and pulling the door. She flung it open. As she did, Charlie raced from his bed and through her legs and onto the porch. Immediately, he stopped.

The porch was clear. Jill called Charlie back, who willingly obliged. She stood for a few seconds, scanning the area. No one could have run away that fast had it been a prank. And besides, what she saw, it was clearly the frame of a big man with a hat. She froze. The older man, the clocksmith, he told her he'd seen a big man wearing a hat standing on the old platform. And Darren, before he fell, he described the same image. A troubled sensation ran down her. She closed the door, locking it and returned to the kitchen with Charlie.

Later that night and after dinner, Jill sat quietly next to Paul. "Can I ask you something?" she said, taking a sip of her coffee.

"Anything."

"Have you had any strange experiences or felt like someone's watching you?" Jill asked.

"No, why?"

"When I came out of the shower today, I could have sworn someone was watching me. I know there wasn't anyone around, I checked, but it was so tangible."

"What, in the bathroom?"

"No, in the bedroom, after I'd had the shower."

"Were the curtains closed?" Paul asked.

"No."

"Well, if you're gonna stand naked and strut about with everything on show, sooner or later, someone will cotton on and watch you."

"What the hell is that supposed to mean?" Jill snapped, furious by Paul's reaction.

"Well, I mean, close the curtains."

"There is nothing on our land in the direction of the bedroom windows; you designed it that way. Privacy without shutting out the view, I think you said. Anyway, it wasn't so much someone looking in, as someone was in the room with me."

"I know, you're right, I did design the house to maximise the privacy. Sorry, but it's been a long day. When did the feeling start?" Paul replied.

"Like I said. I took a shower, came out in my towel, sat at my dressing table and then went to get dressed. That's when I took the towel off, and that's when it felt like someone was watching."

"Did you see anyone?" Paul asked.

"No, not then."

"What do you mean? Not then?"

"After I took Charlie for his walk, I was in the kitchen, and he started growling. When I looked in the direction he was staring, I saw a figure at the door through the glass."

"Who was it?" Paul asked, a little agitated.

"When I opened it, no one was there. But that's not all." Jill took another sip. "The figure I saw was of a man. A tall, broad man wearing a hat. Isn't that who Darren said he'd seen before he fell, and the old clocksmith?"

"I wouldn't pay it much attention," Paul replied glibly.

"That's not all. Have you noticed how cold it is in here?" Jill asked.

"I expect it's the climate control. I'll call them tomorrow," Paul replied, wanting to bring this line of conversation to an end.

"I called them out today, and they said there's nothing wrong. I know this will sound bizarre, but while they were here, it wasn't cold. It seemed to go back to normal."

"It seems fine to me," Paul replied.

"Yes, it only seems to become cold when I'm on my own. I can't explain it."

"I don't know what to tell you. If they've been out, and everything is okay, then..." Paul shrugged dismissively.

"It isn't just that. I haven't said anything, but when we moved in, I thought I heard that nursery rhyme again. Remember, when we first came onto the land?"

"And was it the same child singing it?" Paul asked flippantly.

Jill stood and placed her empty coffee cup on the table. Frustrated by Paul's lack of involvement in her concerns, she decided she would go to bed and call an end to the day. "I'm off to bed. I'll see you when you come up."

"Okay, I shouldn't be too long," Paul replied, his gaze already back on the flat screen.

Jill walked up the stairs and made her way to their bedroom. Pulling the curtains closed, she changed for bed. The cold had gone, and the house felt comfortable. She climbed into bed and pulled the light, cotton covers over her. *'Perhaps this is all in my head,'* she thought, as she lay in the darkened room. *'But why would Charlie behave like that if it was?'* She turned on her side, closing her eyes, determined that, tonight, she would have a good night's sleep, and that tomorrow, she would put these strange things out of her mind.

In the living room, Paul continued to watch the documentary on *The Great White Shark Café Migration.* Outside, the summer sun still hung in the sky. When the documentary had finished, Paul turned off the TV and made his way to the drawing room. He put on one of his vinyl records and sat back in the recliner, the music of Diane Krall smoothing the day away. Elsewhere, the house was quiet. Charlie lay asleep in his bed by the old radiator in the kitchen, and Jill, as she'd hoped she would, had fallen asleep. Outside, a soft breeze blew across the shallow valley, making the grass and tall flowers waft in its gentle embrace.

As the automatic lights began to switch on, the station clock reached nine-thirty. In the study, Paul was asleep, the vinyl record still playing. As he snored softly, a shadow moved across his face. As it did, the crucifix, which Jill had left on the kitchen counter, started to slowly tarnish. As the blemishing darkened, the large handprint, which Jill had seen on the first day, began to appear.

In his bed, Charlie woke. He crept from it, his head down and his hackles raised. His lips curled at the sides, bearing his teeth. Something was spooking him, something that was not meant to be, was here, with them in their home, and only Charlie could perceive it. He moved quietly toward the study, stalking whatever it was, he felt his pack needed protecting from. As he approached the study, he began the same low growl he'd used earlier when this, whatever it was that Charlie could sense, had been at the door. He entered the study and made his way to where Paul sat, asleep. The vinyl finished, and with a click, the stylus arm lifted from it and returned to its resting place.

As the record came to a gentle stop, Charlie's gaze followed the shadow, as it crossed the room towards the staircase. His growl deepened, and he bared more teeth and extended his hackles further.

The shadow moved up the stairs, and Charlie followed, unsure of what to do. He knew something was there, he could sense it, but his eyes saw nothing more than shadows, and he had no sense of a smell. Still, he decided his default, defensive growl and posturing would be the best thing to protect his pack. As he climbed the stairs, the shadow had entered his master's bedroom. He followed it in. It stood over Jill. Charlie watched as the shadow began to form a shape. Now, Charlie could see him clearly.

Part 2
The Happenings

It's nine-thirty. Look deeply into the shadows of the night for the large man in the fedora hat.

Chapter 8

August 3 1942

As August rolled in, and the bank holiday came around again, the village of Thirstonfield celebrated their annual festival. During this time of conflict around the world, life in the sleepy village would continue as usual. The British spirit persisting, even in the face of adversity, was not confined to the cities which had seen much of the onslaught from the Luftwaffe. The country as a whole was determined to continue with a way of life hard fought for over the centuries, and one they were not willing to give up, ever. Jack sat by the cricket pitch on the green, located in the centre of the village. He watched the locals enjoying the festivities as the sun beat down on him. He took another bite from the ham and peas pudding sandwich Anne made for him and felt content. From over the narrow road, and in front of the local pub, the kind man waved to him, and Jack waved back, holding up the sandwich in appreciation. He glanced at the village clock, 1.05 p.m. Jack finished the sandwich with one last bite and laid back on the soft, warm grass. In the distance, music played, people laughed and joked, and children played the games of the day. A soft breeze fluttered the red, white and blue bunting which was strewn across the village buildings. Union flags adorned the larger buildings while small boys ran around with wooden model Spitfires, imagining that they were single-handily beating the *Fritz* war machine and firing the bullet which would kill the evil Fuhrer.

With the sun lowering in the sky and as the heat of day began to ebb, Jack, Thomas, Anne and George made their way back to the farm. Jack, as always, sat in the back of the old

Morris pick-up. By the time they reached the farm, night was almost on them, and George was asleep. Carefully, Jack picked him up and carried him up the stairs and to his bed. After saying goodnight to Thomas and Anne, he returned to his own accommodation which he'd made homely and comfortable to his own tastes. Jack stripped, climbed into bed and reflected on his good fortune before finally falling asleep. The last two years had been very kind to Jack. Life on the Bradbury farm was good. Jack had become close to the kind man and his family. He would often play football with George during the short and infrequent downtimes the farm offered. The red mist which had been a significant part of Jack's life hadn't visited him for over a year, and the thought of what took place on that night two years previous was now a distant memory, and Jack, for the most part, convinced himself it was nothing more than a bad dream. It seemed he'd found his place in life. The war had spread from Europe, across to the Pacific, Africa and as far as Russia. Generally, the kind man didn't talk to Jack about the war. Sometimes, it was unavoidable, specifically when a formation of Spitfires or Hurricanes flew low over the farm. The sound of their Merlin engines heard long before the fighters were visible. This small part of the Yorkshire Dales gave the impression that war was a million miles away, something none of them who worked and lived on the farm new to be true, but all wished and pretended was.

Over the North Sea, just off the northeast coast, a lone Luftwaffe Donier bomber flew through the coastal drizzle and made land over the small coastal town of Saltburn-by-the-Sea. Unseen through the low mist, it found the railway lines and began to follow them inland.

Shortly after, the German bomber happened upon Middlesbrough Station. Hidden by the murk which had not made its way farther inland, the bomber spotted the station's Victorian glass roof glistening in the sunlight through the breaks in the grey cloud. As the pilot circled, waiting for the right moment, below them, the station's staff and customers were unaware of the twin-engine bomber six-hundred feet above, its engines drowned out by the din of the station. On its fourth pass over, the cloud opened enough for a target to be identified and the bombs fell. As the first hit, the pilot noted the time and day of the successful mission. August 3 1942 1.08 p.m.

Doris and Molly were, on this particular day, assigned to the kitchens. The direct hit from the second and last bomb to make its target gave them no time to acknowledge or react to it. Molly was killed instantly by the blast wave which tore through the brick building with ease. Doris was thrown back against the only interior wall not made of brick. Unconscious, she was unaware of the detritus which fell onto her, burying her, filling her lungs. She suffocated while comatose, oblivious to her body's struggle to maintain life in the absence of breathable air. By the time she was pulled from the debris, blooded, dirty and with her left leg all but decapitated, she had passed. Along with and next to Molly, she was laid in a line and covered in a sheet. This, it seemed, was what Doris' life amounted to.

August 4 1942.

Thomas made his usual daily run into the village. While there, he'd learned of the attack on the station the previous day. He'd felt cold. Jack had told him about his mother who worked at the station, and of Molly. Though Jack hadn't told Thomas all that transpired, it was this that had caused Jack to end up on his farm. Thomas hadn't questioned it. Though he suspected there was a lot more Jack wasn't telling him, he'd made the decision to take it at face value. He knew now that while he'd tried to protect Jack from the war, he would have to tell him of the attack. It could be that his mother, and perhaps Molly, if Jack was to be bothered about either of them, could have survived. It could be they were lucky. By the reports coming in, only two bombs made their target. Typical Hun shit, the shopkeeper had said to Thomas. Say what you will, our boys always hit their target, he'd continued as Thomas' mind scrambled to figure out how to tell Jack the news.

By the time Thomas pulled the old truck up to the farmhouse, Jack was busy repairing Anne's washing line. Thomas walked to Jack and put his arm around him to lead him away from the house. He always suspected Jack to have a temper, though, thankfully, they'd not seen it. A man this size wasn't someone you wanted to be around when he did lose it, Thomas had often thought to himself. He told Jack of the attack and watched as the big man lost his legs and flopped to the ground. Thomas crouched beside him, offering what solace he could. He told Jack they could well be okay, only two bombs hit their target. But he could tell Jack was out of focus, he'd heard nothing past his opening line, that Middlesbrough Station had been hit directly.

Jack asked to be left alone, and Thomas obliged him. Once out of sight, Jack struggled to contain the feelings of remorse, of anger and of guilt for not being there. He must know; he needed to be sure if his mother was alive or not. Jack stood and made for Thirstonfield Halt.

***

Charlie recognised the shape that stood over his master's bed as that of a human. Though he could see no details, he had not seen one as big as this before. Nonetheless, his duty was to protect against this intruder. Charlie began to growl the first warning, but the figure did not turn or react. Instead, it lent over the bed and pulled back the sheets, uncovering Jill, who was still asleep. Charlie growled again and bit at the back of this shape's legs, but he made contact only with his own jaw, his teeth snapping together. The shape moved again, leaning over the bed, and this time, Charlie leapt at it and onto the bed. As he did, Jill woke with a start, screaming. The shape dispersed, but not before looking directly to Charlie, who attacked again, but again, bit nothing but air. By the time Paul made it to their bedroom, Jill was sat up with the table light on, and Charlie was sat between her legs guarding her.

"What the hell is going on?" Paul asked abruptly.

"I don't know. I was asleep. I felt cold, and the next thing I knew, Charlie was barking at the corner," Jill replied, still shaken.

Paul turned to the dog and instructed him to get off the bed. Charlie obeyed but did not leave the room. Paul switched on the main light, and Jill shielded her eyes.

"What's that?" Paul asked, pointing to Jill's thighs.

Jill looked to where he pointed. She sensed a chill run through her she'd only ever experienced once, the day she was diagnosed with cancer. On the inside of her thighs, near to her groin, were bruises, and close to her pubic bone were two large handprints. "Holy shit!" Jill jumped back. The shock turned her stomach and caused adrenaline to rush through her.

"How did they get there?" Paul demanded.

"I have no idea," Jill answered, confused by what she could see.

"Well, they're not from me!"

"Honestly, I don't know. I have no idea."

Paul stood, unsure of how to proceed. He could see that Jill was shaken by these marks on her body, but he couldn't decide whether that was shock because they were there or because he'd seen them. "Perhaps it'll come back to you in the morning. You can sleep with the dog tonight." Paul turned and left the room, slamming the door as he did. Jill got out of bed and moved to the full-length mirror. She looked at the black and blue marks, and as she did, a thought occurred to her. Slowly, she pulled off her top. Her breasts had the same bruises, and on her right collarbone, just at the nape of her neck, another large handprint. Jill's blood ran cold. She had no explanation for this. Nothing that scrambled around her mind made any sense. These wounds, or marks, would have taken some force, and while the last time they'd made love, Paul had been more passionate than he would normally be, he hadn't exerted so much force as to injure her like this. And besides, the handprints were of a much larger hand than Paul's. She dressed and climbed back into bed. Perhaps, in the morning, things would be clear to her.

She patted the bed and called for Charlie, who jumped up next to her. Leaving the small table lamp on, they both fell asleep. From out of the corner Charlie had barked at, the swirling shadow appeared again. This time, it was stationary while Jill slept.

As the sun broke through the bedroom shades, Charlie began to wake. He searched the bedroom for any sign of the previous night's intruder, but he found nothing. No smell or scent of any kind. Jill woke, and for the briefest of moments while she regained her thoughts, the events of the night were forgotten. But that briefest of calm didn't last long. Jill walked back to the mirror, pulling down her shorts and lifting her top. The marks were gone. There was no bruising around her thighs or breasts, and the handprints around her throat and pubic bone had disappeared too. Had she dreamt the whole thing, she wondered while she studied her body. It seemed to her that something was off, and it had been for a while. Last night was just another *thing* that couldn't be explained, like the time-shift, as she had come to call it, and the large shadow at the door.

She looked back to Charlie and sighed, then left the bedroom and made her way to the kitchen, convinced that it must have been nothing more than a vivid dream.

Jill sat and began to eat her breakfast and was joined shortly after by Paul. She smiled at him, the events of the previous night now firmly dismissed, but Paul didn't respond in kind. Instead, he ignored her and made his way through to the dining room. Jill was a little perplexed by this. Why he was acting in such a way was beyond her. She followed him.

"Hey, grumpy," she said, trying the light approach. "What's up?"

Paul placed down his coffee and moved his attention from the TV to Jill. "You need to ask?"

"Well, yes, I need to ask, that's why I did."

"You have an explanation for the marks on you then? One that doesn't mean someone else had their hands all over you." Paul scowled.

136

"Marks, I thought that was a dream," Jill replied, unsure in her response.

"A fucking dream!" Paul was becoming angry.

"Yes, look." Jill lifted her top to reveal her torso and bare breasts. "No marks. When I looked again this morning and there were none, I thought I'd just dreamt it."

Paul stood and made his way over to Jill, who lowered her top. "Let me see your legs," he asked. Jill pulled down her bottoms. Again, there were no marks. None on her thighs or her groin. Paul took a step back, as Jill pulled up her bottoms.

"See, I told you," she said.

"I don't understand, what the hell is going on, Jill?" Paul became agitated.

"There have been a few strange things happening. I've tried to tell you, but you didn't want to listen, you just dismissed them," Jill defended herself.

"What do you mean things?" Paul snapped.

"What, you want a fucking list? Okay, how about the clocksmith who said a large man in a hat was looking for me, or Darren who said he'd seen a big man in a hat before he fell. Oh, and then the feeling of being watched, and a large male shadow at the front door. And that's not to mention the dead fucking body we found. There is something not right here!" Jill shouted in retaliation and then continued. "And don't ever accuse me of having someone else's hands on me. That is a red line you should never ever cross."

Paul stood silently. He too thought something was off, but his persistence in completing this project meant he had pushed any doubts and uncertainties to the back of his mind. As Jill left the dining room, she turned back to him. Paul relaxed, thinking she was going to retreat from her outburst. She didn't. "And another thing, it's still fucking cold in here."

Before she left the room, Paul replied, "I'll have the engineers come back out and take a look."

"You do that." Then, the door slammed.

By mid-morning, Paul was in his office. The argument this morning had knocked him somewhat. It was the first time in a long time that they'd fallen out. Not since the diagnosis of cancer had they argued over anything of consequence. Perhaps what to watch on TV or which movie to see at the multiplex, but nothing like this. No matter how he tried, he couldn't explain the marks and handprints on Jill and their sudden disappearance the following morning. He'd seen them, right? He thought as he tried to figure out what they could be. Even Google had no explanation other than that of paranormal or supernatural experiences, and he was a long way off from giving that bullshit, as he called it, any credence or room to grow in his mind. Besides, knowing Jill as he did, if he even suggested that, she would grab onto it. He reached across his desk for his phone. Perhaps it was best to call her, tell her he was sorry. As he reached, he caught his coffee cup, spilling what was left of the dregs across his desk. "Fuck!" he shouted, as he watched it drip into his top drawer.

He pulled it open, taking the now wet contents out and placing them on his desk. The last thing he reached was wedged at the back. A brown wax envelope, and he remembered what was inside. The strange waiver he'd signed when they bought The Halt. Paul checked to make sure Jeff was not at his desk. Confirming the coast was clear, he pulled the now damp piece of paper from the envelope. He read it again. "The previous owners, Mr and Mrs George Bradbury, will not be responsible for any unforeseen acts of disturbance, violence or disruption. Whether they be manmade, natural causes or otherwise."

Disturbance, violence and disruption. They'd seen all of these in one form or another. *'Did they know something?'* he wondered. He grabbed the waiver, stuffing it back into the envelope and left the office; his destination, the Bradbury farm.

***

After Paul had left for work, Jill followed her usual routine. She cleared away the breakfast pots, switched on the dishwasher and showered and dressed. She too had searched Google for any answers which would explain the strange

138

marks and their sudden vanishing. And like Paul, the only results which matched her search criteria were those of otherworldly explanations. And though Jill was the spiritual one, she too was not yet convinced of the idea this was some sort of ghost or spirit. Rather, she decided, it was one of those rare and unusual medical conditions which flash across Facebook every so often or make it on a medical show on National Geographic.

Indeed, the last episode of *Monsters Inside Me* she'd watched had a case where bruising would come and go, though even this straw-clutching didn't involve large handprints. After getting her day in order, Jill decided she would take Charlie for his walk. As she began to get ready, a knock came at the door. "Shit," she muttered, as she dropped his lead and answered it. A man wearing white overalls and carrying a small tool chest and laptop stuffed under his right arm stood before her. On his chest was a red badge, *Renewable Heating Solutions.* It was the company responsible for Paul's over-the-top ventilation and heating system. At least he remembered to call them, she thought to herself in the second it took for her to acknowledge the man.

"I'm here to fix your climate control system. It's making the house too cold?" the repairman said rhetorically.

"Yes, come in. I'll take you to where it is," Jill replied.

The repairman followed Jill to the plant room and went about plugging in the laptop and all manner of electrical gadgets. Jill stayed only until she felt her obligation to be polite had passed. "I'm just inside, come and get me when you're done," she said, leaving him to work. The repairman didn't answer. Instead, he just nodded and smiled.

Jill entered the kitchen to find Charlie sat waiting for his daily run. "Sorry, Charlie, looks like you'll have to wait until Daddy is home. He can take you." Charlie whined and made for his bed, sighing as he lay.

***

Paul knocked on the door of the old farmhouse after leaving a dust-bowl amount of dirt in his wake, as he pushed the Range Rover hard along the rough track, which led from the road to the Bradbury's home. After what seemed to Paul an age, but was likely only a minute or two, George opened the door wearing what Paul was convinced were the same clothes and holding the same green mug as he had the last time he'd visited them. George looked him up and down. Paul thought, just for a second at least, he actually saw the moment when George recognised who was standing at his door.

"Aye?" was all the old farmer said.

"This waiver," Paul started, as he pulled it from the envelope. "What exactly didn't you tell me about The Halt?"

George stood, thinking for a second, and then moved to one side. "Come in, lad."

Paul entered the kitchen and stood by the sink while George shuffled his way in, taking a place opposite Paul. "Let me see," he asked Paul, pointing to the piece of paper. Paul handed him the waiver and watched as the farmer read it over the top of half-moon glasses, which perched halfway along his wrinkled-podgy nose, the brass frames standing out against his red cheeks.

"Well?" Paul insisted.

"It's nothing, lad." George handed the waiver back to him.

"What do you mean, nothing? If it's *nothing,* why did you insist I sign it?"

George leant further back onto the old dining table, which creaked a little in protest at the old man's rotund frame. George frowned, his bushy, greying eyebrows creased over his heavily weathered and wrinkled brow. "Listen, lad, you bought it fair-and-square, and as I remember for a pretty penny too. What happens after is on you and your fiancée."

Paul wasn't sure which to respond to first, but his confusion passed quickly enough. "What's that supposed mean?"

"Exactly what I said, lad."

Paul stood upright and took a step toward him. He was seething. "Now listen to me, you old sod. There's something not right with that place. Now you tell me, or I'll—"

"You'll what, lad? I've shit bigger than you. Now, get off my land, and don't bother coming back." George reached behind the table and lifted a shotgun from under it.

Paul backed down. He figured the crazy, old git would probably use it, and though the law was a little hazy; he was on his land, and they'd been arguing. "I'm going, but you stay away from our home," Paul protested, as he left the house.

Paul climbed into the Range Rover. Still fuming from the old farmer's reactions, he threw the envelope onto the back seat. The waxy cardboard skimmed across the leather upholstery and fell under the front passenger seat.

***

George watched the SUV scurry its way back along the farm track with the shotgun resting across his folded arms and a smile across his face. As Paul's Range Rover turned onto the main road, George Bradbury released his grip on the old shotgun. It hadn't been fired for years, and he had no useable shells for it, but he knew it would scare the *city-yuppie* off his land. As he turned and headed back inside, Mavis came into the kitchen. She'd heard Paul's argument with George. She'd been in the large pantry just off the kitchen when Paul had entered, and she'd elected to remain there once she heard what the subject matter was. She sat at the table. "Was that about the old place?" she asked George, as he put the shotgun away.

"Aye, it was. Seems it's starting up again," George said with a heavy tone.

"We shouldn't-a sold them the place, George."

"We need the money, wife. You know the farm is dying."

"Even so."

George didn't answer. Rather, he shrugged and poured some tea into the old, green mug.

Mavis stood. "Perhaps we should tell them, husband?" Mavis asked.

"We can't tell them. They'll start poking their bloody noses in our business, and then they'll find out about them both. And that secret stays between us. Who knows what folk would say if that came out," George answered with a heavy sigh.

George watched, as Mavis walked slowly out of the kitchen. Sitting, he stirred his tea and looked out across the farmyard through the open door. He remembered how it used to be back in the farm's hey-days of the forties through to the seventies. Since then, they'd struggled to keep it going. The livestock were long gone, as had most of the harvest. These days, farmers were given subsidies not to grow and produce, and when the bulk food suppliers had come to George, the price they offered him didn't cover the cost of the production, and so he'd chased them off.

He knew the farm was dying around him, and there was nothing he could do except wait for his time to come too. And as he drank his tea, he wasn't sure which would come first.

***

"Hi," the repairman announced himself, as he entered the kitchen. "I've checked it again, and I still can't find any faults recorded or current. I'm sorry," he said.

"Okay, we'll see how it goes," Jill replied. "Why he couldn't just have a normal heating system is beyond me," she continued, frustrated and annoyed by Paul's overcomplicating of this.

The repairman didn't answer; he wouldn't be drawn into something that was obviously a cause of contention between the two of them. "Well, if that's all, I'll get going."

"Yes, that's it. I guess there's nothing you can fix if there's nothing actually wrong with it. But sometimes it gets so cold in here you'd swear every damn door and window was open," Jill replied.

The repairman headed through to the front of the house and left. Jill closed the door behind him and returned to the kitchen. She glanced at the clock; it was already time to start tea. Reaching over to the fridge, she knocked her phone off the counter. She grabbed for it but missed, and in some kind of weird slow motion, it fell behind the breakfast bar. "Fuck shit," she shouted.

She turned to Charlie. "What a bloody day, Charlie." Jill knelt and pushed her hand in the small gap between the bar and the range oven. She searched around and managed to put her outstretched middle finger on the phone. After trying to flick it several times, she managed to gain some purchase and began to drag it from its resting place. Just as she could see the phone, she felt something cold move against her hand. She stopped. Nothing moved, she could still feel her phone, but the cold thing was no longer there. She dragged the phone out the rest of the way, then, turning on the flashlight app, she shone it in the narrow gap. She could make something out. It looked like metal, and then Jill realised what it was. The crucifix. How could she have forgotten about it, she thought as she looked for something to reach it. Finally, after using a pasta server for something the designer would never have considered, she rescued the crucifix. She dusted it off and rubbed it against her jeans. She remembered taking it down, because it had tarnished, and putting it on the side the morning she felt she was being watched. "But how did it fall between the gap?" she shrugged. "Never mind, out of sight, out of mind I guess," she said to Charlie. The crucifix was now a mat black, the same as when she'd first found it. She couldn't understand why it kept tarnishing, but after being charged a small fortune, she was damn sure it could stay that way. Besides, she did like the patina look somewhat. Jill took the crucifix and hung it back above the main door. As she did, she heard Paul's SUV pull up.

Jill made her way back to the kitchen and began tea. When Paul entered, he seemed flustered somehow, distracted and distant. Jill assumed he was still carrying the argument they'd had that morning. He did like to brood when they have a rare falling out. But it wasn't that; the thought running around Paul's mind was of the old farmer. Paul could tell there was something he wasn't telling him about The Halt. He felt

143

cuckolded by it, and the fact that when he'd tried to insist, he told him, he'd brought out a gun. He could tell Jill, but then she'd ask why he'd been there, why have contact with him and Paul would have to tell her. And if he did that, she would know of the waiver, and then she'd begin putting two and two together. No, this must be handled delicately. He couldn't risk losing this house, not after the work and money he'd put into it.

"Hi, darling," he finally said, after formulating how to work an angle.

"Hi, you okay?" she asked.

"Yeah, listen. Have you had that feeling of being watched lately? Or any other strange things?" Paul asked.

"Not since we last spoke, why? Seems an odd thing to ask me out of the blue."

He cleared his throat and continued. "Oh, no reason, just curious."

"You think something is wrong?"

Paul hesitated. He was in this lie now, no way out. "No, not at all. Just making sure my number one lady is all good."

"I have thought about calling the police. You know, just in case."

'Shit, shit, shit,' Paul thought to himself, *'why couldn't she just fucking do what she was asked.'* "No, I don't think we should. They'll just say they haven't the manpower." *'Please go along with this,'* Paul thought privately as he finished.

"Okay, I guess," Jill said.

Paul changed the subject. "Anyway, what's for tea? I'm starving."

After tea, and as the light began to fade, Jill cleared away the dirty pots and pans while Paul fed Charlie. It seemed to Paul that Jill had bought his deception, and hopefully, it was now a settled matter. Charlie scoffed his meal while Paul and Jill sat with a glass of wine. All things considered, the day ended much better for them both than it had begun. And the end of day routine was bringing normality back into their lives. Paul finished his glass. It was that time of day before twilight but after the full light of day had slipped behind the hills. Paul looked at the clock. 9.12 p.m.

"Has Charlie been for his walk?" he asked.

"No, I was going to, but the engineer turned up to look at the climate control thingy," Jill answered.

"I'll take him now, while you have a nice bath," Paul said, placing down his glass and standing.

"You sure?"

Paul was already putting on Charlie's blue striped collar. He knew Jill's *you sure* was completely rhetorical, and so he didn't bother to answer it. Instead, he smiled and nodded to her. He led Charlie out the door and turned west, following the green lane where the tracks had once been. Charlie sniffed eagerly, his brass nametag jangling against the metal clip of the long, extendable lead. Paul would go as far as the hill, turn right and then double back to the house.

As he continued, Charlie became more agitated, barking and pulling on the lead. "Behave," Paul snapped at the excited dog. But Charlie kept pulling him. Frustrated, and with more important things on his mind, Paul released the metal clip, freeing the dog. Charlie bolted. "Fuck!" Paul shouted, as the Spaniel disappeared around the corner. Paul ran after him, panting heavily on his full stomach, while his out of shape cardiovascular system struggled to maintain the pace. Eventually, he reached the corner and turned to find an open railway tunnel in front of him. Paul stopped dead.

From inside the tunnel, he could hear Charlie barking. Paul pulled his phone from his pocket and switched on its flashlight. Slowly, he entered the tunnel. With the sun low in the sky and behind the hill the tunnel bore through, he walked across a line of light and dark and was immediately plunged into blackness. He shone the narrow beam of light in front of him, illuminating only as far as a few feet. He walked slowly and very carefully. He turned around. He could see the entrance and the daylight which seemed to stop dead at the threshold, as if it was too afraid to enter the old tunnel. He noticed the stale, thick air which filled his throat and the ice-cold temperature. Turning back, his foot snagged on something and he fell forward, dropping the phone. He stretched out a hand. He had no idea where the tunnel wall was or what he was falling against. Just before he hit the floor and after his knees had bent in preparation, his hand impacted on something cold, wet and slimy. He recoiled it instantly, shaking it to get the putrid stuff off him. On his knees for safety, he looked around. There before him was a small slice of light cutting through the darkness. He reached with his clean hand and picked up his phone.

He pointed it to the ground and illuminated the old, rotten railway track sleepers he'd stumbled over. He moved the small beam to where his hand had been. It was indeed the tunnel wall but it was covered in a green, slimy moss. It stunk, the smell now only registering. Paul coughed. "Fuck it!" he shouted. His words echoed throughout the tunnel. As they finally stopped repeating, another sound broke the silence. A yelping, an animal in distress. "Fuck, Charlie," Paul said, as the reason he was in the tunnel came flooding back to him. Another yelp, and then silence. "Charlie?" Paul shouted the dog's name again. Nothing came back. Desperately, and with panic rising inside of him, he frantically searched, but when the sun finally slipped away and the light outside began to fade, Paul turned and headed back for the entrance. On his phone, the time read 9.30 p.m. Once home, he could, for the first time, see the mulch he'd brought with him. As he stood at the sink washing the green bile from his hands and clothes, Jill came in.

"Christ, what happened to you? If you're this bad, I'd hate to see what Charlie is like," she said, passing him. "Where is he, anyway? I'd better get him cleaned up."

"He ran off into that old tunnel. I tried to find him, but it was too dark," Paul said, clearly distressed.

"Which tunnel?"

"The tunnel, there's only one bloody tunnel," Paul answered, scrubbing his hands harder.

"That tunnel is blocked up. I was there a few days ago," Jill said, confused.

"Well, it isn't, because I went in after him and got covered in this shit."

"We can't leave him out there, Paul, he'll be frightened. We'll go back. I'll get my boots and the torches."

Paul thought about telling Jill that he'd heard Charlie yelp but decided against it. Hopefully, they would find the dumb dog when they got back with the high-powered flashlights Paul had insisted, they needed now they were living mainly off grid. For both Jill and Paul, the walk to the tunnel seemed to take much longer than they remembered. Finally, they came to the bend in the green lane which led to it. They both turned the corner, ready to enter the tunnel, but they both stopped. As they shone the beams of their torches at the tunnel entrance, it was, as Jill had insisted, sealed up.

Chapter 9

Jack stood at the entrance to Middlesbrough Station. All around him was a scene of utter destruction. Though only two bombs had hit directly, they'd caused absolute devastation of their targets. He began carefully walking through the debris field, picking his way over fallen walls and roofs. The smell of burning still hung in the air, filling the back of his throat. The fire service, air-raid wardens and home guard were all in attendance by the time Jack had managed to get back to Middlesbrough. Already, bodies were being lined up, covered in sheets, to protect their dignity and modesty, their clothes burned or ripped in the attack. They were also covered to protect the living from seeing the effects high-explosive ordinance has on the human body. Jack struggled to keep his footing, but loose rubble made the going treacherous. He slipped on one such layer of rubble, and his hand, outstretched to break his fall, landed on something soft and hairy. Instinctively, he looked to see the carcass of a dog, its body severed behind its rib cage. Jack coughed, and he thought he might vomit at the sight and smell of the dead animal, but he held it in, swallowing it back down.

Noise filled the air. People shouting, crying in anger and disbelief that a lone bomber could cause such annihilation. Others cried foul for the lack of air defence, ground batteries and RAF fighters. There were Spitfires stationed only a few miles away, but no one had heard or seen the lone attacker, and by the time the call had gone out to scramble the fighters following the attack, the Donier had long since escaped, following the rail tracks back to the coast. Jim Green, Jack's old boss, recognised him and came over to him. He explained to Jack what had happened to Doris and Molly. He pleaded with Jack not to look, there would be no point, they'd been identified, Jack didn't need to be here. But Jack shrugged him away and made for the temporary morgue. When Jack stepped through the door, he was met with rows of white sheets, all of them giving away the shape underneath. Though there were differing shapes and sizes, it was obvious to him he was facing death in this room, and on a scale he had never considered. He began reading the tags fastened to each big toe on the left foot, assuming, that was, that the body had one. He found the first tag he'd come to see. It read: Molly Thorpe.

Slowly, Jack moved up the table and took hold of the sheet. Gently, he pulled it back, uncovering her to her waist. The left side of Molly had all but gone. The explosion had ripped through the kitchen as Molly was leaving, her right side shielded, as she headed for the door. Another few seconds and she may have survived. Her left side took the full force of the air displacement caused by the shock wave and the heat of the blast. Without making a noise or showing any expression, Jack pulled the sheet back, covering the dead girl. He moved to the next table and checked the tag. Doris Bright. Jack's fist tightened, as he took hold of the sheet. Sweating and with nausea rising inside him, he pulled it back. His heart beat so hard and fast, he believed that it might burst from his chest at any moment. His limbs shook as his adrenal gland released its hormone, readying his body for what he was about to see. Shaking, his right hand drew back the thick cotton sheet. His mother lay, still covered in the detritus which had buried her, she looked gaunt and pale. Jack could see the pain and panic on her face which had registered before she'd succumbed to the blast. Her clothes were torn, and her arms and shoulders were covered in bruises and scratches.

Jack didn't remember covering her or making his way out of the make-shift morgue and then out of the station. He didn't remember walking, in a daze, back to Tavistock Street and to the small house he'd fled two years previous. But now, he found himself there, sat in his mother's chair where he would often seek comfort or to comfort her once his father had fallen asleep. Jack stood, his self-awareness now restored, he made his way up the narrow staircase to his old bedroom.

Other than it being cleaned and the bed made-up, it was exactly as he'd left it. He moved into his mother's room. He stared at the bed. The memory he'd convinced himself was no more than a bad dream came back. As it did, the lie he'd told himself came crashing down, and the realisation and admittance of what he'd done hit him. As it did, Jack passed out.

By the time Jack came around, face down where he'd landed on the bed, night had circled around. Outside, the street lamps sent a warm, soft glow through the open curtains. He picked himself up and walked to the kitchen. There, he washed his face to shake the hazy feeling that was still with him. As his mind cleared, a familiar feeling came back to him. The red mist. Jack's mind became clear; he would avenge his mother's slaying at the hands of the German forces. He would join-up. It would become his personal vendetta in life to kill as many of those *bastards* as he could. But first, he would travel back to the farm and collect something. He left the small, terraced house in the dead of night, locking the door as he did. If he were to make it back from the war, at least he would have a home to come back to. Jack went to the next station along the line which was still operational. By the time he got there, the last train had left, and so huddling under his coat, he sat in the semi-sheltered waiting room and waited until morning.

A little after lunchtime, Jack crept back onto the farm. He didn't want to get caught up in a conversation with the kind man or his wife. He would much prefer to sneak in and back out without them knowing he'd been; it would be easier this way for them all. He entered his room and made for the old trunk he'd been given when he'd agreed to stay on. Opening it, Jack reached to the bottom and found what he'd come back for. His grandfather's Kirpan knife. This knife had already seen action in the theatre of war, and Jack was determined it would again. Placing it in his pocket, he journeyed back to Thirstonfield Halt Station, where he boarded the train which would eventually take him to Darlington. He didn't dare to join in his hometown for fear of being arrested over the Ninnyhammer's disappearance, rather, he would say he'd been working in the area and had only just received his call-up papers following his mother's death. It seemed, he would tell them, she'd kept them from him to protect him from the horrors of war.

By the end of the day, Jack was the latest recruit into the British Army, and the Durham Light Infantry, to be exact. Over the next few weeks, he would be taught how to be the best soldier he could be. For now, the red mist was kept in check. It had become a travelling companion to Jack; they'd forged a symbiotic relationship of convenience. Jack could keep it in check, at least for some time, on the understanding it was let free of its restraints when needed. Jack's size and power had meant that during his basic training it had not been needed. The other recruits had sensed in Jack a torment and an anger which none of them wanted to see, and so while being respectful, and often too polite, they'd all given Jack a wide birth. As his training ended and the battalion's first deployment came, Jack was ready to have his revenge.

***

Paul placed a hand on the cold brickwork which blocked the old tunnel's entrance. He hit his hand against it, bewilderment running through his mind. Jill shone the glare of the high-powered flashlight around the tunnel entrance, looking for any openings she may have missed when she'd walked Charlie there only two days before. But there were none. The bricks looked old, as if they'd been there for decades. "See, bricked up," Jill said, stepping closer. "He must have run around to the other side," she continued, trying to offer Paul an explanation.

"No, I was in the tunnel. I fell over the old track, and that's why I'm dirty," he insisted.

"The tracks have all been removed," Jill said, pointing the beam of light to the ground.

Paul turned to her. "I'm telling you, Charlie ran into the tunnel, I went in after him and fell. Then I heard—" he stopped, mid-sentence.

"Heard what?" Jill asked.

"I heard a dog yelp, and then it went quiet," Paul said, sighing as he did.

"And you're telling me this now? What is wrong with you?" Jill scolded him.

"I didn't want to panic you, what with everything else. I thought we'd find him."

Jill turned and began to climb the steep bank to the left of the tunnel, and Paul scurried after her. She ran over the top and down to the other side, but it too was sealed. "He can't be in here, Paul. This was sealed a long time ago."

"I'm telling you he is," Paul argued.

In the silence, Jill heard a noise. A whimpering bark. "That's him, Paul, that's Charlie." The whimper came again. "We have to get in there."

"It's pitch black. We won't find a way in tonight. We'll come back first light, check then," Paul said.

Jill pulled her phone from her pocket and dialled John Watts. After a few seconds, he answered. "John, this is Jill at The Halt. Yes, hi, listen, Charlie, our dog, he's got himself trapped in an old tunnel, could you bring something over to get through the bricks? Yes, I understand, yes, that will be fine." She hung up and pushed the phone back into her pocket.

"What did he say?" Paul asked.

"He's coming over tomorrow with a *jackhammer,* I think he called it."

"Okay then, let's go back tonight, there's nothing more we can do," Paul said, coaxing Jill away from the tunnel.

Jill made her way back to the house behind Paul. Her annoyance at him was beginning to turn to resentment. It was he that had insisted on buying this place, and it was he who'd insisted on just about every detail.

From the layout of her office, which she hated, to the stupid climate control which can never keep the house at a nice temperature. She watched from behind, as he walked along the green lane. Shortly after they arrived home, Jill decided she would sleep downstairs tonight in case Charlie did find his way home. That way, she could leave the kitchen door open. Paul had resisted the idea, stating that it could invite trouble, or an intruder could sneak in, he'd said. Jill told him to stop being absurd and to go the bed, which after registering his protest, he did. After changing into her nightwear, Jill pulled the duvet from the spare bed and laid on the large corner couch. She pulled the thick covers over her and switched on the TV. If Charlie did come back, he would be attracted by the noise. She flicked through the channels and settled on a movie before fighting the sleep that came. Eventually, she lost the battle and closed her eyes, as the sound of the movie drifted away into the far distance.

She woke at some point a few hours into the early morning, roused by a crashing sound. Outside, it was still dark, the TV had switched itself off and the room was in darkness. Jill sat up and reached for the table lamp, switching it on. Blinking the last remaining sleep from her eyes, she searched the room, looking for the source of the noise which had woken her. Her phone, it was across the room, face down, and from here, she could see the shards of smashed screen. Jill moved over to it and picked it up. She remembered putting it behind her on the couch, so how had it come to be here and broken? She'd dropped it on more than one occasion, and the screen hadn't scratched, let-alone shattered. "It must have taken some force," Jill muttered. As she turned, her peripheral vision caught a movement. Jill froze, and the temperature suddenly becoming apparent to her; it was cold, very cold. In her shallow breaths, she could see it leave her body. She wanted to call for Charlie, he would bark a warning, wake Paul faster than she could. But he was not here.

She moved slowly to the door which led into the hallway. She thought she saw the shadow again, this time for longer, and she made its detail. Human, large and with a brimmed hat. Jill screamed, "Paul!"

A few seconds later, the lights which illuminated the stairs and hall came on as Paul ran as quickly as he could to see why

Jill was screaming. He entered the room to find Jill sitting on the couch, sobbing. "What the hell is it?" he asked.

"It was him, the man," Jill said, through her crying.

"Which man?"

"The large man in the hat, the one Darren said he'd seen, the one the old clocksmith said had been hanging around." Jill wiped the tears from her eyes.

"Where is he? Where did he go?"

"I don't know. When I screamed, he just vanished." Jill stood, holding out her phone. "This was behind me, but, somehow, it ended up across the room, smashed."

"I'm not sure what you're saying, Jill, just calm down. There'll be an explanation for it."

"Like what?" Jill's fear was turning to anger.

"Like, well, you left the door open, so he could have crept in, smashed your phone and left again."

"Really?" Jill replied. "That's it, that's the all-knowing explanation? He fucking crept in, did he? And once in, he thought the best thing to do was reach down behind my back, where he obviously knew my phone was, and then throw it with such force, it smashed to pieces."

Paul had no idea what to say or do. He was losing control of this. The things that couldn't be explained were beginning to mount up. And he knew it wouldn't be long before Jill started with the whole *unnatural, otherworldly* bullshit. He needed to calm her and reassure her. "Follow me," he said. Jill put the shattered phone on the side and followed Paul into his study. "I had this installed while the house was being built. This should put your mind at ease."

"What is it?" Jill asked, sitting next to him behind his desk.

"It's a security system." Paul knew what would come next.

"You fitted *CCTV,* and you didn't tell me?" Jill protested.

"Only downstairs, and it records over itself every day. I didn't see the need to bore you with every detail."

Jill didn't answer him. Instead, she wondered what else he hadn't told her. Nonetheless, she was glad the system was in, or, at least she was for tonight because she could prove to him what she saw. Paul opened the software, and they both watched from the moment Jill fell asleep to the moment Paul had entered the room. From the angle of the camera, the phone could be seen hitting the floor, but the couch was out of view. Jill could be seen picking up the phone and then standing rigid. But no shadow could be seen, and Jill's breath could not be picked up in the dim light.

"See," Paul said. "Nothing. It's more likely you flung the phone in your sleep, then, still half-asleep, you imagined this big man because it's been on your mind."

"But what about the cold?" Jill said, now doubting herself.

"It feels fine to me, but you left the door open, so a cold gust of wind maybe? Are you cold now?"

"No, I'm fine," Jill answered, now aware that she had forgotten about being cold.

"Like I said, a cold breeze, and you had been under the duvet, so you would feel cold," Paul said, impressed by his own reasoning. "Close the back door, come to bed, we'll find Charlie in the morning, and this will make sense." He leaned over and kissed her on the forehead.

"Okay, you're right, I guess that makes sense."

Jill left the study and closed the kitchen door, locking it. After checking the room once more, she followed Paul to bed. In the hours before the sun broke the night's darkness and while both Paul and Jill slept, a shape moved in the darkest corner of their bedroom. It watched as Jill's chest rose and fell as she slept.

The following morning, Jill found herself, with Paul and John, back at the tunnel. John had manoeuvred his Toyota pick-up truck, which held the generator needed for the hydraulic jackhammer, along the green lane. Covering her ears, she watched as John quarried a hole big enough for the three of them to fit through. After fifteen minutes or so of battering the old brickwork, John shut down the generator and grabbed his flashlight. Following John and Paul, Jill squeezed through the gap and into the absolute darkness of the tunnel. She switched her flashlight on. The three intense beams searched through the blackness like a warship's searchlight. Slowly, they moved forward, carefully avoiding the rotten sleepers and rusting tracks on Paul's advice. After a few minutes, John shouted them to a section of the wall which was set back. John assumed it was for workers caught short when a train approached. As Jill and Paul reached him, his light illuminated a dog's skeleton. "Could that be him?" John asked.

"No, this has been here years, if not decades," Paul answered.

Jill wasn't so sure. She knelt in front of the decaying bones and retrieved the collar. It was dirty and threadbare, but even so, in the limited light, she could tell it was the blue striped collar Charlie had worn. In the beams of the torches, Jill noticed a nametag. She turned it around, wiping the decades of dust and loam from it. It read Charlie, and below it, Jill's mobile phone number. She gasped, dropping the collar. "Jesus!" she yelled in shock. "It is him; it's Charlie."

"It can't be. Someone's playing a fucking trick," Paul insisted.

Jill moved the searchlight along the skeleton. On the rear leg, a small metal plate. "And I suppose they replicated where he was run over too? I'm telling you, this is Charlie." Jill bent forward and delicately put the skeleton into a bag she'd brought with her. "There's one way to be sure. I'll take these remains to the vets. They'll be able to confirm this."

John turned to them both. "Well, I'm not sure what's going on here, but this place creeps me the fuck out. Listen, Paul, I know you want me back to finish the shed, but I'm done with this place. Find another contractor." John turned and headed for the small shaft of daylight finding its way in through the hole they'd made. "I'll plug that hole up before I go," he said, his back to them both, "then that's it."

Paul looked to Jill for support in the argument of making him stay, but Jill shook her head. She understood completely why John wouldn't want to come back, hell, she wouldn't. They followed John out of the tunnel and left him while he repaired the hole. Back at the house, Jill informed Paul that she would take the remains to the vets, while he found out when the tunnel had been bricked up. Paul thought it best to go along with what she said and not question the validity of incurring the fee the vets would charge, for what he thought at least, was a foregone conclusion that this simply couldn't be Charlie.

He couldn't conceive how it could be, regardless of the evidence of the collar and metal plate in its hind leg. As Jill got into her car and left, Paul entered his study. After all, it shouldn't take long to find out when the tunnel had been sealed.

***

As Jill reached the veterinary clinic, she felt a great deal of trepidation at what she was going to find out. On the one hand, she believed she had to know, and in fact, she believed what she was holding were the remains of Charlie, though she couldn't explain that just yet. Once confirmed, then she would look for an answer. On the other, if it wasn't Charlie, then where was he? What had happened to him? Jill approached the desk and realised she hadn't thought of a plausible excuse for what she was about to ask.

"Can I help?" the young-ish girl who Jill thought to be in her twenties, and whose nametag read Teri, asked.

"Yes, I wonder if you could identify the remains of this dog. You see, I believe it to my missing Spaniel, Charlie, and I thought perhaps dental records or something." Jill mentally shook her head at herself for stumbling through the request.

The young-ish girl took the bag from Jill and peeked inside, instantly regretting that she had. "Yes, I'll take these through and see what we can come up with. Do we have your details?"

Jill furnished Teri with her details and told her she'd only just transferred from her previous vet. The young-ish girl then assured Jill she would hear within a day and then took the remains away. Jill left the surgery and made her way back to her car. Climbing in, she broke down, crying over the thought of how poor Charlie must have suffered, alone and scared in that dark, horrible place. After a few moments, she regained herself enough to drive home. She pulled up next to Paul's Range Rover and stepped out of her car before heading into the house. She found Paul in his study.

"Did you find out when the tunnel was covered?" she asked, taking her jacket off and placing her bag down.

"Yes, I did. It's amazing what you can find out." He sounded cocky, something else that had begun irritating her.

"And?"

"It's called the Estdale Tunnel, and it was bricked up in nineteen seventy-three. So, there's no way those remains could have been Charlie's. Which is good, isn't it?"

"I don't know," Jill answered.

"How could it not be?" Paul asked.

"Because if they're not, where is he, and how the hell did his collar get around that dog's neck? And, also, why does that dog have the same injury as Charlie and in the same exact place?" Jill snapped.

"I guess we'll have to wait and see," Paul replied, now trying to calm his distraught fiancée.

Jill turned without speaking another word and left the room. She'd had enough of today, and it had only just turned early afternoon. Entering their bedroom, she sat on the end of bed. She felt sick. She couldn't decide if it was because she hadn't eaten or because of yet another thing was being piled on top of her. It seemed to her it was like death by a thousand needles, one you don't notice, but a thousand would kill you. The urge to vomit grew quickly, and as she reached the toilet, what little contents there were in her stomach came up. After washing her face, Jill laid on the bed. She heard Paul shout from the bottom of the stairs that he was going to work, she replied with a single word, and she heard the front door open, and then close. She felt alone and lost. This generous house was empty without Charlie keeping her company, and the thought of what he may have suffered or was suffering if the skeleton wasn't his, was hurting her. *'Fuck!'* she thought to herself, *'this Schrodinger's cat shit can drive a person crazy.'*

At some point, though, she couldn't pinpoint it, she must have fallen asleep. The landline phone on her bedside cabinet was ringing. Dry-mouthed and a little foggy, she reached over and picked it up. "Hello?"

"Is that Miss Goodwin?" the voice asked.

"Yes, who is this?" Jill tried her best not to sound like she'd just woken.

"It's Georgina, from the veterinary practice. You brought in canine remains earlier."

Jill's consciousness came back, as did her attention. "Yes, that's right. You're quick. Have you established if they're a match for my dog?"

"Yes, they are. The dental records and injury records are an exact match. There can be no doubt, Miss Goodwin, this is, or was, Charlie. But we're a little puzzled. The autopsy show's this dog died sometime around the early nineteen-seventies. Yet your dog was seen in your previous practice two months ago for his boosters."

"Thank you for being prompt and for calling me," Jill answered, her mind now on autopilot.

"What would you like us to do with the remains?"

"Huh?" Jill couldn't focus.

"The remains, Miss Goodwin, what would you like us to with them?"

"Please just dispose of them how you see fit but retain the collar for me. I'll collect it when I'm next in the village," Jill answered before hanging up.

There could be no doubt. Somehow, Charlie had entered the tunnel, and somehow, he'd died in there. Alone, and in the dark, shortly before it had been bricked up. A feeling of guilt ripped at her. How the hell could this have happened? Then the millions of *ifs* came. If only she'd stood firm with Paul, not allowed him to buy this place.

If only the heating engineer had turned up after she'd taken Charlie out. *If only*. The two words she'd used more than any other, aside from *why me*, after her cancer was discovered. Those words had haunted her, and now they were back. Perhaps, she thought, the universe hadn't quite finished fucking with her yet. However, she would have to call Paul at work and tell him the news, regardless of whether or not the universe was screwing with them. She picked up the landline phone next to the bed and paused before she dialled. *'How would he take this news?'* she wondered. After all, he was out with Charlie when this, whatever this was, happened to him. She dialled. Shortly after, he answered. Jill told him that the vet confirmed it was Charlie, that there was no ambiguity, their beloved dog was dead, and more than that, he died over four decades ago. Alone, frightened and in the pitch black of the tunnel. The line was silent for a few moments while Paul soaked up the news. Jill had no more to say to him, not at that moment anyway. She would, for now, say goodbye, and let him digest the news as she'd had to. Paul heard the click, and then the deadline tone. He pressed *end-call* on his mobile and leaned back in his chair, tossing his phone onto his desk. He knew Jill would blame him for this. Actually, he thought, she would delight in it. He'd sensed she'd been off with him a little. After those bruisers, nothing seemed to be the same, even though they'd gone the next morning and not come back. As his mind wondered, Jeff came into the office and brought Paul back to where he was.

Jill went to her study. Her blog had been neglected for too long, and she'd already begun to lose her audience. She sat at her desk, staring at the blank screen. Switching tabs, she opened *Edge*. In the Google search bar, she typed *Mysterious time deaths.* She wasn't sure whether or not this would expose the information she was looking for but at least it was a starting place. After trawling through countless pages of science-fiction, she eventually closed in on something that looked promising. Another case, almost the same as Charlie's, had happened a few years back to a family in Dorset. Jill poured over the details of the case. They too had experienced similar strange occurrences, and their dog, a German Shepard, had vanished. The normally obedient dog, running off barking and chasing something. When the owners finally found it, it too appeared to have been dead for a long time, buried in a disused mine, sealed over twenty years before the dog had been born. Jill picked up the phone. She would call Paul, tell him it had happened to another family, at least one she knew of, but then she thought. She placed the receiver back down. No, she would keep this to herself for now. If Paul thought she was beginning to think along these lines, it would cause them to argue.

She scrolled further down the page, finding the contact details for the spiritualist medium who helped them find the dead dog. She saved the page to her favourites and left her study. Her blog would have to wait a little while longer.

As nine-thirty came and Jill dozed in front of the TV, for the briefest of moments, she thought she heard the quiet whimpering of a dog.

Chapter 10

June 6 1944

At eleven-hundred hours, the 151 Brigade, 9th Battalion Durham Light Infantry, stormed Gold Beach. It was D-Day. Jack was the first off the boat, his companion, the red mist, pushing him on. The confusion around him as he ran through the shallow water disorientated him. Explosions rained around him along with the cries of men. Mostly, they began as war cries, shouts of victory long before they were due. Shortly after, they became the cries of pain and of death. Jack kept running over the shattered bodies of the dead. The smoke grenades, designed to mask their approach, made it impossible to see. At one point, Jack thought he'd been turned around by the chaos around him and he was running back toward the sea. But he caught a break in the smoke, and much to his relief, found he was heading in the right direction. The German guns, unable to see their targets clearly, now fired indiscriminately, strafing the beach in rapid bursts from multiple positions. The whistling of bullets which whizzed past his ears, followed by the dull thud as they made contact with the soldiers around him, seemed, to Jack, that he was running through a swarm of metal bees. And at any moment, one of them, or more, would sting him, and he would die. Here on the blooded sand. Against the odds, he made it to the relative safety of the bunker. From here, the German guns could not reach him. He turned, huddled with the other lucky few who had made it across the open beach and watched in horror as waves of men were cut down, decapitated or exploded into a crimson rain when a shell made a direct hit. For the first time since his father and the Ninnyhammer, Jack felt afraid. A tug on his shoulder brought him back. The corporal ordered what was left of this detachment farther up and to the beachhead. Once in the relative safety of the Allied camp, and still shaken, wet and covered in damp sand, Jack sat with a coffee and waited for the adrenaline that had coursed around his body to subside. He'd been in action before this after his basic training finished, but nothing they had told them could prepare anyone for the horror he'd witnessed. As his body came back to him, he began to remember why he was here. The corporal shouted for volunteers, and Jack immediately stood. It was time.

Along a covered tree line, a few kilometres outside of the small French village, *Villers-Le-Sec*, a German 88mm gun position was slowing the Allied advance. Led by their corporal, a small but heavily built man—Jack presumed by his accent to be from East London—Jack, and a small number of soldiers were tasked with taking it out. Its position in the tree line had meant the fighter-bombers could not make a direct hit. But while this was good to guard against the Allied air forces, it proved to be its weakness against a ground assault. They found the gun inactive, its crew taking a break from the relentless bombardment of the advancing Allied forces while the gun itself cooled. They watched from behind the tree line while their German counterparts smoked and drank coffee. They looked well-fed and relaxed, Jack thought. He studied the eleven soldiers who were oblivious to what was about to happen and singled one out. This young-looking soldier, who reminded Jack of the Ninnyhammer somewhat, would be the first to feel his wrath at what had happened to his mother. The corporal nodded, and Jack, along with the small band of soldiers, rushed the position. By the time the German soldiers realised they were under attack, they had no time to reach their weapons. So confident had they been of repelling the advance, they had left their rifles out of reach. He charged him, shouting as he did a cry of anguish, of hatred and of utter rage. The German soldier backed away, his arms raised, surrendering, but Jack took no heed.

He lifted his Enfield rifle and fired a single shot. It hit his target to the left of his heart with a soft thud, spinning the German around. He fell onto his knees, his breath coming in gasps while blood found its way out of his mouth. Jack reached him and, bending over him, he put his large hand on his jacket and spun him around. The German landed heavily on his back, his grey tunic now becoming a wet, dark red. He fumbled into his pocket and pulled out a picture. It was him, the German Ninnyhammer with his wife and children. Two girls, Jack noticed. He took the picture from him and studied it. The young German thought it might bring him some mercy, but the red mist was already controlling Jack. He crumpled the picture and threw it to the ground, stomping it into the mud.

Then, he turned back to the young man who lay before him. Jack straddled his chest and laid his rifle next to him. His fear, to Jack, was palpable, and for the first time since killing the Ninnyhammer, he became aroused. He slid the Kirpan knife out of its sheath and put it to the young man's throat. In German, he began pleading for his life, but Jack took no notice. To him, he was as guilty of his mother's death as the pilot of the bomber. With only an expression of sexual delight, Jack drew the curved blade across his throat. Blood ran freely as the young man coughed, his body fighting for its preservation. His deep-blue eyes widened, as the realisation of his imminent death came over him. He turned his head to where Jack had dropped the photo of his family. The last thing he saw was the crumpled face of his young wife, and as he exhaled his last breath and his eyes became lifeless, Jack ejaculated. The red mist was now firmly in control. He stood over the corpse and wiped mud into the crotch of his trousers, hiding the stains made by his excitement. Turning, he noticed the eleven bodies the gun crew strewed across the damp ground, the gun itself now silent. The smell of cordite filled the air, and in the distance, the rumble of gunfire, and in between, larger ordinance. The order was given to destroy the gun and return to their rendezvous point. Jack's vengeance for

Doris had begun, and as he carved a small notch into the wooden handle of his rifle, he smiled to himself.

That night, Jack slept well, while around him other men cowered and hid from the sounds which filled the air. Most of the other, newer soldiers, gathered around the small barrel fires and behind what few armoured vehicles there were for protection. Jack sought no such comfort in numbers, nor did the protection the armoured steel give them. He had no doubt he would survive this war and return home, his mother's murder, as he now thought of her death, avenged and his bloodlust satisfied. The following morning, the detachment was ordered onward, farther into France and toward Holland.

***

Jill woke from her slumber in front of the TV. The whimpering came again, a soft crying, the same Charlie would make when vying for pity. Blurry eyed, she looked at the clock, 9.30 p.m. "That time again," she whispered to herself, remembering the hour she lost or thought she'd lost. She picked up the remote, silenced the TV and listened as intently as she could. But now, there was just silence; the noise, whatever it was, had gone. Yawning, she turned the sound back on and sat back to watch the end of the show, unaware of the large man in the fedora hat standing behind her in the deepest corner of the room. Paul sat in his study. Things between himself and Jill had rarely been this bad. The events, which seemed to be spiralling out of control, were putting a huge strain on their relationship. Neither of them could explain what had happened to Charlie. Paul believed Jill blamed him directly, regardless of her assurances to the contrary. She was withdrawing again, just as she'd done when the cancer was first diagnosed. The initial empathy he felt was turning to anger at what he believed was her unappreciation for the beautiful home he had built for them. He flicked from tab to tab on his PC screen while drinking the finest malt he'd awarded himself when The Halt was finished. The image from the TV room came on his screen.

He could partially see Jill on the corner settee. She seemed to be moving slightly while the flat screen illuminated the room. Suddenly, a large shadow cast over her. Paul stared closely at the screen. Was he imagining this? He thought. Another movement came over her side. Paul dropped the glass and ran to where Jill sat.

He entered the room, switching on the ceiling lights as he did, to find Jill laid asleep on the settee, her blouse partially open. She woke and stared at Paul who stood over her. Looking down, she noticed her blouse and pulled it closed before she stood and fastened it.

"What's going on?" she asked, not yet fully awake.

"You're asking me?" Paul replied.

"Why did you undo my top?"

Paul stepped back, aghast at the question. "Me? It was like that when I came in. There was someone in here with you!" he yelled back.

"What?" Jill sounded authentic in her bewilderment, and Paul didn't know how to react.

Unsure, he remained confrontational. He'd seen the shadow, it was obvious to him it was a person, and here she was, her top unfastened. He decided to show her what he'd seen. "Let me show you."

Jill followed him into the study. He replayed the footage, and she watched, as the shadow moved around her. As Paul ran into the room and switched on the lights, the shadow disappeared. Jill stood silently. She recognised the image on the screen. "Play it back, slowly," she asked Paul. He started the video again, this time in slow motion. As the figure moved around her, Jill asked Paul to pause the clip. There, standing over Jill while she slept, and in perfect form but without features, stood the large man wearing a fedora hat. Jill felt a chill run through her bones. It was as if her soul itself was frightened by the image she could see on the screen. "It's him," she whispered

"It's who?" Paul asked.

"Don't you see him? It's him. Can you print it off?"

Paul hit the print command. "Yes, there," he said, pointing to the wireless printer.

Jill grabbed the finished print and headed for the door.

"Where are you going at this hour?" Paul demanded.

"I'm going to see Darren. I need him to look at this picture," Jill replied, grabbing the first set of car keys her hand reached.

Outside, Jill pointed the fob at her car and pressed the button, but it was Paul's which signalled its unlocking. "Shit," she said. With no time or inclination to go back for her own keys, she jumped into Paul's Range Rover and set off for the home of the young builder. Pushing the SUV hard, she reached his home a little after ten-thirty. She looked to the house to see it still lit. "Thank God, they're still up." As she opened the door, the floor courtesy lights illuminated, and Jill noticed something jutting out from under the passenger seat. She reached down and picked up the brown wax-cardboard envelope. She looked at it, flipping it over. Then she opened it and pulled out the waiver and read it. It was dated the same day they exchanged the contracts on The Halt, and she was in no doubt it was Paul's signature. She felt her anger at him building for not only signing such an ambiguous document but mostly for not telling her. Especially after everything that had happened. She picked up her new mobile and began to call Paul, but then hung up. She would wait before she told him. Tonight, she had to see Darren.

Locking the car, Jill made her way to the house and knocked on the door. The woman who Jill had assumed was a Susan at the hospital answered. Behind her stood Keith. Jill held out a hand, which Susan shook. "Hi, I'm Jill. I own The Halt. I wonder if I could see Darren for just a minute. It's quite important," Jill said in the calmest voice she could muster.

"Yes, please come in," Susan answered, stepping back and opening the door wider.

"Thank you," Jill replied, smiling.

"Darren, the woman from the job over at Thirstonfield is here to see you," Keith shouted at the foot of the narrow staircase.

Jill smiled to herself at the description he'd given her. A few seconds later, she heard a door close above her, and then the sound of quick, rhythmic footsteps, as they bounded down the stairs. Darren entered the room, looking vaguely worried. Jill stood, and as politely as she could, she handed the picture to him.

"Do you recognise this man?" she asked.

Darren studied it, and then looked to Jill. His expression changed from worry to unease. "Yes, that's the bastard I saw, the one that made me fall off my ladder."

Jill took the picture back. "Thank you, that's all I needed."

"Hang on a minute," Keith began. "If you know this man, we need to call the police. He could have been killed," he finished, pointing to Darren.

"I'm not sure the police can help with this," Jill said, turning to leave. "But if I find out who he is, I'll let you know," she continued, placating him.

Jill said her goodbye and thanks and made her way to the car as quickly as she could. Once inside, she started the engine, drove out of sight of the house and stopped. A thousand thoughts now scrambled around her mind, but one was central to them. There could be doubt anymore that this mysterious man, whoever he was, was at the centre of everything that had happened since they had bought the old station. The nausea came again. Jill opened the door and emptied her stomach on the side of the road. Then, she began sobbing. A little after midnight, Jill pulled up at home. She entered the house through the kitchen door and made her way to her study. There, she slipped the envelope containing the waiver from her bag and put it into a locked drawer. Then, making sure the house was locked, she went to bed. She found Paul asleep, lying in his usual position and snoring softly. She undressed and climbed into bed next to him. Before she was consciously aware of it, she fell asleep.

The next morning, Jill woke as the sun began to climb over the distant hills and stream in through the sizeable picture windows. She stretched out a hand to find Paul's side of the bed empty. Lifting her head from the pillow, she checked the small alarm clock. 10.37 a.m. "Christ, I must have been tired," she said to herself, as she got out of bed and made her way down the stairs. Once in the kitchen, she made herself a coffee and sat at the dining table. As she took her first sip, the doorbell rang. Sighing, and quietly swearing to herself, she answered the door. A middle-aged man wearing an off the peg suit and with a fat gut which hung over the trousers stood before her.

"Miss Goodwin?" the portly man asked.

"Yes. Who are you?"

"Detective Sayer. I'm here regarding the body you found in the old workshop."

Jill stood for a moment. She'd forgotten about that over the last few days, the more recent and more disturbing events taking it from her mind. "Yes, please come in."

The portly man followed Jill through to the kitchen. "You have a lovely home," he remarked.

"Thank you," Jill replied, not wanting to get drawn into a conversation.

"I'll get straight to it then. His name, we believe, was Paul Stokes. Originally from Middlesbrough, he joined the merchant navy just before the war. He failed to return home and was thought to have either run away when war seemed inevitable or fell afoul of some local while on shore leave. His last voyage, if that's what you'd call it, took him to Egypt."

"Do you know how he died? Or who put him up there?" Jill asked.

"We don't know the cause of death; the body was too far gone. Usually, when there's nothing obvious, such as skull fracture, it's usually a soft tissue trauma. The coroner has recorded it as unexplained, but we know he was wrapped up and put up in your rafters immediately after he was killed. So, it's fair to assume that he was murdered."

"Do we need to worry?" Jill asked.

The portly man smiled. "No, he was killed seventy years ago, so even if his killer was still alive, I doubt he'd be a threat to anyone now."

Jill nodded to the portly detective and thanked him. She followed him to the door and locked it. She sat at her PC in her study and Googled the name the detective had given her. After trawling down result pages of Facebook accounts for every Paul Stokes currently or very recently alive, she found an archive site for old newspapers. An article in the north-eastern Gazette detailed the police search for the missing man. It cited his connection with the Middlesbrough train station and went on to say he'd joined the merchant navy, following in his father's footsteps. As she read on, the article confirmed what Detective Sayer had told her. After finding no witnesses to his disappearance and no leads to find him, it was assumed he'd ran away to avoid the potential draft as war became an ever-more reality. Or met his end while on shore leave. Jill continued through the search results. More Twitter, Facebook and LinkedIn accounts filled the pages in front of her, but she was determined to find something. There had to be some link between him and the large man. It was too much to be a coincidence, even though she knew that was exactly what Paul would put it down to. After searching for another hour, she found a site which detailed archived school records. She knew he was from Middlesbrough, and he had some connection with the station, and so she began searching the database around that area.

Eventually, she found him. A student at Linthorpe School, he'd been in trouble on a few occasions for picking on a boy by the name of Jack Bright. It also mentioned his disappearance and the fact that his former victim, Jack, had also vanished shortly after, resurfacing a few years later when his mother, Doris, was killed in an air raid on Middlesbrough Station. Jill opened another tab and Googled Jack Bright. After looking through the usual social media sights, she found an article dating back to 1949. Suspected of multiple murders, Jack Bright was chased at Thirstonfield Halt Station, where, rather than being captured by the police, he jumped in front of the 9.30 p.m. locomotive and was killed by decapitation. The article went on to say that before and after the war, he worked as a farm hand for Thomas and Anne Bradbury. It went on to say that soon after returning to the farm, he ran away and began to live rough in his hometown of Middlesbrough. Below the article was a grainy black and white photo of the Bradbury farm, taken in 1948. Behind whom Jill spotted was a young George Bradbury who she thought looked around eleven was a large man wearing a fedora hat. And Jill instantly recognised him as the man in the photo. A chill came over her at the realisation of what this meant. The pieces were coming together. She had one thing left to do before she could take this to Paul. She must confront George Bradbury about the waiver she'd found. Saving the pages to her favourites, she closed the lid on her laptop and headed for the Bradbury farm.

As she drove through the village of Thirstonfield, the nausea came back in waves. It didn't surprise her that she was feeling this way. The revelations she had discovered would knock anyone for six, she reassured herself. Regardless, she decided to make a detour to the only pharmacy in the village.

Whatever the reason for it, she needed to control it. As Jill approached the counter, she passed through the feminine isle, and a realisation came across her. She hadn't had her period in the last month. In fact, she couldn't remember when she last did have it. She tried to pacify herself again. 'Stress can cause that,' she thought to herself, but she wasn't buying her own sales pitch.

Reaching over, she picked up two self-pregnancy test kits, bought them and headed back to the car. She pushed the shopping bag onto the passenger seat and resumed her journey.

She drove along the track to the Bradbury's farmhouse, pulling up slowly outside of what she assumed to be their kitchen door. Grabbing the waiver from the glovebox, she walked to the door and knocked. After a few minutes, the door creaked open and George appeared. Jill, as politely as she could, held the waiver up in front of him. "Recognise this?" she asked the scowling, old man.

"You found it then," he answered glibly.

"What the hell is this? And what do you know about Jack Bright?" The old man's face changed. Gone was the expression of smugness, and now his old face looked angered. Jill realised she'd caught him off guard. "Well?" She pushed her advantage.

George glared at her. "What do you know of him?" he asked.

"I know he worked for you, and I know he was wanted for questioning for multiple murders," Jill continued. "You know we found a dead man in the rafters of the engine shed, Paul Stokes?"

"I hadn't heard that or the name," George replied.

"I don't believe you. Some gossiping prick around here would have said something. You can't do a damn thing without the whole fucking village knowing," Jill barked at him.

"In my day, ladies didn't swear, Miss Goodwin."

"Swearing, are you kidding me? In my day, farmers don't harbour fucking murderers. How's that for fucking swearing?"

George's face was turning a dark-crimson colour, and Jill could tell she'd hit a nerve when she asked about this Jack Bright. But she could also tell George wasn't going to tell her anything. Not because he was being obstinate, rather, she suspected it because she saw fear behind his anger. George closed the door in her face, leaving Jill without the answers she'd come for. As she turned, she spotted Mavis across the yard, who waved her over. Jill walked to the cattle shed where she stood, only just visible from the house. Still unsure of her motives, Jill decided to keep some distance.

"I heard you," Mavis said, as Jill came close enough to hear her.

"Heard me what?" Jill asked.

"Talking to husband about Jack."

"Do you know anything of him? It's important to tell me if you do." Jill tried to be friendly, sensing the same fear in Mavis as she had in George.

"Follow me," Mavis said.

Jill followed her into the barn and through to the rear of it. Stopping by a door, the old woman pulled a big brass key from her pocket and unlocked it. She entered, and Jill followed her in. Inside, it was partly furnished. A single bed was pushed against the wall, and a pile of old clothes, which were neatly folded and placed, sat rotting at the end of the bed. Next to the bed were an old oil lamp and a pitted photograph, the glass too dirty for Jill to see the picture clearly. On the opposite wall, a tallboy with a jug and basin, Jill assumed was to be used for washing, and hanging above them was a dirty, encrusted mirror. To the left of the basin stood a child's metal spinning top. Around the edges, the nursery rhyme, *Seesaw Margery Daw*. "This is where he slept," Mavis said, distracting Jill from the toy.

"Jack?" Jill looked for confirmation.

"Oh, yes. The police came around looking for him, but they never looked in here. Didn't think to check the back of the barn."

"Who was he?" Jill pushed the question.

"He was an odd fellow. A big man, and a very troubled man. His father beat him and his mother, you see. That was, until he grew up, of course. Sent his father away with a bad injury, George heard him tell Thomas. For some reason, he fled his home, leaving his mother. We never did find out why."

"Did he leave for the war?" Jill asked, her tone softer now that Mavis seemed she was disclosing all she knew.

"No, Thomas kept the war from him. That was, until the Luftwaffe bombed the railway station where his mother worked. Killed her outright, so they say. He joined the army then. After the war had finished, Jack came back to the farm. Thomas and Anne lived for quite a few years after the war. But Jack was different than before, so Thomas used to say. Changed, somehow. He carried a darkness with him." Mavis became upset.

Jill moved to comfort her. "It's okay, he's dead now, he must be."

"It's not that. You see, we all have secrets, and the Bradbury's is…" Mavis stopped.

Jill sensed someone behind her. She turned to see George in the open doorway.

"That's enough! That's enough!" he yelled at Mavis.

Mavis immediately cowered and left the barn. As Mavis left, Jill picked up the fading photo and slipped it into her bag. George turned to Jill.

"Leave this farm, and don't ever come back here. I told your fella the last time he came here holding that piece of paper, you bought the place, you deal with what's there." George stood aside and pointed out of the barn.

With no choice, Jill left the barn and walked to her car. After leaving the farm, she headed home. She had what she needed, for now, at least. She knew who Jack was and his connection to the body, and she knew the Bradbury's were hiding something, though George had interrupted before Mavis could confess. But one question still puzzled her. If Jack had committed suicide, who, or what, was on their CCTV? And who had Darren recognised when she'd shown it to him?

Jill hadn't long been home when Paul arrived, at his usual time. Jill elected not to say anything until after they'd eaten. After all, the information she's gathered today dated back to the Second World War, another hour or so wouldn't make much of a difference. There was also something else she would need to tell him, though she wasn't sure which order her two pieces of news should take. After dinner, Paul went to his study while Jill cleared away. After making herself a coffee and pouring Paul a glass of wine, she went to his study and sat on the large Chesterfield sofa opposite his desk.

"The police came today." Jill opened the conversation.

"Why?"

"Don't you remember, the body in the roof?" Jill replied.

"Oh, shit, yeah, forgotten all about it."

"Seems he is, rather, he was, called Paul Stokes."

"Anything else they know of him?"

Jill explained what the portly detective had told her, and then she told Paul what she'd found on him and the name of the mysterious man in the hat. She waited for his reaction.

"Seems you've been busy today," Paul said, shifting a little in his seat.

"I also found this." Jill slapped down the waiver on his desk. "Care to explain?"

Paul looked uncomfortable. He reminded Jill of a schoolchild explaining some misdemeanour to an intimidating teaching. "It's nothing, something the daft, old sod wanted signed. I didn't want to bother you with it."

"Is that why you went back to see him?" Jill asked.

"How do you know that?"

"Because I went there today to ask him myself."

Paul became enraged. Everything was on the line. He hadn't told Jill; he'd figured he could make it back up. The Halt had gone drastically over budget, and to make up the shortfall, he'd taken money out of the partnership. If she started to have misgivings about this place and wanted to sell, he would lose it all. The Halt and his stake in the partnership. He'd be ruined, financially and professionally. "Why are you sticking your nose in? What fucking good is it going to do?"

"You're kidding, right? I don't have a right to find out what the hell is going on? Is that seriously what you're saying to me?" Jill shouted back.

"Just leave it alone. There's nothing strange. It's all just a series of coincidences and nothing more."

"Then why do we have a photo of a man, who, by the way, two other people have seen, standing in our TV room who's supposedly been dead for seventy-odd years?"

Paul laughed at her. "Here we go with the fucking ghostly supernatural shit. I hate to burst your spiritual bubble, but there is no such thing. When you die, you go in a hole in the ground and fucking rot. As for that photo, nothing more than a trick of the light."

"You are an utter bastard. I wish I'd never let you talk me into this place," Jill replied, becoming upset.

"Talk you into it? I seem to remember you giving me a blowjob when I secured it."

Jill's control finally left her. "Get out! Get out of here! I don't want to be anywhere near you until I decide what to do," she yelled, hurting the back of her throat.

"I'm going, but you're not keeping this place. I'll be back for it."

"Oh, you can have it, lock, stock and barrel," Jill replied, her temper giving way to emotion.

Paul left the house, slamming the door as he did. Jill locked it behind him, putting on the security chain, ensuring he couldn't get back in even with his key. She leant against the door and whispered, "By the way, I'm pregnant."

Chapter 11

October 1944. Nijmegen, Holland

After the failure of Operation Market Garden, Jack's battalion, the Durham Light Infantry, were ordered to a desolate stretch of low-lying ground, known locally as the island. With the Germans occupying the higher ground around the town, the area was prone to random motor attacks and shelling. The conditions in October were, to say the least, atrocious. Inclined to flooding, it was impossible to keep dry, and so, for the next few days, the battalion spent much of its time dodging the German shells and trying to keep warm. Jack had managed to dig a small foxhole and build a fire. Lined with discarded clothes to protect him against the wet, cold mud. For most of the soldiers, this thick, damp sludge was now a constant companion, and while the damp chilled those not lucky enough to find shelter to their bones, the mud weighed on their thick winter uniforms, slowing them, making even the simplest tasks exhausting. As the men's extremities lost their dexterity, some struggled to keep the fires lit or even to eat. Jack couldn't decide which was worse, the hot sun of the summer war or the gnarling cold of winter's fingers, as they reached inside of him, taking away what little warmth he had. He thought of that summer back in Thirstonfield. Laying on the village green, listening to the gayety of the celebrations and the warm, soft breeze which wisped over his face. It seemed now a world away from this grey, desolate and almost monochrome world he now inhabited. The bright, vibrant colours were gone. Now all he saw when he looked around was the despair that war had brought to this place and every other place he'd passed through on the way to the next encounter. As the sun began to slide away and another cloudless October night loomed, Jack pulled the piece of corrugated metal he'd found over the top of his hideaway. This would not only keep him warm, trapping the heat from his fire, but it would also mask the light from it. And that meant not being visible to any German snipers who hunted in the darkness.

Twenty-five miles to the north lay the small hamlet of Hallderen. Defending this area were the ninth and tenth SS Panzer Divisions. Backed up by machine guns and Hanomag Halftrack armoured vehicles. The Durham Light Infantry were once again called on to take out the machine gun nests, while the fifth Canadian armour division and RAF attacked the King Tiger tanks of the SS. The battalion was to approach at the break of day and wait until the Sherman tanks of the Canadian's engaged the much larger and more powerful King Tigers. The assault began a little after eight-thirty when a Sherman fired on a King Tiger. Jack watched, as its shell did nothing but graze the thick armour. The Tiger retaliated immediately, firing one shot which exploded the Sherman into a ball of fire and red-hot debris. Instantly, two other Sherman's opened fire. One made a direct hit on the tracks, immobilising the Tiger. It didn't matter; the King Tiger turned its turret and hit back. Another Sherman blew up, its crew scrambling amongst the burning wreckage of their tank. The first Hawker Typhoon fighter flew in low, firing a salvo of eight rockets. The first six missed their target. The last two didn't. The King Tiger exploded. As Jack watched the tank incinerate, the order was given to attack.

The battalion rushed the machine gun nests. Jack's nest was the closest to their ambush point. He and five other men charged in. He fired his Enfield rifle, taking out a German officer with a single shot to the face. The second German soldier, a younger man, was next. He fired at Jack, grazing his left arm.

Jack dropped his rifle. He was too close to fire and charged him. He struck out, catching the young soldier on the cheek, fracturing it. On his back and dazed, the young soldier was an easy target for Jack.

The Kirpan knife ran across his throat, slicing it with ease. Jack stood while the young man grabbed at his trousers, pleading for help. This time, there was no sexual delight for Jack. The killing of war had become routine and mundane for him. It had lost its pleasure amongst the necessity of it. He heard a scream the likes of which he'd not heard before, not even in this hell. A ball of fire came across the hedgerow the machine gun nest they had taken was positioned behind. Then the rumble of tracks and Jack knew what was coming. He hid behind the ammunition dump which once fed the machine gun. A halftrack fitted with a flamethrower crashed through the hedge. Another fountain of flames spewed from it, catching the men Jack had come to know since D-Day, instantly turning them to fire. Their screams filled his ears but only for a fleeting moment. And after they'd stopped, the smell of burning flesh filled his nostrils. The red mist came across him. As the halftrack moved passed him, Jack ran after it, throwing a hand grenade into the open back. The explosion came a second or so after, killing two of the men in it. The halftrack stopped as Jack continued his pursuit. As the remaining crew turned the flamethrower toward Jack, he leapt into the back. Grabbing the first solider by the throat, he ran him backward, smashing the back of his neck against the sharp, metal sides of the armour, breaking it. He turned to the next soldier who was pulling his Luger from its holder. Jack grabbed him and brought the Kirpan knife up, its curved blade slicing through his stomach. The soldier dropped to his knees, holding his guts in his hands. Jack watched, as he fell face down, his entrails now spilled out across the deck of the halftrack. In the small, cramped cabin, the driver tried to flee, but Jack turned the flamethrower around and roasted him where he sat. With the halftrack on fire, Jack jumped from it and ran to the next target, the red mist driving him forward.

Across from where Jack had joined up with the battalion, the Canadian armour was losing its fight against the King Tigers. The Shermans didn't have the fire power to destroy them, and the Typhoons, though they'd destroyed over half of the Tigers, were now depleted of rockets and fuel. It was decided they would make one last push against them. The machine gun nests were all destroyed, and only the King Tiger tanks now stood in their way. Jack, along with five other men, were ordered to attack the last tank while another assault team would take out the lead tank, creating a road block, making the remaining three Tigers easy targets. They ran adjacent to it, hiding behind the hedgerow which skirted the narrow road. The ground vibrated under the weight of this metal behemoth as its tracks rumbled over the cobbles, tearing them up, as it made its way in search of the next Sherman. Seeing a break in the hedge, Jack ran out from the cover and leapt onto its back. He could feel the heat from its exhausts which protruded from the rear armour. Pulling the pin on his last hand grenade, he pushed it down between the air intakes on its back and jumped off, landing heavily on the ground. The explosion came quickly, and Jack was flung through the air as he tried to get clear. When he hit the ground, everything became hazy. The voices around him were muffled and the sound of the exploding tank nothing more than a distant rumble. Then everything became black and silent. Jack woke sometime later in a field hospital, the right of his face wrapped in bandages where the shrapnel had hit him when the tank had exploded.

***

Unable to sleep in the empty house, Jill tossed and turned until sometime in the early hours of the morning. Partly, it was because the house was once again cold. But, mainly, it was because her mind was scrambling to pinpoint the moment when everything seemed to go wrong. A few months ago, they were happy. They lived what most people would see as an idyllic life, though albeit, it was disrupted by her fight with cancer. But, even so, they had a lovely home, they were happy, and she had Charlie. Now, she was alone, in a house that she hadn't wanted, and was stuck in some kind of nightmarish plot from a bad movie.

And to top it all, she was pregnant. They'd often discussed having a family, but when the time was right, and by any measure, this wasn't it. Eventually, Jill gave up the notion of sleep and made herself a coffee before going to her study. She opened the lid on her laptop and went back to the web page she'd used to research Paul Stokes. Sipping the strong, black coffee as the sun began to creep over the moors, she found a link to Thirstonfield Halt and a small article which described strange occurrences and a local priest who was sent to cast out the supposed spirit responsible. As she read the piece, it was obvious to her that it had been written before the priest's planned visit. As she moved her gaze to the photograph of the young priest, she recognised something he held in his hand. It was the crucifix which now hung above her door. Another piece of the puzzle fitted together. The article mentioned that it was George Bradbury who called in the priest. Now the waiver made sense to her, and she began to understand why Paul had been able to get the place so cheaply, and more importantly, why no one else had bought it. Paul told her that Thomas wouldn't sell it for sentimental reasons and because he didn't want change, but she now understood that wasn't the case at all. Thomas hadn't sold it because of its truth. The truth that it was a place of evil, and whether you believe in spirits or not, a dark and malevolent soul haunts it. Jill drank a big swig of the now cooling coffee and read on. The article referred her back to the page which detailed Jack's death. At the bottom, almost unreadable, was a side note. The name of a police officer Jack had struck that night. She printed the pages off and then Googled both priest and police officer. To her amazement, they were both still alive and living locally. Her mind was made up. She would go and speak to these two men and pay another visit to Mavis Bradbury. Jill felt certain Mavis had tried to tell her something, but George stopped her. Whatever it was, Jill needed to know.

Jill pulled up outside of the St Francis retirement home for priests. The large building, it seemed to her, was once a very grand manor house, set back along a driveway which kept it out of sight of the only road. She reached out and pressed the intercom button located on the solid brick column. "Hello," a voice came over the old speaker.

"Yes, I'm here to see Father Terrance Crowley." The speaker clicked with static. After a few seconds of silence, the impressive, metal gates juddered, and with a rusting squeak, opened. Jill passed through them, parking her car outside what she rightly assumed was the main entrance. She entered the imposing building and was met by an older woman wearing the kind of nurse's uniform she would expect to see in a 1950s period drama. Jill smiled politely and stated who she'd come to see. The 1950s nurse turned and led Jill along a grand corridor and to a room that at one time had been the formal reception room. Jill was shown in. As she entered, the door was closed behind her. In a wingback chair by the open fire sat an elderly man who waved Jill over, inviting her to sit opposite him in the chair's twin. Jill complied.

"What can I do for you, my dear?" the elderly man asked.

"Are you Father Terrance Crowley?" Jill asked nervously.

"Yes, I am."

Jill fidgeted a little in her seat and continued, "I've come to ask you about a service you carried out for a Mr George Bradbury." She swallowed hard.

Jill watched his expression, as the elderly man searched his memory. After some time, he politely shook his head. "I am sorry, my dear. I do not remember that name."

"It was nineteen sixty-seven. He called you and asked you to visit an old train station that was on his land. Thirstonfield Halt Station, to be exact," Jill explained, trying to jog his fading memory.

The room was dark, the large windows were, to an extent, obscured by thick, dark-green curtains. The reflection of the fire danced and skipped across his old face, highlighting the years of smiles and worries which had left their marks on it.

The expression changed, and Jill could tell he'd found something in his memory. "Yes, I remember that place. Tell me, why do you have an interest in it?"

"I own it. I live there," Jill replied.

His expression changed again. The elderly man now wore a look of concern. "Do the Bradburys not own the land anymore?"

"No, they sold us The Halt and some of the surrounding land. Why?"

Concern changed to anger. "I told him never to sell that place. To lock it up and forget about it until the day it crumbled. Only then would that land be clean again."

"Who did you tell? Was it George? George Bradbury?" Jill asked.

"Yes, George Bradbury. I remember him now. An obtuse, little man as I remember, and his wife, Mavis."

Jill opened her bag and pulled out the tarnished crucifix. She held it out toward the elderly priest. On seeing it, he recoiled into his chair. "Where did you find that?"

"On the land by the gate. I've had it cleaned, but it keeps tarnishing."

"That crucifix was touched by the dark spirit which is present on that land. It is forever sullied by the hand of evil. By bringing it here, you have opened this house to that evil."

Jill pushed it back down into her bag. "I'm sorry, I didn't know. But there are weird things happening. Our dog went into a tunnel that was sealed up years ago. When we broke in, we found him dead. He'd been dead for decades. How can that be?"

"Dogs ward off evil; they warn you of its presence. The evil spirit that resides there will have needed to dispose of your dog to move freely. You must leave now. I fought with him many years ago and escaped with my life. I'm too old and weak now to do it again."

"Fought with who? Was his name Jack Bright? The spirit, was that his name?" Jill asked, standing.

The elderly man looked up at her. "He was the evillest presence I have ever encountered. You must not go back there. Do not return. Dispose of that crucifix, for as long as you have it, he is with you." As she stood and turned to leave, the priest said something more. "My dear, the name you gave, Jack Bright."

"Yes?" Jill replied.

"That is not the name I remember."

"What name do you remember?"

The priest didn't answer. He turned away to face the fire and muttered something only just audible to Jill. "I beg of you, do not go back there."

"It's my home," Jill said, as she pulled the door closed behind her.

***

Paul had spent the night at Jeff's house. After storming out following the argument with Jill, he'd driven around for a while, his head buzzing with a thousand thoughts of the events which had led him to that moment. After an hour or so of amnesic driving, he'd found himself outside of his business partner's house. He'd knocked on the door, gave Jeff his side of the events and asked if he could stay there for a night or until he could, at least, *sweet talk* Jill into letting him go home. Jeff had agreed and listened to Paul's ranting and excuses, and though he'd shown his business partner, and friend, sympathy, he hadn't believed everything he'd been told. He knew Paul too well, and he knew Jill.

Paul woke as Jeff followed his morning routine. The pull-out sofa hadn't offered Paul much in the way of comfort, but it was better than the alternative, that being the back seat of his Range Rover. The only hotel close enough was in the village of Thirstonfield, and he knew if he'd stayed there, the local gossips would have dined out on them both for months. Jeff lived partway between The Halt and their office, so it was a good fit. He could hear Jeff clanking around in the kitchen. Paul couldn't decide if Jeff was naturally loud or if it was a not so subtle way of ensuring Paul was up and out. He stretched and made his way to the bathroom.

After urinating, he moved to the sink and pulled off his shirt to have a quick wash before going home. He rubbed the soap into the warm water running from the tap. When he applied it to his chest, he felt an agonising stinging. When he looked in the mirror, he froze. Across his chest, in mirrored writing and carved into his skin was the name Jack. A feeling of horror rushed through his body. He screamed at the shock of what he could see. As his mind scrambled to understand the sight before him, it overloaded. And as his vision became narrow, he felt his body hit the bathroom floor. Rushing into the bathroom, Jeff found his friend passed out on the floor. Turning on the cold tap, he cupped as much as he could in his palms and splashed it onto Paul's face. Instantly, Paul came to. Clambering away from Jeff, Paul scrambled into the corner behind the freestanding bath.

"What the hell is wrong with you?" Jeff asked.

Paul looked at him in confusion. "Can't you see it?"

"See what?"

Paul looked down at his chest. The writing had gone. "I don't understand," he whispered, as he stood and gazed into the mirror, rubbing his hands across his chest.

"Makes fucking two of us, buddy. You gave me a fright," Jeff replied. "You're okay now?"

Paul nodded. "Yeah, it's nothing. I must have dreamt it."

"Go home and get your head sorted before you come into the office." Jeff left the bathroom, closing the door as he did.

***

Jill stood outside of the small, glass porch at an unassuming house in Raisby Close, Middlesbrough. The address she had tracked the retired police officer to. Nervously, she knocked. After a short while, a thin, elderly man opened the glass door. "Yes?" he said softly to her.

"Hi, are you William Dowding? Formerly police Sergeant William Dowding?" Her nervousness came out with her words.

The old man smiled. "I haven't heard that title for a long time. It's just Bill these days."

"Hello. I've come in the hopes that I can ask you a few questions about an incident that happened back in October of 1949?" Jill's words came easier now.

"And what incident would that be?"

"It happened at Thirstonfield Halt Station. A suspect you were chasing jumped in front of an oncoming train." Jill hoped that would open his memory.

"But not before breaking my nose, yes, I remember him," Bill answered, as he rubbed his face.

"Please, it's very important, can I speak with you?"

Bill moved to one side and invited Jill into his modest home. As she entered, a middle-aged woman dressed in a healthcare workers uniform entered from the kitchen. She introduced herself as Bill's care worker and then left. Inside, it was much as Jill would have expected. A life serving in the police force had given Bill a decent standard of living and comfortable home. To Jill, it seemed homely, and she surmised that Bill wasn't wanting for things he liked or needed. She sat on the sofa while Bill muted the unbranded flat screen. Taking a seat opposite her, he sat back, crossing his legs.

"What is it you want to know?" His voice was still soft and quiet.

"The man, Jack Bright, why were you chasing him?"

He thought for a while, and then, uncrossing his legs, he leaned forward a little. "Between the end of the war and forty-nine, there had been seven murders in and around the village of Thirstonfield and in Middlesbrough. On the odd time we had a witness, they always gave the same description. A large man wearing a black fedora style hat." He took a breath. "No one ever saw the killing, of course, but this description always seemed to crop up close to where the murder had taken place."

"But what led you to him. To Jack?" Jill asked.

"We eventually traced the events back to Thirstonfield Village, and a young woman there remembered seeing a man who fitted that description working on a farm nearby."

"The Bradbury farm?"

"Yes, that's their name. Thomas, I think," Bill said excitedly as his memory fired up.

"Go on," Jill said, encouraging him.

"When we went to see Thomas and his wife, he told us who this man was and his story and that he'd fled the farm, but they didn't or wouldn't say why. Luckily, we happened to be at the train station that night and spotted him. He stood out because of his size."

"What do you know of Paul Stokes?" Jill asked.

Bill leaned back in his chair and thought. Rubbing his cheek again. "Yes, I remember that case. He vanished, and we assumed he'd been killed abroad or something had happened to him on ship, fallen overboard perhaps. Why do you ask?"

"His body was found in the old engine shed during the restoration. And it seems he bullied Jack at school. Do you think Jack could have killed him?" Jill asked.

Bill nodded. "Yes, Jack was a violent man. He seemed to get some sort of sick pleasure from it."

Jill sat back in the soft sofa. Surely, there was no doubt. The only thing she needed to hear now was the Bradbury secret Mavis tried to tell her. It seemed to Jill that whatever it was could be, the missing detail which would pull this whole thing together. Jill looked back over to Bill. "Is there anything else you can tell me?"

"There is one thing. Between nineteen fifty-seven and sixty-seven, people began reporting pets and livestock being killed and tortured. We never did find out who was responsible. Some believed Jack had come back, and George Bradbury called in a priest to try and stop it. Strangely, around the same time, it did stop. I'm not a religious man, my dear, I've seen the worst of people and the best, and I don't know if there's such things as spirits and ghosts. But I know one thing for sure."

"What's that?" Jill asked.

"I wouldn't step foot on that land again. Something is off up there, and if you ask me, it's best left alone," Bill said, his words now much harder.

Jill left the retired policeman's house and headed back to Thirstonfield. She wanted to tell Paul what she had found out, and she needed to tell him they were expecting their first child. This news, she'd decided, could only be told face to face. She had one more person to see: Mavis. Once she found out what she had tried to tell her, she would call Paul and ask him to come home. She would tell him their news, and then she would ask him to open his mind and listen to the facts she'd gathered. She hoped, as she navigated the narrow country lanes, that once he had the facts, he would draw the same conclusions as she. If he didn't, or wouldn't, she had no idea what she would do.

Eventually, Jill pulled up at the top of the bank which led down to the farm. From there, she could see George's old truck parked outside the farmhouse. Jill decided she would wait until he went out before making her way down. After sitting for almost an hour, she watched as George came out and climbed into the Land Rover. A puff of blue smoke told Jill he'd started the engine. A few seconds later, she watched it trundle out of the farmyard and toward the hills which backed up around the farm. Once out of sight, Jill set off.

Pulling up outside of the farmhouse, Jill checked one last time. If he appeared now, she figured she could still outrun it in her car, even over the rough track. After reassuring herself she had time, Jill knocked on the door and Mavis answered.

"I saw you at the top," Mavis said, without a hello or any other acknowledgement.

"You did?"

"Yes, that's why I sent George off t' market with some beer money. He'll be gone long enough. I reckon you want to talk some more." Mavis stood back, and Jill entered the kitchen.

She sat at the old table while Mavis made a fresh pot of tea. Without speaking, she brought over two cups, a jug of milk and the teapot, which was wrapped in a thick, woollen cosy. "Let that mash for a while," she said, putting the teapot onto a metal stand. After which, she turned to Jill. "What is it you want to know?"

"I want to know what it was you were about to tell me. I know about Jack, I know George called in a priest, and I've spoken to him, the priest. Why did you sell us The Halt knowing what you do? Is that the secret of the Bradbury's? The Halt, Jack Bright?"

Mavis took a heavy breath and sighed it back out slowly. "No, we sold you The Halt because we need the money. No other reason than that, lass. The farm is failing, it's been losing money for years. But that's no secret."

Jill sat back in the chair, pushing a cup toward Mavis, who responded by pouring the now mashed brew into it with a little milk. "So, what is the Bradbury secret?" Jill asked, pulling the cup back toward her.

Mavis supped from her own cup and then placed it down. "It began in the summer of nineteen forty-five. July 18 to be exact. The day Jack returned from the war."

Chapter 12

July 18 1945

Jack had survived the war, though the facial injury he'd sustained and the resulting scar tissue which stretched from his right ear to his temple, meant he no longer had hair across that side of his head. Rather, he had a raised, angry-looking scar which had been remarked upon as something akin to Frankenstein's monster. Ashamed at his disfigurement, Jack had taken to wearing a large fedora hat after returning home with his battalion and was demobbed early July. He had seen the worst of the war, and he'd carried out what he believed was justice for the slaughter of his mother. And yet, his bloodlust was not satisfied. The red mist which had been his constant companion since he'd first fought was as much a part of him as any other biological piece. It was with him always, only resting when he did. Initially, he'd made his way back to Tavistock Street and to the home he'd fled and returned to when the bombs had fallen. But he couldn't settle in the empty house. And so, he'd made his way back to the farm, hoping that going back there and working for the kind man would find him the peace it once had. And so, now he stood atop the same hill he had when he'd first run away. Below him, the farm, and behind him, Thirstonfield Halt. The station had grown while he'd been away fighting and was much busier than he remembered. As the long shadows of the summer afternoon stretched out before him, he walked down the hill and across the farmyard to the house. George, who was now eight, ran out to meet him, shouting to his father, Thomas, as he did.

Thomas came out, looking to see what the commotion was, and when he saw Jack, he welcomed him with open arms. The kind man called to Anne, and she gave Jack a hug. This was the first physical female contact he'd had since that night. The night he'd fled from home. He felt her body push against his and her breasts squash between the two of them. Jack felt an excitement run through him. He wrapped his huge arms around her and hugged her as once he had Doris. His left arm across her shoulders, the right in the small of her back. He spread his fingers and felt his little finger follow her curve, eventually, resting on her left buttock. Anne pulled away from him, still smiling and paying no mind to where his finger had stopped. To her, it was nothing but a misplaced hug, but to Jack, it was a clear signal of intent, attraction to him and acceptance from Anne for physical contact.

***

Mavis took another sip. "Seems things would return to normal, as they had before the bombing, and before Jack had gone to get his revenge. But Anne could see he was a troubled soul by what he'd witnessed in Europe. And then, there was that hat. After the war, he insisted on wearing it. Never took it off. And it was always tilted to the right as if to hide something. We never did find out what. After a week or two, he began confiding in her the horrors he'd witnessed. He told her he'd seen friends burst into flames at the hands of Nazi flamethrowers, and men explode into a bloody vapour. Sometimes, he'd found a piece of a man, not a scratch on it, while the rest of him was nothing more than a tarn of red pulp." She poured herself some more tea. "Anne decided to help Jack come to terms with it and began spending more time with him. They began to form a close friendship. That was, until a particular winter's night in nineteen forty-six."

***

191

November 1946

A storm was hitting the moors hard. High winds and strong, driving rain meant that no work could be carried out. In the distance, thunder could be heard rumbling across the moors. By late afternoon, as the sun began to retreat, Jack found himself in his bunk. The sound of the thunder, wind and rain lashing the side of the barn brought with it the flashbacks that haunted his dreams. The sound of the storm took him back to Holland and the foxhole he'd hid in. He curled up on the bed and gritted his teeth, banging his fists against his head.

Then the door opened. It was Anne. Seeing his torment, she ran to the bed and sat beside him. She grabbed his wrists to stop him hitting himself and calmly spoke his name over and over.

She wasn't to know that Jack had mistaken her kindness for affection and that in Jack's mind, her attempts to make him feel better were a clear signal of physical attraction. Nor was she to know what Jack had done to his mother, Doris, or that the red mist had control of him. He sat up and took hold of her arms. Standing, he spun her around and pushed her down onto the bed. With one large hand holding her down, he unfastened his trousers. Anne pleaded with him, begging him to stop, but Jack tore her clothes from her. She yelled for Thomas, but the storm drowned out her cries. Jack spun her around. With her cries now muffled by the bed sheets, he entered her and began fucking her hard. With his lust for the feel of a woman around him unsatisfied since that night, he let go what little restraint he still had. After ejaculating, he let her go. She ran crying, her clothes shredded, from his bunk and to the house. A few moments later, while Jack found peace on his bed, the door opened again. This time, it was Thomas, and he was carrying a shotgun.

***

"What happened?" Jill asked, pouring some more tea.

"Thomas chased him from the farm. He vowed if he ever saw him again, he would shoot him. Nine months on, Anne gave birth to Arthur." Jill could see the sadness in her eyes.

"Please, carry on," Jill said softly.

"Arthur grew up not knowing he was the bastard son of Jack. No one did, not even George. Thomas and Anne couldn't have stood the shame. Times were very different back then, lass. But he was like his father. A troubled and wicked boy." Mavis stood and filled the stainless-steel kettle with fresh water before putting it on the range stove. "As he grew, things began happening to the animals. Some of the villagers believed Jack had come back after killing himself. I told George it was Arthur, but he wouldn't have it, not then, anyway."

"What do you mean, not then? What changed?" Jill asked.

"After they had him committed to St Luke's hospital for the insane, Thomas told George that Arthur was the one killing and hurting the farm animals. Up until then, they'd told him men were sneaking onto t' farm. The night they came for him, he was eighteen. It was a stormy night, and late. Thomas had insisted they came at night, to stop anyone seeing them. They arrived at nine-thirty sharp. He kicked and screamed when they put the straitjacket on him." Mavis took another mouth full of tea and continued. "George visited him at the hospital, but Thomas and Anne disowned him. They never saw Arthur after that night."

"You said he was troubled?" Jill asked.

"Yes, the devil himself, if you ask me. He told Thomas and Anne he could hear a man's voice telling him to do things. He became more aggressive as he got older and bigger. By the time he was fifteen, he was bigger than Thomas. They tried to treat him at St Luke's, but nothing worked, he just got worse."

"What did he do?"

"He broke the legs of Thomas' favourite Collie and gutted some of the livestock. That's not to mention what he did to some of the local pets. That's when Thomas had had enough and had him taken away."

"That's what Bill Dowding was referring to when he said animals were being hurt and killed. It was Arthur, not some ghost of Jack?" Jill said, helping Mavis with the clean teacups and plates.

"Every time George went to see him, he was in that straitjacket. The staff were too afraid of him, you see. George would tell me Arthur would just sit and rock back and forth and sing that damned nursery rhyme. *Seesaw Margery Daw, Jack has got a new master. He shall work for a penny a day because he can't work faster.*" Mavis stopped talking and stared into space, her eyes dim and her brow clenched. "One day, George came home and told me the staff overheard Arthur pleasuring himself while fantasising about killing someone."

Jill shivered. "What happened to Arthur? Is he still alive?" she asked.

"No, he died during the electric shock treatment when he was twenty. Only then did Thomas tell George what happened on that November night. That Arthur was the bastard son of Jack," she continued. "Anyway, before that, George called in a priest to exorcise the old station. By then, it had been closed."

"But what about all the strange things? Are you saying you don't believe Jack's spirit is with us, that it was Arthur?"

"Oh yes, Jack's here, all right. He wants to keep that place for himself. Before he committed suicide, he caused us one more heartache."

"What was that?" Jill asked, taking a piece of homemade coffee cake.

***

October 1949

Jack had lived rough since being chased from the farm. His home had been taken over, sold after the war when he'd failed to claim it. With a national housing shortage, any homes believed now to be vacant because of the war were reclaimed for the families in need. He had nowhere to go. The nights were turning cold again. He earned what money he could the only way he could. By renting himself to people who wanted someone else to pay for an indiscretion. For a few shillings, Jack would beat whoever it was. The more severe you wanted the beating to be, the more it cost you. On this particular day, he'd made his way back to Thirstonfield. While waiting for the last train, he'd gone to the village pub, made eye contact with a woman and followed her across the fields. He hadn't recognised her, why would he, she was Thomas' niece, and he'd only met her once before when she was young. He'd introduced himself, but she'd refused him instantly. He was going to let her go; today wasn't a day he needed the thrill or sexual delight from killing. But when she'd told him her name, the red mist had come back. He found the opportunity to take revenge on the Bradburys. Moments later, she was dead, and Jack was making his way to the station.

As the police closed in on him, he'd jumped onto the track. He wouldn't be taken alive and hanged for his crimes. He would die on his own terms. Bring to an end this life of misery, bane and of hurt. His body registered nothing of the hit from the train before his head was decapitated from his body. Jack's death, it seemed, unlike his life, was painless.

***

Mavis became upset. "He swore to Thomas as he left, he would get a Bradbury. And he did, that poor girl."

"Did Jack know about his son?" Jill asked, washing the cake down with fresh tea.

"No, he never knew Arthur. He wouldn't have known Anne was pregnant. It was for the best, really. If he'd known, there's no telling what he'd have done."

"So why the kid's toy in Jack's bunk?" Jill asked.

"Arthur used to play in there. After he was committed, George threw everything out, but I guess that slipped his mind. You see, when his father told him, George locked the door and forbid anyone from entering it."

"That's why he reacted so angrily the other day?" Jill said.

"Yes, dear. He won't tear the room down for fear of Jack coming here. He believes if he leaves it be, Jack will stay at the station." Mavis took a sip of the hot tea. "You see, lass, this is the Bradbury family secret. And now, you know. I'm sorry for what comes next."

Jill felt a cold run through her. "What do you mean, what comes next?"

Mavis smiled to her. "Once you know of the secret, the secret knows of you."

Jill felt angry, foolish and deceived. This old woman, who Jill believed was befriending her, had played her. She had unburdened herself onto Jill, something she knew no one in the village must ever know. Even if Jill went to the village gossips with this, no one would believe her. She was still an outsider. She stood and finished her tea. "Thank you for your time, Mrs Bradbury. I'm going to put a stop to this nonsense once and for all."

Mavis smiled at her. "You do that, dear."

Jill climbed into her car and began the journey home, ready now to call Paul and tell him everything she'd found out. Even he, the biggest cynic she'd ever met, couldn't deny this much evidence. As she joined the main road, she pressed his speed dial. It rang.

"Hi," came the reply.

"Hi, where are you?" Jill asked.

"I'm at home. I needed some things and a shower. I'll be gone before you get here," Paul said submissively.

"No, stay there. I need to talk to you. There's something I need to tell you and something you should know."

Paul hesitated. "I can't fight anymore, Jill. I'm exhausted."

"Me neither. Please just wait for me."

"Will do." Paul hung up.

***

Mavis lifted the old teapot from the table and carried it over to the sink. She emptied the contents of the cold tea and tea bags and rinsed it. Turning, she made her way through to the living room and sat by the fire. She gazed out the window she'd looked out of every day since marrying George back in 1961. Before long, the warmth of the fire and the comfort of the chair meant Mavis slipped into a deep sleep.

When Jill got home, she parked her car in the garage and entered the house through the connecting door. The electric garage doors closed behind her. She found Paul in the kitchen. She had thought about what and how to tell him and decided that she would keep the news of the pregnancy until the end. Firstly, she would tell him what she'd found out and that she wanted to call in the spiritualist medium who'd helped the German Shepard family.

Jill made a fresh coffee and poured Paul a mug. Setting it down opposite him, she began. It took her almost an hour to explain what she discovered. Everything from the other dog through to the Bradbury secret. "What do you think?" she asked Paul.

"About what?" Paul asked.

"About everything, what I've just said."

Paul sighed heavily. "I think these events, or whatever they are, have fired your imagination. I think you're seeing things where nothing exists. It's all just coincidence. I keep telling you that."

"So even the nursery rhyme, which I told you the first day we came here I heard a child singing, is a coincidence? Even though, at that point, we didn't even know the fucking Bradburys, let alone their secret," Jill argued, becoming ever more frustrated.

"I don't know what to tell you," Paul answered, shrugging. "I guess you need something in your life, especially now you've given up on blogging and your website. Looks like all the financial responsibility is on me while you chase spirits and ghosts, none of which actually fucking exist. But you know what does exist? The mortgage, the bills, that's what's real!" Paul shouted back.

"You want real? Here's real. I'm pregnant. How's that for fucking real?"

Paul stopped dead. "You're what?"

"I'm pregnant," Jill replied, in a much calmer tone.

"How, when?"

"I guess that first night here."

Paul bowed his head and ran his fingers through his hair. Jill could see small beads of sweat collecting on his brow. "What's wrong, aren't you excited?" Jill asked.

"Yeah, of course, I'm just. It's nothing, don't worry," Paul stammered his answer.

"What is it?" Jill asked.

"Nothing, it's fine, hun, honestly. It's great news." Paul moved over and hugged Jill, kissing her. Then, he made his way upstairs to change.

Jill made her way to her study. There, she opened Edge on her laptop and brought up the web page for the spiritualist medium and called him. Though Paul hadn't wanted Jill to call him and still didn't buy into the whole ghost-spirit argument, she decided to at least talk to him. Too much had happened that simply couldn't be explained, even by Paul, who normally thought he had a good reason for things. She knew this was against his wishes, but she was past the point of caring. This was their home, and soon, they would have a family. She would do whatever it took to keep them safe. After speaking with him, she cleared her browsing history and moved to Paul's study where she found him sitting behind his desk. His nose, as always, buried in the screen of his laptop.

"The conversation we've just had," she said, as sweetly as she could.

Paul looked up from his laptop. "Which one?"

"The one about Jack and the Bradbury's," she reminded him.

"Oh Christ, not this again," Paul remarked.

"Well, I've called the spiritualist to see if he'd come and check over The Halt."

"Check the house. What does that mean?"

"He helped that other family, remember, the one I told you about." Jill's tone was disarming.

"For fuck's sake, Jill, the last thing I want is someone snooping around our home," Paul snapped. "And how much will this cost?"

Jill looked puzzled. "Is that what is bothering you? The cost?"

"Well, how much?" Paul asked again.

"He'd charge one hundred and fifty pounds because he's come up from Beverly."

"You're kidding." Paul stood, slamming his laptop lid.

Jill became defensive. "All the way through this project I've given you free reign on everything. From the ridiculous heating system, which doesn't work, to the over complicated lighting system, which I can't for the life of me figure out. But I spend that on something which could really help us, and you blow a fuse. Anyway, I haven't booked him yet, I've only spoken to him and he thinks he can help us."

"Well, you can call him back and tell him thanks, but no thanks," Paul shouted. As he finished berating Jill, his phone rang. He looked at the screen; it was Jeff. "Hi, Jeff, yeah, sure. What now? Okay then, I'll be there soon." He turned back to Jill. "Jeff needs me at the office."

Paul stormed out of the study. Moments later, Jill heard the SUV fire up and drive away. She watched Paul's Range Rover head up the drive. She hadn't noticed at first, but a storm was building from the east coast. Outside, the rain sprayed through the porch lights in sliver shots, while the wind rocked the hanging baskets and the old station clock. As Paul joined the main road and headed to the office, one thought kept running through his mind. How the fuck was he going to afford a baby? His credit line was full, the bank was all but empty, and that included the overdraft and he knew Jill would expect a lot of money spent on a nursery. And then, she'd want her family to visit, and that meant finishing the engine shed. A sweat ran down his back. He couldn't tell Jill about their financial situation. He'd promised her The Halt was affordable, well within their means, he'd said. But it hadn't been. For all intents and purposes, they were now broke. On the main road, Paul was pushing the Range Rover through the building storm. The high beams lit the road ahead, but even on their maximum setting, the wipers were having difficulty clearing the window. As he rounded a corner, a flash of lightning illuminated the dark road. In that instant, he saw a man standing in front of him. A tall, large built man wearing a hat. Paul blasted the horn, but he didn't move. The Range Rover tried to swerve around him, but the speed it was carrying made it unstable, and it began fishtailing. Paul fought with the wheel, but eventually, the Range Rover caught the ditch and flipped over. It rolled down the embankment, coming to a stop on its nose. Inside, Paul hung unconscious from his seat belt. The airbags had deployed, but he'd hit the interior several times. Blood dripped from the open wounds, and his right leg was broken. When the car had hit the tree at the bottom, Paul still had his foot pressing hard on the brake pedal. The impact shattered his tibia and fibula. From the road, the black Range Rover had disappeared. Only when a flurry of rain passed over the crash site could the faintest red glow be seen from its taillights along with the intermittent orange flash of its hazard lights. On the roof lining by the sunroof control, the red SOS light began flashing. While Paul slipped in and out of consciousness, the car sent a rescue message.

As Jill sat in the study, she felt the house, once again, become cold. She yawned and looked at the clock. 9.30 p.m. She was waiting for Paul to come home before she went to bed. But, so far, she hadn't heard from him since leaving for the office a few hours earlier. As she sat watching the TV, she thought she heard the distant sound of a dog barking. And again, it sounded just like Charlie's bark, the one he used to get attention. She shivered, pulling the fleece throw around her. She felt sad for their little dog. What an awful death it must have been for him, trapped and alone in the tunnel. A tear rolled down her face. Another noise replaced it and brought her mind back. She recognised it as the sound of Paul's SUV. *'At last,'* she thought, *'he's home.'* She smiled to herself. He must have calmed down by now. A knock came at the door.

Confused why Paul would knock, she stood and made her way to the door. When she opened it, two police officers informed her that Paul had crashed and that he'd been taken to James Cook University Hospital in Middlesbrough.

Jeff sat waiting for Paul at their offices, unaware of his car-wreck. In front of him on the screen, Jeff had discovered Paul's financial anomalies and the bridging loan he'd secured against the business which was due at the end of the month, which he knew Paul couldn't pay. He picked up his phone and tried Paul's number. Again, there was no answer. He tried Jill's, and she answered. "Hi Jeff, can I call you back?"

"I need to speak with Paul, it's urgent," Jeff said.

"Jeff, he's been in an accident. I'm at the hospital now. I'll call you back." She hung up.

After waiting for him to come out of surgery, Jill was taken to the ward where she found Paul lying in traction. His right leg was pinned. She sat beside him, holding his hand tightly. He was battered and bruised. "What the hell happened?" she asked, through her tears.

"You were right all along," he whispered, his voice sounding harsh and forced.

"What about?"

"I saw him. Standing in the road," Paul replied.

"Who, Jack?" Jill asked.

"Yes, the man you described, the one Darren saw. I saw him. I swerved, lost control and crashed," Paul coughed and spluttered his words out.

Jill wiped the tears away and nodded.

"There's something else. When I was at Jeff's, I saw his name carved into my chest."

Jill pulled back the blankets, expecting to see this mutilation.

Paul took hold of her hand. "It went almost as soon as I saw it. Just like your bruises." He coughed again, wheezing as he inhaled. "Go and get that spirit guy, find a way to fix this. And Jill, I'm sorry." His apology was only just audible, his voice now almost gone.

Jill leaned over and kissed him. Then she left the ward and made her way back home. Once there, she called Richard Durant and asked him to come as quickly as he could.

It was the morning after Paul's crash. Jill had been to see the wreck being recovered earlier that day and wondered how anyone could have survived the obvious ferocity of the impact. The once gleaming Range Rover was now nothing more than a mangled wreck of aluminium and plastic. She'd been handed Paul's personal items, including his phone, which in her haste she'd stuffed into a bag along with his Ray-Ban's and briefcase. Later that day, she began preparing for Richard Durant. As she finished making the house as welcoming as she could, a knock came at the door. She opened it. A short, fat man wearing overalls and holding a clipboard met her gaze.

"Yes?" Jill asked.

"I'm looking for a Paul Sullivan or a Jill Goodwin."

"I'm Miss Goodwin. How can help you?"

"I'm here to repossess one Toyota C-HR, Registration."

Jill cut him off. "What do you mean? Repossess."

"The lease hasn't been paid for five months, so the finance company wants it back. I have a court order." The fat mechanic, as Jill had decided he was, showed her the court order. It was there in black and white, so she had no choice but to hand over her keys and let him take it.

Jill watched as he drove her car from their garage and loaded her car onto the truck. As it pulled away, she heard Paul's phone ring. She rushed to the bag and pulled it out. It was Jeff. Jill decided not to answer, rather, she would let it ring off. After a few intros to Paul's favourite James track, the phone became silent. She unlocked it and checked his messages and emails. She found the emails from the finance company threatening to repossess both cars if the back payments on the leases weren't made by the end of last week. She found other emails too. Some from credit card companies she didn't know they had cards with and which were all maxed out, and one from the bank threatening to close down their overdraft for being thousands over its agreed limit. As if she hadn't enough to contend with, it seemed Paul had been lying to her. Still, she would deal with this another time. Today, or rather tonight, it was about Jack Bright.

A little after seven, at the time they had planned, Richard Durant arrived. He was a bald man of average height and slightly more than average weight. "Jill Goodwin?" he asked.

"Yes, you must be Mr Durant?" Jill extended a hand.

"It's Richard," he said, shaking her hand.

"Please, come in. I'm sorry it's a bit cold, the heating is playing up again."

"Thank you, hell of a night, isn't it?" he said, walking past her.

As it was last night, a storm had come in from the east coast. And Jill felt a menace in the air.

Part 3
The Rescue

Chapter 13

November 2017

Richard heard Jill close the door behind him, shutting out the sound of the rising storm. He removed his coat and hung it from the only spare hook on the grand cloak stand which stood adjacent to the heavy front door. Turning, he smiled at the nervous woman, Jill, who stood before him. As with so many people who had not undergone this before, she looked unsure and somewhat regretful that she'd called him. He'd experienced this, many times before in his years as a spiritualist medium. Jill led Richard through to the sitting room and offered him a seat in front of the large, open fire. She sat opposite him and leaned toward him. Though she was anxious of what this night might bring, she felt a sense of devout enlightenment about this man. It was almost tangible to her, and it eased her fears.

"I hope the fire is okay? It's the only warm room in the house," Jill said.

Richard answered in a soft, calming tone. "It's fine, thank you. Before I begin, I need you to relax. Keep your mind as clear as possible and focus only on the light of God and all positive things." Jill sat back in her chair, and Richard took a deep breath as the storm intensified and the rain hit the triple glazed windows like the shrapnel of a thousand needles while lightning flashed, and thunder rumbled. He began.

"Jill, I need to ask. Have you or Paul dabbled with any devices or spells designed to entice the spirit presence?"

"No, I wouldn't know how to. What devices?" Jill asked nervously.

"Ouija board, for instance."

"No. Paul wouldn't give anything like that the time of day, and I wouldn't go anywhere near something like that," Jill answered assuredly.

"It is of the utmost importance that, whatever I ask, you are open and honest with me. Do not keep anything from me."

Jill nodded. "Yes, of course. There is something you should know in the interest of being open and honest."

"Yes?"

"I'm pregnant. Does that matter to this? Is my baby in any danger?"

"No, it's not, and you're not. Why don't you tell me why you called me," Richard said, taking out a notepad and pen.

Richard began taking notes while Jill explained what had taken place. Everything from the gust of cold wind on the hot summer day they found The Halt, through to Darren having his accident, the clocksmith telling her a large man in a hat was looking for her, as well as the dead body in the engine shed and its connection to this Jack, and, of course, Charlie. She talked about the time shift and the large shadow at the door. The fact when she was alone the house never felt warm. Richard listened as she became more distraught as the timeline moved forward. Paul's experience of the name Jack carved across his chest, his car crash and the Bradbury's secret. She told him of the priest, and of the crucifix, and the old policeman she'd visited.

"May I see the house now?" Richard asked, closing his notebook.

Jill nodded and stood, pointing the way from the sitting room to the kitchen. Richard followed behind her. As he did, he opened himself to the spirit world. Richard could already begin to feel a presence. It was male, and powerful.

As he followed Jill out of the kitchen and up the stairs, he began to get a sense of how big his physical form had been. Richard could feel this was a big man. He wasn't afraid in his later life, but in his earlier years, he had been very afraid, though, of what, he wasn't yet sure. There was something else. Something Richard couldn't focus on, but this large, menacing spirit was afraid again. Not for the same reasons he had been afraid as a child. This was something different. Richard stopped in Jill and Paul's bedroom. His presence here seemed strong, and yet it wasn't the epicentre. He turned to Jill.

"Have you felt him in here?" Richard asked.

Jill hesitated. "Yes, when we moved in and since," she said.

"I need you to open up to me, you have to be open to me," Richard insisted.

Jill became uncomfortable. "The first night here, we made love. Paul felt heavier than he usually did. I put it down to being tired. After, I turned to him, and I swear it wasn't Paul lying next to me. But when I blinked, it was. It was Paul." Jill paused, embarrassed slightly. "I didn't pay it any mind, but when I started researching this, I read articles about spirits taking over the bodies of the living." She took a gulp. "When it first happened, I didn't know who was lying next to me. I hadn't seen his face before. Now I've seen Jack's photo, I know now it was him. I haven't told Paul. I don't know how he'd handle this, especially after the accident."

"And you're pregnant because of that night?" Richard asked.

"Yes, that's right. Why?" Jill asked, the uneasiness clear in her voice.

Richard changed the subject. "Since that night, have you sensed anyone or thing?"

"When I've undressed or showered, I've felt like someone was watching, but in the room, not outside. Then there was—" she stopped.

"Carry on," Richard said.

"I woke to Charlie barking, and when Paul came in, I had marks on my chest and thighs. The next day, they were gone."

"We'll carry on downstairs."

Richard followed, as Jill led him back to the sitting room. He could sense the negative energy increasing inside the house. A slow, sickening feeling began to crawl over him, and waves of nausea washed through him. As they reached the sitting room, Richard's stomach began to knot. He knew this feeling well. It was an ominous sign in anticipation of the negative spirit. Before he sat, he turned to Jill. "Do you have anything that belonged to this Jack Bright?"

Jill reached for her handbag and pulled out the decaying photo frame. "I took this from the place he stayed on the Bradbury farm." She handed it to him.

Richard took the photo frame from her. He rubbed the decades of grime and dust from the glass and looked at the picture hidden beneath. Then he looked back to Jill. "Did you look at this?" he asked, handing it to her.

"No, I just slipped it in my bag." Jill took it from him and looked down. Her eyes focused on the picture as her mind scrambled to comprehend what they saw. Staring back at Jill was a likeness to herself she did not believe possible.

"Who is this?" Richard asked.

"This was Doris, his mother. I researched her but never found a picture, only a description. She was killed in an air-raid. That's why Jack joined the army. He'd hidden from conscription on the farm." Jill placed the picture down. "Do you think he sees me as her?"

Richard didn't answer her directly. Instead, he asked her another question. "I would like to see where you found the body. For some reason, I'm being drawn to that place."

She looked unsure. "It's getting pretty bad out there."

"I need to go where I feel the spirit will be."

"We'll need our coats, and I'll get a couple of torches."

Outside, the storm was hitting the open land hard. The station clock creaked on its mounts, and the wind whistled around the gable ends of The Halt. To Jill, it sounded like the ghost of some old steam train announcing its arrival. Pushing against the wind and driving sharp-cold rain, they reached the engine shed. Left empty since the police removed the body, Jill unlocked it and slid the considerable, wooden door across. They shone their torches inside. "I'll get my car," Richard shouted against the storm.

Jill had understood him, but only just. She watched him, nervous and frightened he wouldn't come back, that he would jump into his car and disappear. Leaving her to whatever it was that had drawn him to the shed. She felt relief when the high-beams of his car turned to face her, and he drove into the engine shed.

He climbed out and gestured to Jill to slide the heavy door shut, which she did. With the storm, somewhat at least shut out, and the interior illuminated by the xenon headlamps, they put their torches on the car.

Richard walked in front of his car. The wind rattled the old roof while large drops of collected rain dropped from it, splashing into larger puddles with almost orchestral timing. The headlamp beams cast shadows around the old building, and his breath left vapour trails as he exhaled in the white light. It seemed to him that it was much colder inside the shed than it was in the storm.

To his right was the inspection pit, and Richard felt a strong draw to it. He moved over to it and stood atop of it and looked down. "This is where you found Darren?"

Jill moved closer. "Yes, he'd fallen into it and impaled himself on the knife," she answered, not moving any closer.

Richard could sense her fear of the dark space below him. He turned and walked back to the middle of the shed. Now behind him, his car headlamps silhouetted him and cast an oversized shadow of him against the old walls.

He felt a weight begin to push him down, and the vibrations of negative energy began to pulse through him as if every atom he was comprised of was vibrating a warning to the evil he now sensed. He knew Jack was with them. "I will now open myself to the spirit world and attempt to investigate the disturbances you've experienced. I should inform you that I have a spirit guide with me who relays information from their world. He is called Thunder Cloud and was once a Nez Perce Native American. By opening myself, I will allow the spirit world to see me and communicate with me. And I with it."

Richard turned to Jill. "He's here. Jack is with us."

On hearing this, Jill felt a rush of warmth which tingled through her body to the ends of her toes and fingers. Adrenaline rushed around her, her senses heightened and she

211

became aware of a presence, as she had done so many times since living in this place. "Where is he, can I see him?"

Richard responded quietly. "When I speak to the spirits, I use infused thought. You won't hear me, or Jack speak aloud. When I need you to talk to him, I'll ask you. Only I will be able to see him using my third eye." Then he signalled for her to remain calm and perfectly quiet.

Richard turned to face the direction the headlamps were pointing and moved forward slowly. Outside, the storm seemed to be getting worse. The old roof rattled in protest at the wind, and where the old building had gaps in its walls, the wind and rain whistled through them. The time between the lightning strikes and thunder were becoming shorter, and the thunder had intensified. Richard stopped dead centre. In his mind, he began. *"Who are you? What is your name? Why are you still present here, disturbing the lives of the living?"* No answer came. Richard repeated his questions. This time, his manner was more demanding. *"Who are you? Why are you disturbing the lives of the living?"* Still nothing.

Jill moved a little closer to Richard. He held his hand out, gesturing for her to stand by his side. Jill moved next to him.

Richard demanded again. *Who are you? What is your name?* This time, an answer came.

The voice in his head was deep, and it was full of menace and vehemence. *"You know who I am, seear mortuorum. Or should I call you, cunt?"*

Richard took another step forward. *"I demand you tell me your name. I represent the eternal light and goodness of God. I can offer you help."*

"What can you offer me, cunt?"

Richard took another step. *"I can guide you into the eternal light. Now, tell me your name."*

"You want my name? My name is Jack."

"Why are you here, Jack?" Richard asked again.

No answer came. Only the sound of the storm could be heard. Jill moved closer to Richard. "Has he gone?" she asked.

"No, he's still here with us," Richard answered, staring intently ahead.

Jill noticed his glare. "Can you see him?"

"No, not yet, but I think he will show himself eventually to my third eye."

As he spoke, Jack's voice came back into his head. *"Why are you here?"*

"To help you, and to stop you." Richard answered and continued. *"You must stop tormenting the living. This is their world, their home now, this is not where you belong. You must go into the light."*

Richard felt a pressure wave push on him. He could feel Jack's growing impatience and anger toward him. The nausea began to rise, and the knot in his stomach tightened. *"You must leave now. This is my place to be, not theirs. Leave now. This will be your last warning."*

Richard summoned his strength. *"Spirit, I represent the eternal light and goodness of God. Although I walk through the shadow of death, I fear no evil, you cannot harm me, for thou art with me."*

Richard heard a laugh. It was an evil, deep laugh, the likes of which he'd seldom heard before. As the laughter continued, a dark shadow began to form in front of him. A ball of black cloud began to swirl around. It began forming a shape. Before Richard stood the apparition of Jack Bright. Richard began again. *"Spirit, I represent the eternal light. The Father, Son and Holy Ghost. You cannot harm me because I am of God and all things good. I now—"*

Jack cut him off. *"I warned you to leave, cunt, and you haven't. I will have fun with you before I kill you, then I will have this place and Jill to myself. As it should be."*

"Spirit. He who dwells in the shelter of the Most High, who abides in the shadow of the Almighty." As Richard began to reprise Psalm 91, Jack became furious. From across the shed, a spanner flew at him. Jill shouted to Richard, who moved just in time. The spanner hit the car windshield, smashing through it, burying itself in the passenger seat.

Richard began again. *"He who dwells—"*

213

Jack moved forward. As he did, his dark energy swirled and twisted around him. Debris on the floor circled him like a miniature twister. *"You can offer me nothing, there is nothing I want from you. Fuck off, leave this place or I'll kill you like I did the old clocksmith. I'll stop your heart as I did his."*

Richard took a step forward. *"I can send you to the eternal light. There you will find peace."* He turned to Jill. "Say something to him, Jill, tell Jack he has no place here," Richard shouted his command to Jill, as the storm now seemed to be right on top of them.

Jill looked to where Richard was pointing. She felt a fear run through her. It was the same she had felt before but magnified a thousand times over. Gathering what strength she had, she shouted over the wind which now gusted through the gaps in the old building, "Why are you here?"

Jack replied to Richard, *"This is my place. And she reminds me of my mother."*

Richard relayed the message to Jill. "But I'm not your mother. I'm not Doris," Jill said softly. Her fear becoming less, as she spoke to him. She couldn't explain it, but for some reason, now that she could talk to him, her fear was subsiding. She felt drawn to him somehow as if she knew he would not harm her.

"This is my place," Jack repeated. Pointing to Richard. *"This man cannot help me, and he cannot help you."*

Richard turned back to Jack. *"This is not your place. This is for the living; this is not for you."*

Jack's hostility rose again. The dark energy increased, and the swirling cloud began shaking the old building. Richard and Jill fought to keep upright against the wind. It seemed to her that the storm which raged outside had found its way in. But Richard knew it was Jack. Suddenly, it was gone along with Jack, and the shed became calm. The storm once again was confined to the outside. Richard searched the shed. He could still feel Jack's presence. Their torches blinked and switched off. Then, the car headlamps began fading and brightening, and Richard knew Jack was affecting the car's electrical systems. The headlamps then extinguished, and the shed was plunged into darkness. "Richard," Jill shouted. He turned toward her to reassure her. As he did, the headlamps switched back on. Brighter and brighter until the high beams seemed to fizzle and crack. The indicators flashed randomly, and the stereo system began to play. Richard turned to face Jill and saw Jack's apparition standing behind her. "He's behind you," Richard shouted as the dark, swirling cloud began again. Jill turned and screamed.

"I can see him," Jill shouted. Fear poured through her words.

Richard realised he too could see him with his own eyes. *'This shouldn't be,'* he thought to himself. But Jack was visible to them both. The dark spirit of Jack swirled and moved around Jill, circling her, smiling down on her as he did. Jill stood frozen to the spot, unable to move as the fear overran her cognitive thoughts.

Richard shouted to Jack, "Spirit. He who dwells in the shelter of the Most High, who abides in the shadow of the Almighty." This time, he said it aloud. There was no need now to use his infused thought. Jack, it seemed, had manifested into a physical form. Jack spun around and glided toward Richard. As Jack spoke for the first time, they heard his voice. It was an ominous, deep voice. It sounded unnatural and strange. As if he alone had the voice of a thousand demons, all yelling at once. "You cannot help me. You want her for yourself like her last nebbish. I'll get you out of the way too. I'll have her to myself, and I'll fuck her again."

Richard repeated himself. "Spirit. He who dwells in the shelter of the Most High, who abides in the shadow of the Almighty."

Jack's rage increased. As it did, he became larger, and the dark, swirling cloud whipped and churned around them both. Jack roared at Richard. As he did, the car's electrical system overloaded. The lights blew out, and with a crack of sparks, the shed became dark again. Richard and Jill pulled out their phones and switched on the flashlights. Shining their narrow beams to where Jack had last been, they could see the dark mass of cloud as it whirled in and out of the light. Richard repeated his verse. "Spirit. He who dwells in the shelter of the Most High, who abides in the shadow of the Almighty."

Jack shouted across him. Repeating himself. But this time, there was a change in him. "You cannot help me. You want her like the last one. But I'll have her to myself, and I'll fuck her again like I did—" he stopped. His face changed from anger to regret.

"Like you did who?" Richard shouted over the noise of the dark cloud. "Who did you fuck, Jack?"

Jack turned back to Jill, his energy becoming calmer. The mass of whirling cloud abated, and Jack's manifestation now floated calmly in and out of the flashlight beams. The torment and rage had gone. "That's why she died. I killed her. I killed my mother." His anger subsided, as his remorse increased.

Jill moved a little closer to the now calm spirit before her. Gone now was the dark cloud and squall it had brought to the interior of the shed. "No, Jack, your mother died in an air raid," she said.

"The bombs may have killed her, but I'm the reason she was there that day." Jack's tone was now sorrowful.

"What do you mean? You were on the Bradbury farm when it happened," Richard asked.

"I couldn't help myself. I couldn't stop myself," Jack answered.

"Couldn't stop what?" Richard asked.

"I fucked her. That's why I ran away. That's why she was working that day."

"Have you missed her?" Richard asked, sensing a change to the spirit before him.

Jack turned to him. "Yes, I wanted to tell her I was sorry for what I'd done to her. But I never got the chance."

Richard saw his chance to send Jack into the eternal light. "You can be with your mother for eternity, Jack, once you have received the help you desperately need. You must have the help to come to terms with the negative purposeful intentions you exercised in your life on Earth. You must confront the regret and remorse of your wicked acts and thoughts. Then, and only then, can you have eternity with your mother."

The large spirit which stood before Richard now looked broken. His shadow began to shrink, and Richard could hear a soft sobbing. He looked at Richard, his tone now soft. "I want to be with my mother."

A brilliant white light appeared behind Jack. The interior of the shed glowed. Jill and Richard shielded their eyes. As they became used to it, they saw a silhouette materialise. It was Doris. Jack turned to the light and began walking toward it. Richard whispered to Jill to encourage him in. "Jack, enter the light, be with your mother," she said.

Jack stopped a few feet away. He turned back to Richard. "Beware the other."

"What is the other?" Richard replied.

"The other spirit that dwells. Biding its time, watching and waiting." Jack smiled to Jill and then turned back to the light as Doris beckoned him to join her. He took one last step, and as he did, the light vanished and the shed became dark again. Only their phones offered some relief from the pitch black of night.

Richard turned to Jill. "He's gone."

Jill felt the relief the moment he spoke those words. She walked to Richard and hugged him. "Should we go back into the house?"

"I think that would be good. I need a stiff drink," he replied.

Jill pointed to his car. "What about your car?"

Richard looked at the metal spanner lodged in the passenger seat and the smoke marks on the bodywork left by the burning electrics. "I'll have it recovered tomorrow, but first, I need that drink."

Jill smiled. "Of course."

Richard followed Jill out of the shed and back into the storm. Once she'd closed the shed door, they made their way over to the house. Inside, it was warm. Jill noticed it immediately. It was the first time since they had moved in that the house felt at all cosy. Jill walked Richard to the kitchen where she poured him a whisky before making a fresh coffee for herself.

She felt relaxed and for the first time, The Halt began to feel like home. She glanced at the clock. Nine twenty-three, p.m. It had taken nearly two and half hours for Richard to convince Jack to enter the light, and she could tell he was exhausted.

"I sensed a fear in Jack. There is something he is scared of," Richard said, sipping the coffee.

"Jack? Scared of something. I find that hard to believe," Jill replied, smiling.

"He mentioned the other. Does that mean anything to you?"

"No, why? Should I be worried? It is over, isn't it?" Jill became nervous again.

"Yes, it's probably nothing, don't worry. Often, when spirits go into the light, especially spirits like Jack, they'll occasionally say something as they leave. A parting shot, if you will. I'm sure it was just him having the last word, nothing more."

"But you said he felt scared."

"Yes, most probably of going into the light," Richard reassured Jill, though he wasn't buying into his own response. Jack had been afraid of something he'd called The Other. Richard knew it wasn't entirely down to him that Jack had gone into the light so willingly. He'd sensed a relief from Jack when he'd stepped into the light, and not just because he had been reunited with his mother. He changed the subject. "You mentioned a crucifix?"

"Yes, I'll get it for you." Jill went into the hallway and brought back the tarnished crucifix. She handed it to Richard. "I need the loo, be two minutes, then I'll call Paul. Tell him the good news."

She came back into the kitchen from the utility room where the small toilet was located to find Richard sitting where she'd left him. She sat and picked up her coffee. She looked at him, ready to smile and ask him some more questions. When she saw his expression, she hesitated. He had a look of dread on his face as if something sinister had invaded his mind. "What is it?" she asked him

"This crucifix, where did you find it?" Richard asked.

"One the ground outside. Why?"

"This has a different energy to that of Jack. It's darker, somehow more powerful." Richard's hands trembled as he placed it on the table. He looked to Jill. "Do you know of anyone who would wear a straitjacket?" Richard asked, his voice beginning to tremble. "Anyone that would sing nursery rhymes. Particularly this one." He began to sing it. "Seesaw Margery Daw."

Jill felt the dread rise again. As she did, the house became cold, very cold. She looked at Richard. "Arthur," she whispered.

As soon as she spoke, Richard was lifted from his seat and flung across the kitchen. He landed heavily on his left arm. Jill heard the crack and the cry of pain. She rushed to him. As she picked him up, he was pulled away from her and hurled onto the kitchen counter. The coffee pot and toaster were sent sprawling across the floor. A sound behind her made Jill turn just in time to see the oven become detached from its wall mounting. It collapsed onto the ground, the door smashing into small shards of needle-sharp glass. The fridge opened, and the contents were splayed around the kitchen. She turned back to Richard, his nose blooded and his eye cut. Jill helped him up, and they ran from the house. Outside, Richard turned back to look through the open door. In the hallway, he saw a man. He was bigger than Jack, taller, broader and heavier. The straitjacket ripped from his shoulders. His mouth opened, and a malicious sound erupted from it. As it did, the front door slammed shut. Richard grabbed Jill and spun her around. The storm still raging. "We need to get out of here, but you'll have to drive. Do you have a car?" Richard asked, cradling his arm.

"No, we'll have to make it on foot." Jill's words only just made it to Richard. Supporting him, they turned and began to walk.

Jill pointed to behind the house. "Over there is Little Ayton station. We should make the last train." Her words were almost lost in the howling gale which surrounded them.

At the top of the rise, Jill took one last look at The Halt. Then, she turned and walked over the brow of the hill. A little before eleven, they reached the station at Little Ayton. She rested Richard on a long, metal bench and bought two tickets from the self-service machine. Around ten minutes later, the small diesel train pulled alongside the platform. Jill helped Richard onto the train. It was almost empty. Just a few late-night stragglers on their way from the coast to the town of Middlesbrough.

Chapter 14

I was sat on my own, on my way back from visiting my aunt in Whitby, when the couple sat opposite me. The thing that struck me about them was not that they looked dishevelled. It was clear for me to see that the clothes they wore were of a high quality. No, what struck me was how utterly exhausted and frightened they looked. With a small jerk, our train set off. I observed the woman as she watched the small station disappear from view. She could see nothing now but her own reflection and that of the carriage we sat in. Outside, it was pitch black. The wind and rain still battered the sides of the train. She turned to her companion and asked him, "Are you okay?"

"I will be," he said, holding his injured arm, which looked broken to me.

She sighed and turned to face the direction of travel. She caught my tired, old eyes. I smiled politely. The woman nodded and half-smiled back. Sensing a small, but obvious, connection, I leaned forward. "So, what brings you on to this late and last scheduled train?" I asked her.

She looked at me with a dead stare. "You wouldn't believe me if I told you."

"You'd be surprised what I'd believe, Miss," I answered.

Sometime later, and as the train pulled into Middlesbrough station, she finished telling me her story. When the train had stopped, I stood, nodded respectively to them and left. I've never been one for ghost stories, I've always thought myself a man of science. But after meeting these two strangers on that stormy night and hearing their tale, I always check the shadows at nine-thirty.

***

Ten months later, Jill and Paul lived in Ingleby Barwick, a housing estate not far from Stockton-on-Tees, where Paul had managed to secure a new job. His previous partner, Jeff, had bought Paul out of their business, less his debts, when the details of his financial discrepancies became known. Unable to obtain a mortgage, they now rented a pleasant four bedroomed house. There was another reason why they now lived in close proximity with their neighbours. It was the feeling of security in numbers living on these new developments brought. Unlike the country, it never really became dark, and no matter what time of night it was, there was always the sound of people and cars to keep the silence away. Jill had begun her blogging again, and that, as well as their newborn son, Daniel, kept her busy. There was also another new addition. A cross-terrier named Timber.

Jill and Richard had kept in touch since that night, and when Jill had come home with their new son, she had Skyped Richard to share their good news. Richard, of course, was delighted for them both. And the newborn boy looked healthy and perfect.

It was only when Jill had mentioned the birthmark which stretched from his right ear to his temple that Richard remembered in detail the face of Jack Bright and the scar he kept hidden by the fedora even in death. Jill had bared the birthmark no mind, so confident was she that when his hair grew it would be covered. Richard had smiled and agreed. He chose not to tell Jill of the scar he'd seen when Jack had appeared in his third eye, convincing himself it was nothing more than coincidence. And besides, they'd been through enough without him causing her unnecessary worry over something he was certain would prove to be nothing of any importance. The Halt itself was repossessed by the bank, and Paul had had to declare bankruptcy. After everything they had been through, this seemed a smaller problem to have. Life, it seemed, was now normal. The things they had once seen as big problems they mostly ignored or laughed off.

Her pregnancy had thankfully been a normal one, and Daniel was born at a healthy weight of nine pounds and four ounces on May 28 at nine-thirty a.m. Though, financially, they had lost everything, they could at least begin again as a family. For the most part, Jill only told her closest of friends what had happened to them. As always, one or two believed their story while the others simply placated her. For everybody else, their story was a familiar one of overstretching their finances for the perfect home and life and an unfortunate accident which had left Paul with life-altering injuries.

"One day," Jill had said to Paul one evening, "I'll write a book about what happened to us."

Paul had smiled at her and raised his wine glass. "When you do, make me taller and give me a six-pack."

***

April 2021

Following the repossession of The Halt, the bank had failed to secure a private buyer. It had sat on their stock for four years before the Railway Heritage Trust managed to raise the funds needed to buy it. It was only then that the restoration work to bring it back to its former glory as a working station could begin. It would be turned back from the once contemporary home Paul had made it to an accurate replica of what it would have been in its prime back in the forties. Complete with four-miles of track and the reopening of the Estdale Tunnel. The plan eventually was to have a working steam train running the line. As work began, five of the workers were charged with clearing the kitchen diner. After Jill had ran from The Halt, neither she nor Paul had returned, choosing to leave everything behind.

As they began clearing the kitchen, one of them, an older, thin man called Bob, spotted the crucifix under the kitchen table. He picked it up and rubbed the dirt from it before slipping it into his pocket. Returning to clearing the units of the kitchenware and rotten food, he began singing, "Seesaw Margery Daw Jack has got a new master."

One of his colleagues turned to him. "What the fuck are you singing?"

"It just popped into my head," Bob replied.

"Ya fucking Doyle, you'll be singing Humpty Fucking Dumpty next."

The End.

Epilogue
By
Steven Ellington

As a spiritualist, one of the most fundamental teachings and understandings is that of universal energy. This infinite matter is the very building block of life, in fact, everyone and everything is made of universal energy. As a capable and experienced spiritualist medium, one of the most fundamental practices is the awareness and interpretation of the varied types of universal energy.

Whether it is energy of a spirit person, meaning the continued existence of a living present consciousness or the energy signature of a person existing in the physical dimension, or indeed residual energy, the energy vibrations within the fabric of an existing building's atmosphere or the surrounding area where a building once stood. Everyone and everything inadvertently impacts the unseen ocean of universal energy, forever engraving imagery from their actions, emotions and even the continued or once physical existence. Energy simply impacts energy, and because you cannot destroy matter, it means it is forever permanently etched in time, in the way the image created by light is forever imprinted onto a negative.

When you think of a typical, haunted location, you would understandably envisage images of spooky, old manor houses or ghostly castles. But any building or place that has been inhabited by people for lengthy periods of time will, without doubt, be subject to some kind of spirit activity. Either by spirits who return from the spirit world in visitation, to spend time in familiar surroundings, or spirits who wish to spend time with loved ones or by spirits who remain grounded, trapped in the physical dimension of Earth. It is highly likely, therefore, that any property or place steeped in time will have some degree of spirit activity. These places may include homes, places of work such as offices and factory's, military bases, hotels and inns, and, of course, old manor houses and castles. Quite frankly, the list is endless. Where people have once lived, or worked, for many varied reasons, it is highly likely their spirits remain to linger or continue to visit, and most certainly, their once physical presence will be forever imprinted into the fabric of a building's atmosphere as residual energy.

It is surprisingly common due to nothing more than pure pent-up frustration for spirits to often attempt some form of interaction with the physical environment of a former Earthly place of residence, which they may still regard as their own, and wish to protect from new occupancy or alteration. Or, merely attempt to preserve a customary way of life by continuing to interact in recognisable surroundings. But when changes inevitably occur to a place that may have been a home or place of work for many years, changes that a spirit may not entirely agree with, or approve of, it is all too common for spirits to begin making a nuisance of themselves.

They may move small inanimate objects, leaving the occupants puzzled as to their whereabouts, intentionally create noise, tapping on walls, for example, stepping heavily across floors, closing doors with a degree of force, stamping up or down a flight of stairs. Such occurrences are all types of common spirit activity, as spirits try in vain to make their presence and frustrations known. As a result, often unnerving and frightening the unfortunate occupants, who if sensitive to spirit energy may also sense a noticeable unseen presence.

But no matter how well a spirit recognises such a place, how clear the spirit's memories of everyday customary activities are, or how affectionate the recollections, it is a place in which a spirit in the physical sense can no longer partake. It is a place in which a pure energy form without the physical body no longer belongs. A spirit in visitation is simply a living unseen consciousness observing the everyday activities of people now in occupancy.

While most spirits who either are in visitation or grounded simply observe without attempting any form of interaction, some spirits simply cannot help themselves. Over the years, I have helped many individuals in their own homes, places of work, pubs, hotels, in fact, all manner of properties, find peace from the disruptive activity of inquisitive, frustrated and sometimes obstructive spirits. While most spirits are nothing more than curious as to the changes and alterations new owners may be undertaking, other spirits have not taken too kindly to new inhabitants occupying former properties especially when changes and alterations begin. This type of investigation work involves spending time in the property to gain an in-depth understanding into the type of spirit activity as well as attempting to communicate directly with the spirit to discover their identity as well as the reason and purpose for their continued presence and interaction. I often have to perform rescue work by patiently reminding and informing the spirit in question that they no longer belong in the physical dimension of Earth and gently nurture, guide and help them pass over into the spirit dimension, much to the relief of the building's occupants who are left in peace and whose lives can return to some form of normality.

A building or area of land where a building once stood without the presence of spirit activity can also offer much in terms of memories, images and events. All that happens within the confines of a building are forever absorbed within the fabric of its atmosphere, even if the building no longer remains. Daily mundane activities, for example, are forever etched within its fabric. I often observe past events played back to me like a movie when investigating historic places or areas. In the physical sense, a particular event or activity has taken place and is confined to the element of times past. In a spiritual sense, however, as far as universal energy is concerned, it is forever recurring, and therefore, still happening now in the present. The more highly emotionally charged a particular past event, the more evident it is in the present within the fabric of energy that influences the building's atmosphere.

Whenever we use an inanimate object such as jewellery or a piece of furniture, by touching it on a regular basis, we involuntarily infuse our own energy within it. It is possible, therefore, for an inanimate object such as a piece of furniture to record the emotional, mental and physical state of a person who touches it on a regular basis. As a spiritual medium, I can interpret this energy using a technique called psychometry. Any inanimate object that comes into regular contact with a particular person, including jewellery and clothes, can quite easily record the individual's Energy Signature and indeed memories.

Understanding and interoperating the varied universal energy types is paramount when working as a spiritualist medium to maximise the information present within the fabric of an existing building or an area where it once stood. Inanimate objects as well as communicating directly with spirit souls who continue to occupy and visit places they once resided, or remain close to loved ones, currently existing within the physical dimension.

Through the regular, disciplined practice of various meditation techniques, I have developed and use the following abilities to channel and interpret the many forms of universal energy.

Clairsentience:
The ability to sense manifestations that are not of tangible physical structure such as the presence of spirit residual energy and the ability to sense atmospheres.

Clairaudience:
The ability to hear words and sounds that are from dimensions beyond the known physical dimension of Earth, such as words spoken by spirit.

Clairoma:

The ability to smell beyond all that exists in the physical dimension of Earth such as the residual energy of a building or a smell related to spirit communication such as flowers, tobacco or fragrances.

Clairvoyance:

Regarded as second sight, the ability to see beyond all that exists in the physical dimension of Earth such as seeing spirits, seeing past images of how places once looked, remote viewing and observing visions of the future.

Afterword

A thought from M.E. Ellington.

I continue my race against death. A race that began the instant I was born, and one I have so far continued to win. Though I know one day, it is a race I will lose.